Legacy of S[

A story of the Bristol Channel

JOHN GILMAN

First published 2000 by Marine Arts Publications
(Deckchair Books)
"Seascape,"
Robin Hood's Bay,
Whitby. North Yorkshire.
YO22 4SH United Kingdom.

ISBN 0-9516184-3-1

Legacy of Smoke.

Front Cover painting © by Nick Cotton.
Line drawings © by John Legge, Gordon Macfie, John Gilman.

Printed by
Crewe Colour Printers Ltd.

Dedication

To all the families who lost their loved ones in the waters of the Bristol Channel during two bitter wars.

Acknowledgements

My grateful thanks to all seafarers and dwellers along the coasts of the Bristol Channel for many memories recorded here. All the stories have a basis in recorded history, verbal tradition or remembered anecdote. All the places are still there to be discovered, hopefully with as much joy as the writer has experienced over many years.

In the morning watch of the 16th January 1940 the tanker Inverdargle was torpedoed and set on fire by the U-33 off Glenthorne in the Bristol Channel. It is believed there were no survivors....

CHAPTER ONE

Jill shivered and stopped. She'd often wondered what her reactions would be when confronted with the house after so many years. Nevertheless as they drew level with it in the sharp, early winter dusk it came as a shock.

Martin stopped in mid sentence about ten paces ahead and looked back. Jill turned and smiled weakly. She had never told him. Even after thirty-eight years there were still some things that remained hers alone. Of course she'd come close to spilling it all out on many occasions but had somehow managed to choke it all back. Martin had never given her the slightest indication that he had a psychic side or a tolerance of spiritual issues whereas Jill had a long history of experiences that she'd learned to keep to herself; especially this story which had a bearing on their relationship at the outset. Strange how some individualities remained despite long years of harmony and sharing so many things together.

They moved on their way. They had parked the car in Westfield Place where Martin had once rented a bed-sit, one of many bed-sits and flats that became the familiar backdrop to their shared student days in Clifton and Redland. They crossed the busy approach to the suspension bridge and climbed to the Observatory and then on to the Promenade before joining the top of Bridge Valley Road and the edge of the Downs. This was familiar territory. Here on hot summer days they had sprawled on the grass surrounded with books and papers as the many examination and assignment deadlines drew closer. Here on chilly, breath-visible mornings they had met up

4

on their way to lectures and later lingered to watch the tea-time dusk snatch the last of the day over Sea Walls down to the distant, smoke-hazed muffled lights of Avonmouth.

Martin halted again in mid-stride. Sharing in the animated recollections of their days together before they were married was a tonic and he felt boyish again. The years of responsibility had been weightier than he cared to admit and it was a relief to find another way of relaxing. They were good together; always had been and yet he felt that it was his place to take the lead and make the rules. It was probably something to do with the way he had been brought up. Not that they lived a regimented regime but he sometimes realised that he was putting the brakes on for both of them.

Jill was obviously thoughtful about something. It was that damned house. Ever since they'd passed it she'd dropped out of the conversation, lost the thread or just fallen silent. Something had happened there. Something that had had a marked effect upon her at the time and yet she'd never mentioned it. Of course he'd noticed, couldn't fail to. However if it had been important to their relationship he knew she would have mentioned it. At first he suspected that it might have been another man she'd known before him. Later he'd thought that perhaps something bad had happened there in her earlier days. After all she'd lived in nearby Redland for years before he came on the scene. There were certainly some funny characters about in bedsitter-land in those days. Perhaps someone had frightened her badly.

'Oh look,' he announced somewhat awkwardly. 'Worrall Road. Do you remember Anglesea Place and the Palace? That crazy, tumbledown wreck of a house where so many fantastic characters lived? I'll bet its now all done up and highly respectable.'

Jill quickly realised. 'Wasn't that where they burnt the banisters and half the floorboards one winter just to keep warm?'

'And there was Simon who had an elegant Rolls Royce and Roger who was an actor.'

'Several actors lived there. Remember how when we saw them on the television we said, 'Oh look, remember when he was a student?'

It had been their intention to walk across the Downs via the tunnel ventilation tower and on up to the top of the Blackboy Hill. However the walk had become a meander as they remembered who had lived where and the associated crowded incidents that had seemed so important all those years ago. They'd both promised to come back to Bristol one day and to walk the remembered streets, visit the familiar pubs and to search for the houses whose internal dimensions were, barring subsequent alterations of course, as well known as their present home in Brook Street, Macclesfield.

Martin reached out his hand.

'Shall we see if the Port of Call is still there?'

They turned diagonally right and paused before the stream of evening traffic allowed them to cross Upper Belgrave Road and drop past Cheyne House into narrow Wesley Place. They were soon into the village at the top of the Blackboy Hill, a unique settlement probably no more than two hundred and fifty years old and crammed into an absurdly small area bounded on the west by Sutherland Place and on the south by Worrall Road. Opposite the top of York Street they descended through the garden and across the High Street to stand at the top of Quarry Steps by the garages. Behind them the old High Street bent steeply upwards whilst below them fell precipitous Quarry Steps and Belgrave Hill all tucked away under the impressive, towering rise of Belgrave Terrace and its sister blocks overlooking the Downs. Glancing to their right and upwards to the high, silhouetted outline of the buildings that lined the road they seemed an extension of the ancient cliff face itself as if sculptured into the limestone scarp that began the Downs plateau. Vaulted above the grey, ochred and lime-washed lifted blocks with their random squares of mellow light the last trails of blown out salmon sky contrasted with the growing darkness that crouched among the tumbled collection of mews and terraced buildings scree below. Here the lights had gained authority and lent an air of purposeful security to the community embayed below the crags. It was a case of elevated elegance dropping into a homely working township within a hundred yards or so, a pattern repeated all across the city but in few cases as abruptly as here.

They must have stood there for several minutes before Jill broke the spell.

'What I don't understand is why it hasn't changed. It's exactly as I remember it all those years ago.'

'Well there's a few new roofs here and there and a newish block of buildings just below but, yes it's not altered much.'

'Here we are standing where we stood nearly forty years ago and it's we who have changed. It's like a time-slip looking out here.'

Martin sensed that Jill was about to become philosophical.

'It might look the same on the outside but behind every window they'll be living in the present.' He put his arm on her shoulder.

'Let's see if the inside of the Port of Call has escaped the latest wave of pub décor.'

They turned their backs on Quarry Steps and wandered up to the top end of York Street to the curved brick wall of the old outside toilet that in their days was open to the skies. The Port of Call didn't disappoint them. It was exactly as they had left it. The same windows and the same double fronted door looked out onto the crest of the tiny street that plunged within a few yards, like a waterfall, into the mainstream of Blackboy Hill.

The Port of Call was a survivor. Originally two cottages it had expanded into its present form by the middle of Queen Victoria's reign when it boasted two bars. The Public Bar, always the more popular, was separated from the Saloon or Private Bar by the Jug and Bottle just inside the front doors. By far its most popular host had been Rowlie Glass who with his wife Kit was responsible for giving the house its genuine nautical flavour. Rowlie had been a 'club-swinger' in the Royal Navy before retirement and had, like many of his oppo's, collected a number of items that enhanced the character of the place. There were lamps for the swinging, ancient ship models and numerous pictures and prints of ships long gone to their last resting places in Davy Jones' locker or some forgotten scrap-yard. In her younger days Kit had been a popular mannequin in the city and by the fifties the pair had made the Port a focus for a lively group of artists, writers and business folk. When Jill and Martin had known it in the early sixties the Public Bar, with its row of kilderkins mounted behind the bar, was always full of folk who appreciated good company and equally well kept ale.

They entered the familiar front door and turned automatically left. Of course they didn't expect to see Rowlie Glass or any of the other personalities that had contributed to the life of the old place but they were delighted to see that some of the pictures had survived and that the overall character had not been altered. A quick glance showed that the Jug and Bottle had been demolished and that the two bars had been run into one. The changes had been practical and whilst it was now an up-to-date, comfortable and welcoming house, sufficient remained of the old atmosphere to reassure and support its origins as a village pub with a character of its own. Rowlie wouldn't feel out of place here and the company seemed as outgoing and friendly as ever.

'There's a pen and ink drawing of the old Public Bar here that was here when I used to help out.'

Jill remembered.

'Of course, you actually worked here for a while didn't you?'

'Just for a short time. Rowlie took pity on me when I was between bed-sits and offered me a room in exchange for help in the bar. I used to look after the quiet bar so Rowlie could stay with his friends in the busy one.'

'I was living at Redland Close in Elm Lane then. I remember two or three of us coming in to see you. We never got any free drinks though I know we tried!'

Finding seats in the window, Martin ordered and soon

returned with two glasses of beer and a packet of cashew nuts. Clifton had not disappointed them. If anything it was better than they remembered it. Many of the large houses had been renovated, cleaned and decorated and were looking as if they were in single ownership rather than being split up into flats and bed-sits as was the case in the sixties. They were surprised at one particular house that in their day had a large student population, not the best guardian of its architectural heritage. It had obviously passed out of that era and become a classic example of restoration and much as it must have been in the eighteen twenties with its stonework cleaned, woodwork repaired and its historical detail meticulously restored.

'The prices are a bit of a shock aren't they?' Commented Jill.

Martin nodded.

'Perhaps we ought to have stayed here rather than constantly moving. Our Clifton garden flat would buy three houses in Macclesfield!'

'Predicting house prices and shifting fashions in districts is a job for those with lots of capital. We've never been in that league.'

Martin smiled ruefully.

'Perhaps we shouldn't have come back.'

'You wanted to see the exhibition that your friend has set up and I wanted to take a trip into the past. Anyway, we're here now and I think it will prove interesting for both of us.'

'Going back is against the tide of life isn't it?'

'You mean it's fighting the current.'

'Yes, everyone tells you that you can't go back and if you do, when the trauma of first doing so has been felt, it's either smaller or the nostalgia is lacking.'

Jill ran her fingers through her short grey hair and locked her hands behind her head.

'Or is it that we've matured and the view, long over-painted with imaginative replays, is lacking the colour that the mind has given it?'

'Oh I agree that memory can play some strange tricks,' nodded Martin. 'But then I would argue that there is no one single reality to begin with and so it is not surprising that folk can never agree about the past.'

Jill was already beginning to think about her own perceptions and about the possible outcome of their visit to Bristol. For her it was a kind of pilgrimage to a past experience, a glimpse into her past and to seek confirmation that what she had discovered about herself and other figures in a drama had, in fact, taken place and were a part of a wider reality. It was not nostalgia but the challenge of discovering if the perceptions of yesterday were valid or had she been privileged to experience some kind of dream which was essentially the property of others? All our pasts contain ghosts but were these projections a product of her imagination as Martin would think or reconstructed layers of memory like an old retouched painting that now deceives in its apparent veracity. Had she indeed experienced that adventure all those years ago? Visiting the past is the most dangerous of all voyages not least because our guides are untrustworthy.

'Well?' Martin was querying. 'Where have you been? You haven't been listening to a word I've been saying.'

'Sorry.'

'I was thinking that I'd like to spend a couple of hours

at the exhibition and then, if possible, catch up with Peter and talk about the research implications. Is that all right with you?'

Jill was thinking that this would leave her free to take a certain walk and to do some thinking on her own.

'Fine. We could meet up for lunch in that little place we noticed in The Mall, say about twelve thirty?'

'That sounds okay. Would you like another?'

'Not for me but you get one if you like. I'm fine sitting here for a while. It's just like old times.'

Martin pulled himself up from his seat and crossed to the bar. Jill watched the familiar set of his shoulders as he moved with a grace that belied his years. He was a fine man, tall and slim with a good mop of wiry hair. He still carried the air of authority that had taken him to positions of responsibility in two careers. Perhaps his only fault, or at least his most obvious fault, was his lack of imagination or the grace to admit that there was room for other that a purely scientific method of enquiry. He was a good man nevertheless and Jill felt that the decision she had made when still not much more than a child was the right one for both of them. Neither of them had regretted it and perhaps most of the race was now over and they could afford to indulge in a few frivolities; his to take an interest in the achievements of his colleagues and her to discover whether or not she had seen a particular ghost.

She glanced around the room. Apart from the way the youngsters were dressed it could have been at any time in the last few decades. It was certainly strangely familiar being back and she felt she wouldn't have been surprised if one of her college friends was to drop in and greet her. This journey intrigued her and she had the oddest feeling that she was again to be involved in that story which had remained with her all these years. A bit like a deja-vu feeling but not quite, that intuitive prompt that something is waiting to happen and there is an inevitable certainty about it. She'd felt it before and it had always been the precursor to some unusual incident or significant development in her life. If pressed she'd almost say that she'd been drawn back for a reason but all her years with Martin had made a more cautious woman of her. Perhaps wisely so for if something was really in the air it would carry more weight when it did occur.

'Here you are, I got you one after all. You were in one of your pensive moods.'

She smiled up at him. For a second or two he was the boy she was dating and she thought how lucky she was. Time had started its game.

CHAPTER TWO

The morning stretched, sharp and bright under a high, pale cloudless sky; the early frost soon melting out of the long tree shadows and leaving all the subtle undulations of the Downs landscape etched like an engraving cut into frosted glass. A rare day.

Jill had preferred to walk across from the hotel, giving herself time to think about that distant but poignant episode of her student life. Unlike today it had been a warm late evening in the June of 1961 and just about here where the ground dipped into a shallow ravine among clumps of broken yellow grasses. The path, one of many small veins that appear and disappear with the seasons, ran along the higher of the two banks before joining with the main artery as it swept out of the tiny valley. Yes, it was about here that it had started all those years ago. She slowed and being unable to sit, stood and allowed her gaze to gauge the ambience of the place, scanning as if it were a scrolling, flickering computer screen for any vestiges that might remain hidden to this present. Could she feel it? Was there any trace of the drama still extant for her or anyone else to grasp? The still cold of the early morning pressed about her and the traffic, like the surge of a distant tide, washed insistently from the nearby road. The incisive cries of a group of aggressive school children as they swung their bags at each other attempted to snatch her back to a present reality.

She had been walking home from Vicki's flat where two or three of them had been discussing just what Mrs.

Michael had been asking them to do earlier that day. She could remember very little of what the lecture had been about but there had been that expectation of a piece of work and books were in short supply necessitating a sharing of resources. Not a bad plan they had found, as ideas pooled were usually instrumental in clarifying the issues in question. That day's Education lecture had, strangely enough, been on the subject of perception.

She'd got to just about here when the soft night stilled around her. She'd recognised the feeling. A sudden chill goosed the flesh of her bare forearms as if a breeze had gusted low across the dry grass and yet it remained a warm, lazy evening with just a hint of impending thunder perhaps later in the night. She'd then had the knowledge that she was not alone, as if separated in some way from the reality around her whilst remaining very much aware of where she was. Of course she'd recognised the feeling. It had happened before. Many times.

It had been then that she became aware of the figure silently moving from left to right about twenty yards in front of her. She also remembered the thought that flashed into her mind at that moment. Why had this particular figure impinged on her consciousness when just seconds ago she'd been aware of many, in couples and singles making their way across the Downs? The figure had passed on its way across the rough ground towards a clump of immature trees and disappeared beyond them at the edge of Upper Belgrave Road, leaving her with an unmistakable feeling of sadness and desolation that had such an effect it left her in tears. Within seconds there had been again the buzz of traffic, a lone blackbird's song and the shrill cry of two youngsters calling out to each other as they parted. The spell, if you could call it that, had broken.

She was familiar with the pattern. It had been her companion for as far back as she could remember. In fact she had grown up with the ability to see more than was seen by her peers. Of course it took some time before she realised this. She wasn't aware that she was any different from anyone else until she began to share her experiences with her family and then her friends. She'd told her mother first, or rather asked her who the little girl was that often stood in her bedroom looking at her. Her mother had smiled and said that it was Magi Nation. This had seemed a reasonable explanation but Magi never said anything, just stood there, her hands folded in front of her. It was her father who had questioned her a little more thoroughly and asked how the little girl was dressed. When the details had been duly noted, her father had put his arm around her and told her that she was a clever girl to be able to see some of the pictures of the past and that probably the little girl she had seen had lived in the house a long time ago. He had also told her never to be frightened and that in most cases the people that she would see would not be aware of her.

From that time forward she had been aware of many such people. An incident she remembered clearly was to become known as the 'green shoes' episode and one that her mother teased her about for years. It was also the incident that taught her to keep a still tongue about these things, apart from her father who continued to be interested and told her that she had a valuable gift. When she was about five years old she had regularly been taken to a lady who lived just around the corner in Aberdeen Road.

She'd always been called Aunty by her mother but as it turned out she wasn't her real Aunty but a close friend of her mother who was happy to look after a lively youngster for two afternoons a week. The house was a large one on four floors but she always played in the front room on the ground floor, first right after climbing the steep stone steps and walking along the cool tiled hall. The room was fitted with a large, long-piled Indian rug with an exciting pattern. It seemed as if there were animals and adventures woven together in reds and browns and she loved to crawl about on her hands and knees pushing through tangled thickets of bamboo, wading impossible rivers and coming face to face with the amazing creatures that inhabited this magical kingdom. One sunny afternoon she was following one such pictorial adventure when she became aware of the arrival of a pair of green shoes. The shoes were particularly noticeable as they paced up and down through her jungle world. She didn't notice much about the lady, just her legs and of course the shoes that trod so carelessly through her game. After a while the shoes left and she played on until it was time for a drink and a biscuit. The 'green-shoes' lady interrupted her play on more than one occasion, never said anything and usually left shortly before she had her afternoon drink. As the legs were the only other contact she had during the afternoons she had asked Aunty who the lady was with the green shoes only to be met with a puzzled stare. When it was time to be collected she remembered how Aunty had told her mother that she had a very 'maginative child.   'There's no-one else lives here see. As you knows, I lives alone.'

The next impact of her imagination left no question of

17

whether she was hallucinating or dreaming. They had just moved house, around the corner into Cotham Hill and at first it seemed strange to walk on past Number 15 West Park and then to turn right and head for their new house. It wasn't new of course, but another large square Victorian family house on four floors only this time it was bigger and it had a lovely walled garden full of mature established trees. Not a huge garden but an intimate glade, a surprise when one thought of where the house was, in the middle of a large city. She liked to think of it as a secret garden, not only because no-one suspected it was there and it wasn't immediately apparent from a cursory glance at the property but because it felt so delicious to be there. There was a feeling of welcome security, a sense of delight. It quickly became her favourite place

One day, after coming home from school, she headed for the garden and sat for a while at the foot of an ancient pear tree. Allowing the peace of the garden to slowly overcome the clatter of the day she relaxed and allowed her gaze to wander among the dappled, multi-coloured movements of the bowing and shifting branches towards the small mounted sun-dial in the centre of the lawn. She remembered how the wind was pushing and pressing and how the sky seemed miles high above the boundaries of her world. She didn't feel at all alarmed or surprised when she noticed a shadow had somehow strengthened and she was looking at a young boy, probably some three or four years older than herself. He was standing somewhat to the right of the sundial and was watching or looking at someone older or taller than himself. His head was held slightly alert and his hands were held aside from his body as if he had just dropped something. He seemed totally unaware that he was being observed. After a minute or two, he slowly and quietly slipped from view; just wasn't there any more and she knew that her privileged view had ended. She was now quite convinced that she'd seen one of her shadow people and felt that the time had come to share her experience with someone who would understand. Her father was the closest.

'It's a gift,' he'd said. 'Quite a few folk have it. Animals too. You may find that one day it could lead to a greater understanding of the world we live in and the nature of this strange thing called time.'

The shadows had flitted persistently throughout her teenage years and she had often been aware of the tides of emotion that had washed about the transient figures. By the time she was eighteen she'd become accustomed to a wider and more challenging environment whilst at the same time she'd learned to distinguish between the present and the often pressing images from the past. Once, on the Suspension Bridge, she cried out as she saw a young man drop away into the air from the wrong side of the guardrails. It was his fear and despair rather than her shock that hit her the hardest and she had to go and satisfy herself that it wasn't happening before her eyes.

On this occasion it had been the same, the flood of emotion as the figure passed before her was almost overwhelming and she had to choke back the feelings that swept over her. It was as if she was experiencing the mind of the figure and becoming a part of the trauma that had occasioned the spectre in the first place.

Of course, that was only the beginning of the matter.

After seeing the lady crossing the Downs she had turned and gone on her way but not without trying to recollect what she had perceived. The lady was in her middle years and dressed in dark clothing with some form of scarf or hood over her head. She was very much wrapped up in herself and didn't seem to be aware of her surroundings. That she was anguished was certain and she carried such an aura of hopelessness that it almost tangible.

With all thoughts of lectures and essays put aside, Jill could thing of nothing else as she plotted her way back across the Downs to her bed.

It was to be a week later before she saw the figure again, only this time in broad daylight. She had just been into the Refectory for lunch and was walking back up to the top of the Blackboy Hill. Resisting the temptation to pop into the Port of Call for a half, she pressed on to the corner of the Downs where she thought she'd sit for a while and read a couple of chapters of her book. She'd had the feeling that there was someone about when she'd passed the corner of Apsley Road but had shaken it off, It didn't do to switch into her sensitive mode in the middle of a busy street.

As before, she become aware of the figure against a normal contemporary background. There were several folk about, some eating sandwiches on the grass and others strolling along the path that struck out diagonally from where she stood. The spectre was again in dark clothing and she'd noticed that it seemed to strengthen as it moved on a set course across the uneven ground towards the main road. That no-one else was seeing it was obvious as the shadow passed through a group of students who were sitting on the slopes of a slight rise just one hundred yards from her. Despite the distance there was that slight shift in perception, a blurring of the edges of time and she knew that the accompanying waves of emotion would soon impact upon her. She had then made the decision that was to bring home the full meaning of the story re-enacting before her. She followed the ghost.

It had taken only a minute to slip behind the tragic image that swept slowly before her. She had clearly seen that the lady was wearing a dark, belted, full-length woollen coat and a navy blue headscarf. Her right hand held the lapels of the coat together at the neck whilst her left clutched the broken strap of a square, blackish leather handbag. Although she was obviously on course for a local destination she managed to look lost and lonely; a solitary figure in any landscape and quite at odds with the surroundings she now walked through. She remembered thinking at the time.

'This is why the older ghosts stand out so distinctly in the dress of their day whilst it's much harder to distinguish the more recent ghosts in their modern dress, except of course there is always the slightly altered dimensions that I've recognised as pertinent to every sighting.'

Just before the Downs gave way to Upper Belgrave Road, the ghost had paused and almost faded from sight. She had stopped too, about two or three yards from the troubled figure. Then, as if her resolve increased, the shade sharpened into a firm outline, crossed the road and entered the front door of a substantial house to the right of the Terrace. Committed now, Jill had crossed the road just a few seconds after the last of the lady had melted through the panels of the door, and knocked.

CHAPTER THREE

The length of time before she heard footsteps coming down the hall to answer the door seemed interminable. What had she done? What could she possibly say to whoever opened the door? When it did open her fears left her for she was confronted with a small, gentle, smiling woman of some fifty summers who merely asked if she could be of any help. Jill remembered that not being rebuffed or scowled at had made all the difference and she felt able, albeit a little hesitantly, to ask if she might pose a personal question.

Still holding the door with one hand, the woman looked long and hard at her and then, quite deliberately said,

'I think you'd better come in.'

As Jill stepped across the entrance hall, the woman's voice came back to her over her shoulder as she led the way into the sitting room.

'I'm not in the habit of inviting strangers into the house you understand but I can see that this is no ordinary visit.'

Jill had hastened to reassure. 'I'm not trying to sell anything,' she blurted.

'I'm sure you're not my dear. I can see by your face that you have something on your mind. Now, how can I help?'

Jill had stood awkwardly in the doorway of the comfortable sitting room. It was a far cry from the student accommodation she had become used to.

'Oh, I'm sorry,' smiled the woman. 'You must think me very rude. Do sit down and make yourself comfy. My name is Angela Vickery and I've lived here for over twenty years.'

Jill remembered again how she had felt and even now she wondered how she'd had the nerve to barge into a strange house in the middle of the day. It all came back to her.

'I hope you will forgive me for banging on your door like this but I've just had a rather strange experience and felt compelled to follow it through.' She'd broken off lamely and glanced quickly around the room before sinking thankfully into a chair.

Miss Vickery had quietly assessed the situation and smiled encouragingly.

'You take your time young lady and I'll put the kettle on.'

After the tea and some delicious home- made cakes had made their appearance, the two of them had settled to talking.

'So, what was this experience that brought you to my door?'

Jill had felt a little more at ease. 'Since I was a child, I've had the gift of seeing people who aren't a part of the present world. My friends would call them ghosts but I have come to see them as glimpses of past lives. These snapshots from the past are always accompanied by the feelings of the folk involved and I have often become very upset by the fear, anguish or hurt that these folk are carrying.'

Miss Vickery had leaned back in her chair and raised both hands to her face, cupping her cheeks whilst looking straight at Jill.

'And you have seen someone close to this house?'
Jill had nodded.

'Tell me exactly what you saw. Don't make anything up. Be as accurate as you can and maybe I'll be able to tell you something more.'

She remembered shivering before attempting the reconstruction of all that she had seen. All the while Miss Vickery had remained silent but her hands had slipped around to cover her mouth.

Jill's fingers had been unsteady as she reached for her cup.

'And this lady came into your house just a few seconds before I knocked.'

'A few seconds before you knocked I was thinking of her.... My sister, my poor little sister.'

Miss Vickery looked up.

'I don't think that there is any doubt. You saw my sister today. This was her home until she died. It was all very tragic.'

A silence spread between them. Miss Vickery had paled. Jill was definitely regretting her naivety in blundering into what was obviously a sensitive situation. It was the older woman who rescued the moment with the skill that came of long concern for others.

'Oh, you poor love. I don't think that there is any doubt that you have met my sister. The description of her and her state of mind is uncannily accurate. I nursed her here you know, before she died. It was a terrible waste of a life. Poor Annie, she was widowed at the beginning of the war and never really recovered. Oh, I know that many were braver and carried on but Annie couldn't come to terms with her loss and it was just too much for her. She used to walk across to Sea Walls most days and look down the Avon always believing in her heart that her

David would come home again. She never accepted that he was dead. Yes, there was always that air of sadness and despair about her, almost unworldly she became. Just as you describe.'

Jill had never picked up on the close details of one of her shadow people and was struck silent for a while. Angela Vickery continued, looking beyond her into a past that was still too close for comfort.

'Our father died at the beginning of the fifties and mother was living in Watchet but I was housekeeper here for Miss Peath John and she needed me to stay on. It seemed right that Annie should come here to us after that awful winter of 1940. I looked after her. She never really worked again. Just seemed to live in a tragic, broken world of her own.'

'Oh, I'm so sorry. I've brought all this back to you.' Jill suddenly felt the responsibility drop upon her. She still felt an intruder.

'No, don't fret, I've often wondered if such grief over so long a period was able to cross to others. It hurt me terribly but I had a job to do and had to be strong for everyone. Looking back, it was this that kept me on an even keel right through the war and after.'

'Has anyone else seen her?'

'There was a lady from Pembroke Road who couldn't believe that Annie had died because she saw her regularly crossing the Downs for weeks after the funeral. She came to see if she could help. She thought that Annie looked so unhappy. I had a job to persuade her that my sister had, in fact, died months before.'

Jill had pressed gently. 'When did she die?'

'A little over two years ago now. She'd not been eating properly for some months. Then she became quite poorly though still insisting she should go out for her daily walk. She went down quite suddenly. The doctor said she'd just lost the will to live'

Jill had just nodded silently and wondered to herself if her actions might be construed as selfish. She had been shaken back by Angela's gentle smile.

'You seem really concerned my dear.'

'Oh, I am but I've never actually followed anyone before and it has come as a bit of a shock to discover the reality behind the sighting. I've felt it you understand but not really grasped the terrible hurt it must have been for those close to that person. I'm sorry.'

Angela looked at the slight, sensitive girl before her and was struck by the remarkable similarity to her sister. They were very much alike. In fact that had been the reason why she had felt able to invite this youngster in. And, if she cared to admit it to herself, just before the knock came at the door, she thought she'd heard her sister cry out to her. She'd never been much of a one for paranormal things but perhaps there was a strange kind of logic in the visit. It was certainly something to make her think.

'Perhaps Annie wanted you to know. She was every bit as sensitive as you and a very loving and kindly person. David was the great love of her life. In fact he was all her life from the time they met in 1938. Look, my dear, you come back tomorrow afternoon and I'll tell you her story. I'll get some of her things to show you. It may be a way we can both try to understand how she struggled through the years. I used to get quite impatient with her sometimes and wish she could have let go of the past.'

Jill had got up to leave when Angela had put her hand on her arm.

'I shall never tell this story again. There's no-one left who'd want to hear it. Perhaps the re-telling has something to teach us both so please come back and we'll look at her life together and try to understand how and why it ended as it did.'

Jill had found the courage to place her hand over that of Angela and in that second she knew that she wanted desperately to hear the story out and to try to bring some comfort to this lady. Angela was still speaking.

'For me to remember the good times and for you to learn what it was like to lose a lovely young man in the springtime of his life...in that awful winter when so many youngsters went to the bottom of the sea. Will you come?'

Jill had nodded. She'd thought that in some way it was right. She owed it to herself and the strange gift she'd carried all these years and she owed it to this lady to respond and to hear the story through. She started to leave the room and Angela followed her to the door. Jill ventured.

'Have you ever seen her since...since she died?'

Angela opened the heavy front door and stood to one side. She put her finger to her lips.

'Tomorrow,' she smiled, 'tomorrow.'

Of course she'd go back. Although at first she had felt very much on the edge of the story she'd nevertheless been touched by the shadow of Annie Vickery and engaged by the warmth and concern of Angela who had, without doubt, taken her experience to heart. Whether she liked it or not she knew that tomorrow afternoon she would go back to the house.

Jill remembered little of the walk back to her road. She knew it was much later in the day but was surprised to learn that two hours had passed since she had knocked on the door. By the time she had completed her journey she had already resolved not to tell anyone of her visit, not even Martin who would be calling round later that evening. Minutes later, normality struck her as sharply as her afternoon's adventure as she entered the shared kitchen to find two day's washing up, no milk and piles of ironing, papers and books on every chair. She was back.

That evening they had gone to the ABC cinema on the Whiteladies Road. She hadn't been able to concentrate on the film or really distance herself from her earlier experience. She knew it was unfair on Martin who had kept giving her sidelong glances all evening. He didn't say anything but she was aware that her mind had not been wholly on her date. He was quite visibly put out when, later, she had told him that she needed to have the next day to herself. He'd wanted to know what was going on as previously they'd arranged to have a meal together in the evening. She'd tried to reassure him that everything was fine but something had cropped up that needed her full attention. He'd still wanted to worry at it and she felt it extremely difficult to be pulled both ways. She wasn't even sure it had been the best plan to keep some things to herself. Would he still like her if he knew she had a tendency to see ghosts in the everyday world? Worse, what would he think if she told him she'd spent the afternoon following a ghost across the Downs? No, she would keep quiet, at least until she had the opportunity to see where this particular sighting would lead.

They'd parted late that evening, she feeling a need for the security of his arms and he finding reassurance in her willingness to be close. Already they made a good pair, learning how to be generous and understanding of each other's needs. There were upsets of course, and sometimes the intensity of their relationship caused some unnecessary jealousy but Jill had quickly learned to defuse the more obvious situations with a glance or a quiet squeeze of the hand. Coming straight from home to student accommodation with its freedoms and limitations was something they all had to adjust themselves to. All in all, Jill had thought that they had managed pretty well.

The next afternoon had been fine and warm. She had set off for the Downs in good time and managed to smile off any attempts to discover where she was bound. She soon found herself passing the ornamental ventilation tower close to the top of Pembroke Road. She remembered how some of the theological students from Latimer House on the corner were in quiet and earnest discussion whilst a group of drama students from the house opposite were out on the edge of the Downs loudly practising voice projection. The contrast between the serious and the extrovert was obvious and yet she knew some of the tricks that one or two of the theological students had got up to painted a different picture. She had to smile.

Naturally she had been wondering whether or not she might catch a glimpse of Annie Vickery on her way to the house but nothing out of the ordinary impinged on her consciousness. All was quiet with nothing at all visible to suggest that the day would not continue to unfold as it should. A few mare's tails were pasted on an impossible blue sky over the Water Tower and a fitful breeze had begun to tremble the higher leaves of the sparse clumps of greenery. There were few walkers about despite the generosity of the day.

It was a pretty house, pretty that is in contrast with the high, rectangular bulk of the Terrace next door and the harder lines of the property that all but touched on the other side. There was a gable to the front which lifted the neat stonework and the dressed and sculpted limestone mullions and dripstones. A turned limestone ballustrade topped the first floor bay and a symmetrical range of delicately worked foliate carvings placed the building in the top ranks of the stonemason's art. She had noticed that the name of the house was carved into the gateposts on either side of the path that curved to the front door.

It all seemed very normal as she walked up the path. A stone face stared at her impassively from the first floor until she passed under the semi-circular stone porch and reached for the knocker on the sturdy door, fast in it's shadow. She'd just been about to knock on the door for the second time when it happened. That strange stillness, the sudden slight shift in natural values. It was so subtle that she was almost unaware it was taking place until out of the strangely empty quiet came a cry; a cry so lost, so tragic, so appalling it clawed at her and sent her dropping against the door-frame. The door swung open. Angela, white faced, looked full at her. Jill started to pull herself up.

'My God, did you hear that?'

Angela exhaled slowly and nodded.

'I heard it yesterday, just before you came.'

She reached out to Jill.

'Are you all right?'

Jill had made an effort. She felt drained of all energy.

'It was exactly as she reacted when I told her of the news of David.'

Jill still felt faint.

'I've never heard anything like it before! It was dreadful.'

'I can only think that she wants you to know, to share with you in some way. I think you've got a part in this somehow although I confess I don't know what. Are you sure you're all right?'

Jill had taken a deep breath.

'Yes, okay I guess. Thanks.'

Angela tried a weak smile.

'I'll put the kettle on. Meanwhile, go on into the sitting room. You know where it is. I've put out some of her things.'

Jill had stopped.

'It's all right. After yesterday I think of you as one of the family. Really it's all right.'

Jill had walked into the elegant sitting room. A Pembroke table had been set up in the centre of the room with one flap extended. Two chairs were set to the table and a tea trolley was at hand. On the table were some books, some old newspapers, certificates, documents, photographs and an open box containing pieces of jewellery. At the edge of the table lay an ornate silver frame containing the photograph of a young girl of about seventeen. She was smiling up at whoever was taking the photograph and in the background Jill could make out the seaward end of a pier and part of a paddle-steamer just out of focus. She was, Jill had to admit, very much the same build as herself and as far as she could see, she had the same colouring. She had taken up the frame and carried it to the window to catch the light. The smiling face looked into hers and she knew that she wanted to know, to understand and to follow whatever it was that had drawn them together.

Angela came in.

'That's her.'

Jill had met her gaze.

'Yes, I know.'

'Sit down my dear and I'll try to do her justice.'

The cold of the winter morning had penetrated her clothing that, if she cared to admit, was more suited to travelling in cars than walking about on the Downs on a chill, frosty day. She'd been years away, back in her student days and Lord knows how long she'd been standing there. The house was over to her right and she knew that she'd have to go and look at it one last time. There was just that hint of something in the air that was strangely familiar, or, as she ruefully thought, familiarly strange. She'd have to wait and see.

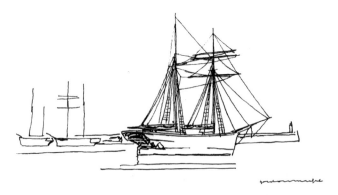

CHAPTER FOUR

Angela looked across the table, warmed yet saddened by the assembled memorabilia of her shared past. Unconsciously brushing back a strand of white curly hair from her forehead, she smiled and began.

'We were both born in the seaport town of Watchet. Myself in the December of 1907 and Annie in March 1917. We lived in a tall house in Anchor Street and I remember Annie was born in the little room over the hall. I had longed for a brother or sister so I was overjoyed when Mrs Sully came downstairs and announced that I had a sister. Father was away at the time on a trip to the London River and so I helped mother with all the thousand and one jobs that you need to do when a new baby arrives in the family. Mother was quickly up and about and it seemed only days before we were wheeling Annie proudly along the Esplanade.

Father came home the following week and we invited the neighbours and his brother captains to a party in order to 'wet the baby's head'. Father was Captain William Vickery, master and owner of the tops'l schooner Dancer. He'd been luckier than many of his fellow captains for he'd been at sea during the mighty gale that destroyed most of Watchet harbour at the tail end of 1900. Dancer had been in Ireland and had returned to find a smashed harbour and many vessels reduced to firewood. Our uncle's schooner Hematite was battered to pieces and there was very little left to sell on as recompense. It was a dreadful time for everyone in Watchet. However father was able to pick up on several contracts from his brother and so carry on.

Annie was born in the war years which were tricky times for all seafarers. In some ways it was a mixed blessing for there were rich pickings for those brave enough to take freights to France and hopefully dodge the U-boats. Shortly after Annie was born, the schooners Perriton and Florence Muspratt were sunk by submarines. Both were shelled and folk were killed. Both vessels had Minehead and Watchet crews on board and it was an anxious time until the survivors were able to come home. Losses from Bristol and Cardiff were higher; it was a lottery but the lucky ones collected enough from the high freights offered for coal voyages to France to enable them to invest or lay money aside for leaner times.

Of course father had some near misses. One of the problems was whether to go in a convoy or not. Mother always urged prudence and told father he was always to go in convoy but it took time to discharge the dozens of vessels that arrived in a convoy and independent craft could often make two voyages in the time it took to turn around in a convoy. In the early years it had been a matter of choice but as the U-boat campaign intensified, the convoy system came into being and it was the foolhardy skipper who risked his life and his vessel to sail alone. There were some captains who took no notice of official orders and remained obdurately self-reliant throughout the war. If they were lucky, they prospered.

On one occasion, father had not waited for the convoy. He'd sailed early in order to secure a return cargo from Plymouth after discharging at Paimpol. If he'd waited for the convoy to form up in Barry Roads he'd have missed the Plymouth cargo so he decided to go ahead of the other vessels and be discharged before the others arrived. All went well until on the return leg about ten miles off Start Point they sighted a U-boat on the surface. One minute the sea was clear and the next she was sitting there with her gun's crew closed up for action. It all happened so quickly hardly anyone had time to do anything but make away from her as fast as possible. The gun cracked. There was a puff of smoke that fell away downwind. A column of water leapt into the air just off the port bow. The submarine now had the range and father ordered the boat to be got ready and the upper tops'l set. The next shot sounded louder, the shell whistling low over the capstan and just missing the fores'l.

Knowing the fate of the Perriton only months before, father thought that this was the end and sent the Mate below for the few valuables on board. Just as they were at the point of heaving to and leaving her, the U-boat broke off the action and motored off on the surface. When not more than a cable from the Dancer the U-boat skipper shouted to father through a megaphone, pointing to the westward, "Saved by your Royal Navy this time Englishman, Good luck!" Then the noise of his heavy diesels picked up and he swept away with a salute.

No longer feeling helpless, the crew gave vent to their relief.

"You can bugger off!"

"An' you'd better do it quick or our lads'll have 'ee!"

Looking out to the westward they could make out the smoke and the bone in the teeth of a destroyer heading their way at speed. Dancer made it back to Watchet with the Plymouth cargo but it was a month or so before he told mother. Another day, when in a convoy this time, father was second in a line ahead to enter harbour when the ketch in front of him hit a mine in the buoyed channel. They were dreadful days and the risks were high and yet father and the others saw it as their part in the war. Other lads from the townships of West Somerset were in the minesweepers and at the front. No-one was idle.

After the war and after the frantic action of years, trade slackened and freights slumped. It became difficult for father to get cargoes. Many brave lads were glad to accept work where it was offered, however difficult or far from home. Captains were shipping as able seamen and we started to eat into the few pounds we had managed to put aside.

The twenties were quiet in Watchet. The number of vessels in the harbour dropped and it was a rare day when Dancer was in her home port. Father was working her out of Bristol, Cardiff and Swansea and that meant few home visits. Mother started helping out in a newsagents shop in Swain Street and so I was left to look after Annie for the greater part of the day. We became great friends even though I was that much older than she was.

I laugh when I think of it now, but we both had a passion for ice cream. Father started it before the war when we went to a fair at Dunster. He'd said, 'We'll see if we can find the hokey-pokey man.' Of course I hadn't the faintest idea who he was until father tracked him down and sang me a little song that goes like this,

Hokey pokey, penny a lump,
That's the stuff to make 'ee jump.
After that I was hooked on the stuff and spent far more

than I should have done. When I was left to look after Annie, we would try as hard as we could to persuade someone to buy us a couple of cream cornets from the little shop on the corner of Anchor Street and Swain Street. I used to eat mine but in those early days Annie used to wear hers.'

Jill grinned.

'I've got to admit I love it too.'

'As I said Watchet was a quiet place and there were no folk to be wary about. Lots of us children used to go for a paddle and a dip from West Street beach, not that it was much of a beach but we all enjoyed it. If we stayed or strayed further afield there were always the old captains or longshoremen, fishermen and boatmen who knew us and would shout out, "Time you youngsters was gettin' 'ome." Home meant thinking of something to eat and mother was a great one for making a feast out of a few bits and bobs. We used to have Fair Maids, that was grilled pilchards, and if we were lucky there was Stargazy pie with all the fishes heads peeping out of the crust. Mother used to tease Annie and say that the heads were for her.

The fishing was very important in those days and the Watchet fishermen were very careful not to tell anyone where the best fish were to be found. Mr Besley always said to father, "You don't want to give away your bread and butter." In those days fish was a valuable food and a little effort setting up nets on the foreshore could make a lot of difference. Some of the locals went for conger. Glattin' it was called and you went down with a dog and a great piece of iron known as a glattin' hook. I was always a little frightened of the conger as they could thrash about and give you a mighty whack. Annie was terrified one day when we came upon Mr Besley catching a huge one well down the beach below West Street. He'd shouted, "Stand well back!" and it was flexing and lashing about with its tail all in a frenzy. Even when we thought it was well and truly dead Mr Besley had warned us, "Clear off now, will 'ee! This is man's work." Nasty things congers. Best left in their pools. I don't like the taste of them anyway.'

Jill joined in.

'Never tried it.'

'Don't! Stick to salmon!'

She smiled and carried on.

'One of the highlights of our childhood was always to welcome father home from one of his voyages. Sometimes he'd leave Dancer in Bristol and come home by train for a few days. On the rarer occasions when he sailed Dancer home to Watchet the whole family would go down to the Eastern Breakwater to meet him. We'd crowd into his small cabin and have some dark coffee sweetened with condensed milk and if we were lucky there'd be a present for us from Bristol. He'd then proudly show us over the vessel and point out any new additions that made her tidier, smarter, or more seaworthy. She was an old girl, built in Bideford in 1868 but built well and good for many more years yet. She was also a good sailer. Father had never considered having an engine fitted though he was beginning to realise that vessels without engines, however good they might be, were no match for the steamers and the auxiliary ketches and motor barges that were taking the majority of the cargoes still going by sea. I suppose, looking back now, they were sad days really. We were looking at the very end of the sailing ship era and very soon there would be none left.

In the summer of 1927, we both went with father and helped to handle Dancer on a trip to Ireland. She was then running without tops'ls and was rigged as a ketch. The idea was that with us on board father could manage with himself and a mate and so save on crew for a month or two. At first I worked with the mate, learning how to steer and mark the points of land as we made down the Channel. Annie, only ten, but able, was appointed cook, coffee maker and general deckhand. The first few days were quite hard as we were unused to the fewer hours sleep and the motion of the vessel tended to make us a bit queasy. However after three days we settled down to a routine that seemed to work well for everyone. Father was full of jokes and good humour and never seemed to notice that there was not a great deal of work done. The mate, Billy Escott was patient and helpful and soon he felt confident to leave me at the wheel for hours at a time. Annie soon came up with some of the old favourites from home and we all enjoyed kettle broth, potato jowdle, and other exotic items provided they could be made from potatoes, onions, bread, bacon and corned beef or fish. The variations were imaginative and born of long practice. The snag was when it came to running out of one or two of the main ingredients or them going mouldy or stale. Then it was a challenge.

That summer went well and the four of us made several trips to Ireland including one up the Shannon to Limerick which was lovely. Father knew lots of folk, agents and local carriers and we had some splendid evenings with music and singing lasting well into the night.

'Don't get the wrong idea,' said father. 'It isn't always like this. It's mainly for your benefit, so don't go telling your mother that I'm living the life of Riley when I come to Ireland.'

As I said, that summer was one to remember, the weather was mainly fine with light westerlies, the make-shift crew coped well and there were no mishaps except perhaps when I dropped a bucket of grease from the gaff and narrowly missed Billy below on the deck. He wasn't very polite.

Annie blossomed. She loved the sea and when not below preparing food for us all or the endless mugs of steaming coffee, she'd come up on deck and help out with washing down or cleaning brass and paintwork. Above all she loved the wide skies, the rocking horizon, the ever changing shades of shifting green ocean and the cries of the seabirds as they dived for the scraps she threw over the side, not that there were many for we were as hungry as they were. Like us, Annie soon coloured up and leaned down with the fresh sea air and exercise. All too soon, the holiday was over and Annie had to start back at school. It was fourteen for leaving in those days although attendance was pretty poor at harvest time or when fruit picking came along. As September came in, Dancer made up for Lundy and then along the Exmoor coast past the North Foreland and Hurlstone Point, to lay up in Blue Anchor Bay to wait for the tide. The next day, we made Watchet harbour and the crew split up to go their separate ways. Annie cried.'

'Did many girls go to sea in those days?'

'Oh yes, though often finding life quite hard. There were many women at sea through the twenties and thirties and several husband and wife teams that ran vessels between them. Anyone who jibed that it was unlucky to take a woman to sea got short shrift and a right mouthful to go with it. In Gloucester Docks many of the motor barges and narrow-boats were crewed by women and very good hands they were too. After my experience, father decided to sign me on permanently and so on the next trip I went as AB and cook, Billy as mate and father as skipper. Of course he only had to pay Billy but my needs in those days were minimal so it didn't matter whether I had anything or not. Annie felt very left out of things but as mother continued to work at the newsagents there was plenty to do at home after school was over.

For me, life was full. There was work on board and work in harbour. Trying to be cook and work on deck was a juggling act and when I thought the day's work was done, there was cargo to load or dig out. Coal was the worst. It got everywhere, in you ears, up your nose and your clothes became black. Father liked a tidy ship so after loading or discharging coal, the whole vessel had to be cleaned from stem to stern. Yes, life was pretty full. I didn't see much of Annie until the Christmas when we made every effort to get back into Watchet. Two other vessels made it home that year and father said it was a grand sight to see ketches and smacks in the harbour again all dressed up with fir-trees lashed to their top-masts.

Dancer needed some repairs to be carried out so after Christmas father moved her up to the Cot-of-the-Quay out of the way so that the shipwrights could get at her. It was not serious but it meant laying out more of our meagre reserves. However it did give me a chance to get out and about with Annie for a week or so while father fretted about the loss of time when he could be earning his living. We ranged up and down the coast looking for ammonites, alabaster and dunnage off ships. It was surprising what came ashore from ships though we never found anything exciting. The weather turned quite nasty in the January of 1928 and put an end to our wanderings so for the rest of the break and before school started again for Annie, we cooked up some of the dishes that I'd found on my trips away. Mother was quite taken with our 'oggies' which, of course, I'd discovered in Plymouth. We'd soon given them an added ingredient or two and they made a tasty meal for all of us.

January was also Annie's birthday and so we had a party in Anchor Street and all Annie's friends came. Billy came too and so did several of the old captains who were uncles and grandparents. It was one of those traditional parties with singing to the piano, all those lovely old songs that you never hear any more. Billy had a lovely voice and sang 'The Bristol Sailor' on his own. Afterwards, the menfolk got their pipes out and enjoyed a drop of Arnold and Hancocks which always went down well when the old lads were at home. Mother seemed to be very content to see her family around her and although she said little, her eyes spoke volumes.

That was to be the last real happy time we all enjoyed in our old home for as the year grew older, the fates seemed to line up against us.'

'Why, what happened?'

'It all started with the next trip on which father had agreed to take a cargo of coal to a little beach half a mile to the westward of Dingle in Dingle Bay. We left Watchet for the Eley River on a Friday. Now, very few sailors like to sail on a Friday because everyone will tell you it's unlucky. Sailing on a Friday with a woman on board was asking for it, or so the doom merchants declared. But father had arranged to load on the Saturday morning and so we duly slipped and proceeded out of Watchet harbour late on the Friday night with a sharp nor'easterly giving us a short choppy sea and little comfort. The wind was contrary and so, after tacking about off the Culvers we made Barry Roads by the early hours and anchored to wait for first light. At daybreak, the wind went round to the east and we managed to get into the Eley River. There, we loaded under the tips, cleared up the mess and having a good wind we ran down the Channel making near seven or eight knots. It's a pretty straight run to Mizen Head and we were doing very well despite the intense cold and the occasional soaking. As I said we were doing well and were thinking that we should soon be picking up Mizen Head when the wind started to increase. It wasn't a case of slowly building up but it swept up in squall after squall bringing flurries of snow and sleet with it. The seas built up too until one minute we were being carried forward on the giant crests and the next we found ourselves pitching and jolting in the huge dark troughs between. It was becoming frightening.

By supper-time, the wind speed practically doubled and shifted back to the nor'east. It was now blowing a full gale. Father ordered the mains'l and the heads'l to be shortened and all other sail to be taken in. By now it was so cold we could hardly move and the canvas was frozen into iron. It took the two of us over two hours to secure her for the storm that was, without doubt, going to have its way with us. Hoving to was impossible. The only sensible course was to run before the weather and hope that it would blow itself out before too long.

For three days we ran out into the Atlantic, taking it in turns to take the wheel. There was little thought of getting anything warm inside us. A handful of bread or an onion was all we could snatch. The galley fire was awash, our bunks were awash, the cargo was taking water and we were in trouble. On the third day Dancer started to break up. The bulwarks went first; just swept away clean leaving no trace. Next went the boat despite being doubly lashed down. Father then detailed Billy to the pump and we took the wheel together preferring to have something to hang on to for great seas were sweeping across the deck and anything that was not securely bolted down was swept away. Dancer was now almost submerged what with the weight of water below and the welter of white about her deck. Father was shaking his head.

"She'll not take much more of this!"

We were all tiring; too cold to think and too weary to work her much longer. Yet we couldn't leave her, there was no boat and if there had been we could never have launched it in such a sea. Our only chance of survival lay in sticking it out until the gale blew itself out.

In the middle watch, just when our hopes were at the lowest level, the wind dropped quite suddenly and the sea moderated to a sullen swell. We had survived. The pumping had to go on because the timbers were strained but at least we could light a fire and get some hot coffee down us. It was a case of one pump, one steer and one cook until things improved. With the first distant line of dawn under the breaking clouds, the wind took up again from the west. The freak easterly had gone. We put the helm over and turned her around. Our estimated position was, so father said, about three hundred miles west of Ireland and a lot of hard work to see us in safely.'

Jill swallowed. It was difficult to think of this lady undergoing such an ordeal and surviving.

'Then what?'

'Five days later we sighted The Skelligs off the south-west tip of Ireland and made up for Dingle Bay. When we got in, we were surprised to receive an enthusiastic welcome. They laid on a warm meal for us and a carpenter came on board to see what could be done in the way of emergency repairs. Apparently two local vessels had been reported lost in the gale and another had been wrecked within the bay despite it being sheltered from the east. We were a curiosity; the vessel that had survived the gale. When he was rested, father surveyed the damage. We'd lost about a third of the cargo and the rest was still waterlogged. The bulwarks could be replaced as could the boat but father reckoned that the damage to the timbers would need looking at by a shipwright to assess whether any major repairs would need doing.

My hands had been so cold for so long they were not able to do any work. I couldn't even hold a knife and fork! Billy said he ached from head to toe but of the three of us, he was the fittest and strongest. A few whiskies soon had him right for anything. Father worried me as he was not a youngster any longer and the strain of being responsible for all our lives had told on him. He was far from steady and the local doctor told him that he needed to rest.

It was the local captains who found a practical though

painful solution to our problems. We had virtually lost the cargo, were uninsured and had extensive repairs ahead of us and no real reserves in hand. They said, "Any vessel that could survive that gale must be a tough little craft. We'll buy her off you as she stands." And so it happened that after much pacing and many sighs, father decided to sell her. It was heart rending for him. Dancer had been his life for more years than he cared to remember. She had seen him through the war years and through the leaner times that had followed. He hardly dared to go home without her. Still, he realised that he would probably never get a better offer and from a pragmatic point of view it would set him up until he could find a berth on another vessel.

So it was that we came home to Watchet by train after sending mother a telegram from Taunton.

"Oh, William," she smiled, "it's high time you gave up struggling to make a living out of a sailin' vessel. Those times have passed. Now you get yourself a nice comfortable job on a steamer. They're the future now. But first, get yourself fit and well and have that rest you've promised yourself."

So for a short while we were a family once more. I decided that I would not go to sea again but try to find a decent job closer to home. Annie was delighted to have us back and soon it was just like old times and we were sharing everything together, even the odd ice cream.

Father did manage to get himself a job, rather a good one as it turned out. He went as mate on the Bristol steamer Domino and after a month was appointed master. Mother could now leave the newsagents and I could take my time looking for a suitable position. It was still a case of father coming home occasionally by train but it slowly became clear to all of us that a move to Bristol would be sensible. And so it came to be that father was looking out for a house where we could all be together.

This must be awfully boring for you,' said Angela with a concerned tilt of the head. 'Let's break for a cup of tea and you can look at some of these photographs. Look, here's Dancer in Watchet harbour and here's father and Billy on the Esplanade.'

She got up.

'I know that we are talking about my little sister but I felt that you ought to know the family background. To be worried for someone at sea was very much a part of her life from the beginning.'

'No, please don't think I'm bored. On the contrary, I'm fascinated. I've been to Watchet once and fished from the harbour. No, please go on.'

Angela smiled and continued to move on her way to the kitchen.

'I could do with a cup of tea.'

Jill reached out and picked up the photo' of the vessel that had survived the great gale of 1928. She stared at it.

'Who would think that a simple picture could hide such a story?'

Angela bit her bottom lip.

'There's worse to come.'

CHAPTER FIVE

'That summer we left the Anchor Street house and moved to Cumberland Road Bristol. Several other captains lived in the road and it was convenient for father to get to Domino's regular berth only a short walk away. Mother soon adjusted to the move and welcomed the change in status. There was a big difference between being a struggling master's wife in Watchet and being a captain's wife in Bristol. Of course she missed all her old friends but made many new ones who introduced her to a far wider selection of shops and services. Not having to go out to work was also a blessing. Annie didn't fare so well. It was a wrench for her to leave her friends at St Decuman's School and to be plunged into a much larger city school where she was an outsider. She wasn't bullied but she found it difficult to break into friendship patterns that had been established for some years. I think that in the end she gave up trying and just concentrated on getting through each day as best she could. She was a bright, sensitive girl with plenty of imagination and did well at everything she found in front of her. Her teachers thought well of her and one in particular, a Mrs Wring, used to encourage her to write and for a while Annie began to keep a family diary. I found it once and she read me some of her thoughts and observations. They were good and certainly better than I could have done.

Well, life soon settled down in our new house. It was a roomy, sunny building, terraced of course, with a bay window on the ground and first floors. There were five bedrooms if you included the attic and mother soon had the place looking shipshape. Father was home every ten days or so for a visit and stayed until he was due to sail which was usually about three days. Sometimes he stayed longer if they were busy in the City Docks and Domino had to wait for a further day to load. Oh, there was something else about the house; it was supposed to be haunted. The neighbours on the right of us had been there for over thirty years and told us that our house had always been a seafarer's home and that it was haunted by the ghost of a sea captain. I think that mother took this with a pinch of salt, father laughed and said that he'd be in good company then and I certainly never saw anything unusual there. Annie however said that on three occasions she had been awakened by a rough hand shaking her shoulder. Each time it had been exactly five thirty in the morning. I remember mentioning this to our neighbour and she said, "Oh, didn't I tell you, that's what the old sea captain does. He shakes his crew when the vessel is due to sail." I never told Annie this and I don't think she mentioned it again. Perhaps the ghost, if there was one, realised that no-one was going to take any notice of him.

As for me, it was time to look for a job and I looked in the Evening Post each night to see if there was anything I could do. I felt after my seafaring days there was very little I couldn't tackle but I didn't want to go into any of the factories or warehouses. In the end I saw an advertisement for a shop assistant where some nautical knowledge would be of advantage. I was intrigued and the next day went along to the address which turned out to be on the other side of the Floating Harbour on Mardyke Wharf. The firm was a small chandlers supplying everything for the modern, and not so modern, vessel. The owner, a Mr

Scase, tried to catch me out to prove whether or not I really did have any knowledge of the sea.

"Tell me young lady," he said, lifting his chin, "How many ropes do a sailin' vessel carry?"

This was one of the questions that father used to ask so I was able to answer,

Two, a boat rope and a bell rope, all the rest are stays, sheets, lifts and braces.

"'Ave you been to sea or something?"

Yes, with my father on the Dancer.

"Right, one more question, what's the difference between the deck watch an' the watch on deck?"

This was another of the catch questions that every AB is taught and so I could answer that one too.

The deck watch is the ships chronometer, though father only ever used his watch and chain, and the watch on deck is the crew not lucky enough to be turned in down below. We worked the ship with three of us and so we were on deck, so to speak, all the time.

Mr Scase nodded.

"You've bin to sea all right. Can you tell a bit o' manilla from sisal or paraffin from white spirit?"

I should hope so, I replied, or we'd soon be in trouble!

"Right," said Mr Scase, "you starts tomorrow at eight. I shan't always be here so you'll have to get on with it. Do right by me an' I'll see you all right. Okay?"

And that was that. I was a working girl. I later discovered that he knew all about Dancer and the gale and how we had kept her afloat with a makeshift crew. He proved a good employer, always paid regularly and we managed to keep the ship afloat when many other small suppliers were going out of business. As he said, he wasn't always there; he'd be in one pub or another but that was where a lot of business was done in those days. The skippers used to come on down to me with their orders to be made up for collection by a member of the crew before sailing. I stayed there for some years.

In the next years Annie blossomed into a charming, mischievous and captivating young lady. She found a new friend during her last year at school and the two of them used to dress up in the height of fashion and parade up to the Centre on a Saturday. Her friend had a portable gramophone and most evenings they danced to the same three or four records until poor mother didn't know whether to laugh or cry. She was happy enough now she'd settled down after the move and was looking forward to leaving school and starting work.'

Jill smiled.

'Things haven't changed much then.'

'Ah, but it really was harder then. There was not a lot of choice in the early thirties and most youngsters were well pleased to get any kind of work. Father considered himself extremely lucky to have landed the job he had for many of his contemporaries had to be satisfied with far less. Mother seemed well settled and of course I was like a pig in muck among all the gear and tackle in the sheds at the wharf. My job was the easiest of all and I was left well alone to manage the store. I even sold a mast-head light to father one day.

Annie's choice of job didn't surprise us. She found it on her own and went up to town for an interview before we had the chance to voice our advice. She'd landed a position as a trainee cook and kitchen-hand at the Randolf Hotel in St Nicholas Street and she was due to start at the beginning of the next month. She expected it to be tough at first and was well prepared for the hard work that would be required of her.

"However tough," she laughed, "it won't be as bad as sharing scraps with the seagulls and washing up in sea water."

As it turned out it was every bit as hard as she had thought. She found herself in a large, noisy, frantic explosion of action where folk seemed to be engaged in a dozen tasks at the same time. It was all heat, clatter and shouts with a lot of coming and going in between. As she expected, her first job was to clean and wash up a great pile of dirty pans and dishes and as soon as that was done there was another pile. Her apron was soon soaked through and the sweat was running down her face but at the end of the day she remained undaunted. As the hours had passed, she'd noticed that one or two glances had shot her way and she wondered what was up. At half past six, her shift was over and the evening staff took over. Her last task was to scrub down the chopping boards and draining boards and mop the floor over. She'd thought,

"Not as bad as cleaning Dancer after lying under the coal tips!"

Father's training had stood her in good stead and she felt that whatever they could throw at her, she'd do her best to master it. Before she left, the lady in charge called her over.

"You're a hard little worker to be sure. Worth two of the idle little madam we sacked last month. Would you really like to learn how to cook?"

"I would indeed," replied Annie.

"Well, we're not a big concern but we've got a good reputation. There's folk here that have been in the game for a long time and their knowledge is worth having. Whether it's sauces or courses, sweets or treats, you'll learn it all here."

"When can I start learning?"

"You'll be on the vegetables by the end of the month and next month you'll start to learn puddings. We're famous for our puddings. Oh, and there's a tradition here, you're entitled to a pint of ale a day while you're fourteen rising to three pints a day when you're sixteen. Write what you want on the slate and the pot-boy will bring it down for you."

Annie came home that night exhausted but well pleased. She persevered and worked hard and as the months went by she advanced through each department learning a host of useful hints and tips as she went. The cook-in-charge was a Mrs Paterson, they didn't have a master-chef, and she had been at Warwick Castle for years and ran the place like the professional she was, with an eye for detail and a flair for excellence.

There's not much I can say about the next few years. We all worked hard and were glad to do so for, as I said, they were lean years and there were many good folk out of work. Ships were idle and crews laid off and most days you could see groups of seamen and dock-workers lining the Narrow Quay hoping that they might catch some work on an incoming freighter. There used to be a notice board there by the swing-bridge that announced the incoming vessels and their berths and there was always the early bird there to glean the information. Even those in regular employment had their wages cut and father suffered a loss of thirty percent per calendar month for a while. It was the same for everyone and we all got on with it.

By 1936, things started to get a bit better and we began to think of having a holiday away. Mother had made a few trips back to Watchet but it was more difficult for us for our jobs were valuable and time was something we didn't ask for. Yet as the nation's fortunes slowly improved, that sense of urgency relaxed a bit and the larger firms and businesses began to give a little. Yet I suppose it was just when the larger firms were beginning to see the light at the end of the tunnel that small concerns like Scasey's were coming to the end of their usefulness. Scasey had been staying away longer and longer from the business and the reason was that he was having to range much further away from his regular haunts to gain orders. The sad day inevitably came in the early summer of 1936 when Scasey told me that he was closing the shed for good and that I could take whatever I wanted for myself in lieu of wages which he could no longer pay. After a long look around the ancient and familiar stock I selected a cabin oil lamp and went home to consider where I might be needed in the future.

They say when one door closes another opens and so it was that I had the stroke of luck that was to become a blessing to both Annie and myself. Looking again in the Evening Post, I saw a small advertisement that looked promising. It said: Lady requires a live-in companion who is able to be both practical and supportive. So I applied and received by return post an invitation to visit this house and meet the owner Miss Peath John. She turned out to be a lively, interesting, eccentric and intelligent old dear who had suffered a serious injury to her right arm when living in India before the war. She had dispensed with the services of several helpers over the years and was almost in despair at finding someone honest who didn't seek to remove things from her house or pry into her affairs. I remember suggesting that it might be a good idea if we got to know each other first and that, as I wasn't in a hurry, we leave decisions until we were both sure that the position would suit us. I remember also suggesting that she write to father and to Mr Scase in order to verify my honesty and character. This was duly done and over the next fortnight I visited regularly and discovered to my satisfaction that I truly liked her and thought that I could very well perform all the duties she required. Her story would make a fascinating book on its own for she had lived in both China and India and had had some fantastic adventures. However, the outcome was that I would move into the house, run it and see to all the practicalities. Alternate week-ends would be free and provision for an annual holiday would be made.

We soon became great friends and it grew into one of those relationships where mutual trust and companionship overcome any barriers that might be thrown up by an employer-employee situation. I was to learn that her young man had been drowned in the Ganges whilst attempting to rescue a child and also that her father had been a Lieutenant General in the Indian Army. Her injury had been caused by a sword cut but she'd always stopped short the story at that point as it had been a particularly shocking and traumatic incident which was painful to recount even after a gap of many years. Oh yes, we were close enough for me to give her a friendly squeeze or a hand up when she needed it and close enough for me to share some of my fears and thoughts about the world with her. She proved an excellent employer and I know that she became genuinely fond of me as I was of her. I recollect one particularly hot evening after I'd been there for a few months Miss Peath John called me to this very room and said,

"How much do you think you should give someone if you wished them to be loyal to you?"

I remember answering. I don't think that you should give them anything. Loyalty is earned through respect and that is the legacy of trust.

"Thank you," she answered. "That's a very helpful answer. Now, what do you think I should do with all this?" indicating a pile of documents and papers on the table.

That depends on what they are. I'm afraid I don't know what you have there.

"Money, shares, land and property, all left to me from my father's estate. You see, I'm quite wealthy but prefer to live here quietly and simply. I have no time for gadding about or being flamboyant. My needs are few so what do I do with all this?"

I think I would place it where it could bring the maximum amount of support or help to needy folk. There are so many who are in need through no fault of their own, especially in these difficult times.

"And how would I know who they were?"

There's the difficulty. You'd want to know which charities are meeting genuine needs and which are only paying lip service to the cause and taking out large sums for administration or officer's salaries. From my experience the Shipwrecked Mariners Society and the Lifeboat Institution are worthwhile bodies that are doing a great deal of good.

"If I was to ask you to help me support one of these charities in the future would you do so?"

Of course I would.

"And be discreet, so that no-one else would know?"

You can count on my support.

"Thank you."

I'd almost forgotten that we'd had this conversation but some years later I had cause to remember it and understand that she was far more perceptive than I'd given her credit for.

In 1937, mother, Annie and I went on the first real holiday of our lives. Father was away with Domino and sent a telegram to wish us well. Our destination was Minehead and we'd booked into Stargroves with Mr and Mrs Harrison in Quay Street. I suppose we were all excited but Annie was over the moon. It was the first time that she had gone back to West Somerset since the move and she was looking forward to seeing all the familiar places once more. Mother had made several trips and I had been down to Watchet twice on business to the Swedish steamer Gertrud to deliver supplies. I suppose we both wanted this to be special for Annie. She'd worked so hard and we were very proud of her. She was still at the hotel and they thought very highly of her.'

'So holidays were pretty special then?

Angela nodded.

'So special we remembered every moment and treasured them. Shortly after eight-o-clock on that Saturday morning we all went by bus with our suitcases to Temple Meads Station and lined up with hundreds of others for the early morning express to the westcountry calling at Taunton, Exeter, Dawlish, Teignmouth and stations to Cornwall. We were to change at Taunton and take the branch line for Minehead leaving from Platform Two. Although we had come from Somerset it was still magical to be there on the platform waiting for the train to whisk us away in clouds of bright steam along the talkative metals to our holiday destination. Father had recommended we stay with Mr Harrison as he knew him from his visits to Minehead in Dancer. He said that Mr Harrison had a splendid motor and would be able to take us on some trips around the area.

At eight forty-five precisely the train thundered into the station causing a sway of passengers to reel back from the platform's edge. For a moment or two it was all bustle as everyone heaved and clambered aboard with their cases, bags, grips and parcels. Then the whistle shrilled and the first throaty chuff sent a jet of white high into the canopy above. We were off.

We all managed to find seats in the same compartment and after hefting our cases onto the rack above, settled down to the lulling, reassuring rhythm of the wheels as they tut-tutted and chattered along the lines to the accompaniment of the repeated looping patterns of the telegraph wires that swept in an everlasting wave alongside the carriage windows. On board it was all chatter and laughter, all eager anticipation as the holiday began to bite. Such a simple thing is catching a train and yet at that moment when it begins to move there is that excitement that is hard to describe. Well that was the way of it in those far off days

Taunton came all too soon and we were off again down the platform to find the Minehead bay. The train was waiting but this time it was no express with a mighty locomotive but five carriages pulled by a meek little tank engine. After what seemed an age in which we peeped into more than one compartment to gaze at the displayed photographs above the bench seats another great express rumbled into the station and ejected its band of holiday-makers. This time there were more for the Minehead line and we were soon well packed in and awaiting the start of the last leg of the journey. Annie had the seat by the window and she couldn't resist the temptation to release the heavy leather strap that let down the window panel and lean out.

"The guard's getting in and he's waving his flag. We're off!"

And indeed we were, slowly at first but gradually gathering speed out of the town, under the road- bridge by Taunton School and along the sidings towards Norton Fitzwarren. Isn't it strange how all the little details of a simple thing like a railway journey can come back to you after so many years? I remember how mother was anxious that Annie pull up the window to stop the smuts coming in and how Annie kept sticking her head out and giving us a running commentary on what she could see.

The stations rolled by under the brown brows of the Quantocks and the Brendons each name being repeated by the passengers as they counted off the stops to where they were going. Each was evocative of its history and surroundings and carried a romantic aura that was both shared and personal. Stogumber, Crowcombe, Williton and then our own dear Watchet where the train leaned around the cut in the rusty cliffs to reveal the harbour and the sea like the curtains being pulled back on a favourite play. The Gertrud was at the Eastern Breakwater and the Rushlight was under the harbour wall in her usual berth. There was an air of activity about the place. I remember several folk waved as they waited to cross the line as we slowly rumbled to a halt at the platform. A dozen of the passengers stepped down from the train, some goods were loaded, then there was a hoot from the little engine and we were off again under the railway bridge and on to Kentsford where we stopped to allow a train to pass in the other direction. It was packed with holiday-makers all at the end of their time. I thought, Here's an example of happiness going one way and sadness going the other. They are all at the end of their holiday and are taking their memories with them and we are all anticipation of what might lie ahead. Folk waved from each train and in a moment or so their train had glided by, there was a jolt, the two worlds were separated, and we were on our way again. Washford was next and no-one alighted. A green bus motored by on the road to our left and we wondered who would get to Minehead first. At Blue Anchor the sea came into view again and we could see a few caravans parked in the field next to the beach. After stopping to allow a dozen or so folk to leave the train and a motor-coach to pass up the road by the level-crossing, the gates slowly swung open and we puffed valiantly on past cows standing like statues in the flat green fields as the smoke from the engine billowed about them. Then it was over another level-crossing and into Dunster station. Annie looked out of the window for the millionth time.

"I can see Minehead straight up the line, we're nearly there!"

Conygar's tower rose above the wooded cone of Dunster's western extremity and the lesser Penny Hill crouched under Hopcott and the sweep of russet moors led on to Minehead's familiar headland and the hotels and houses that clustered at its foot. We were indeed nearly there. As the train tripped and skipped the last clattering mile the passengers all started to move at the same time. Bags and cases were lifted down, coats and parcels tucked under arms and carrier bags and handbags slipped over wrists so that as the long platform rose to meet us we were all ready for the rush to secure some form of transport to our various hotels and boardinghouses. Then as the train squeaked to a halt and the final hiss of steam announced the end of our journey, our troop of intrepid travellers clambered from the train to the accompaniment of the slamming of dozens of doors and set off to the ticket barrier and the taxis, buses and cars waiting in the station yard. We need not have worried about transport for Mr Harrison was waiting in the yard with a big black Wolseley motor and after enquiring if we were the party for Stargroves, took our cases and drove us the short distance along the sea front to Quay Street.

Our first real holiday had begun and why it proved to be so significant to this story I shall tell you.

CHAPTER SIX

During the five or so minutes that it took to drive along the sea front to Quay Street and park outside Stargroves, Mr Harrison was already explaining that he would be available should we wish to take his motor on any trips around the area. He seemed a friendly, open and warm-hearted man and we all took to his smiling ways and thought we might indeed take up his offer when we had settled in. Stargroves was an ancient, whitewashed, quay-side house with comfortable, smallish beamed rooms and uneven floors. It was obviously very old and was part of the quayside community of buildings that were once engaged in seafaring in one form or another. The house reminded mother of the Anchor Street property but I thought it was closer to the cottages at the bottom of West Street albeit a lot bigger. Just over the sea wall at the Quay head opposite lay the ketch Emma Louise. Father had often been in harbour with the Emma Louise and knew the Rawle brothers who owned and sailed her. Like the Dancer she was also kept in tip-top condition. Father had said that steady local contracts had enabled her to keep going when many others had no work to do. It was a tonic to see her there. She had obviously just entered the harbour on the tail end of the tide and would have to wait for the next tide to move up to the crane for unloading. I thought I'd like to go and have a look at her, out of professional interest you understand. She still had her topmast and jib-boom so had probably not yet been fitted with an engine.

After settling into two rooms, mother in the smaller

room and Annie and I in the larger one, we tidied ourselves up and set off along the promenade towards the
town. We knew the town fairly well having lived in
nearby Watchet for most of our childhood and of course
mother had been born locally and so knew all the towns
and villages along the coast in some detail. However,
we were now on holiday and were determined to be holiday-makers and enjoy ourselves.

About half-way along the promenade we heard music
and we soon caught up with it in the Jubilee Gardens
band-stand at the bottom of the Avenue. A lady was playing a squeezebox and two others were accompanying her
with a banjo and a guitar. It was a catchy Irish jig and
played with some energy and spirit. There was certainly
a crowd listening beyond the wooden trellis that had been
erected to enclose the audience and block out the traffic;
and those that hadn't paid to sit down on the deckchairs
within the area. We stayed a while and then looked out
the notice board that detailed the weeks programme. Miss
Ivy Benson and her Girls Band were the main players
but guest appearances by other bands and ensembles were
advertised. Thursday promised to be a good day with
Dorothy Holbrook and the Harmony Hussars appearing
in the evening.

"We should go," said Annie.

Let's see what else there is, the Queen's Hall always
has a visiting company. They might have a good play on
this week.

"Yes, and there's a cinema, a new one in the Avenue,
they'll have the latest film to see."

"Right," said mother, "lets do it all. We'll make a list,
a plan and set out all the things we want to do and if any

one of us sees anything that they think we'd all enjoy they can write it down on the plan."

We moved on past the Bungalow Café and the Strand Café towards the Queen's Hall but the temptation was too strong to pass Fortes Ice Cream Parlour and we all trooped in and ordered knickerbocker glories.

"Now the holiday has begun!" smiled Annie. And we all agreed, it had.

In retrospect I suppose that there is always that golden edge to the world of yester-year. I couldn't tell you whether the sun was shining or whether it was dull. Certainly we all re-lived each happy moment of those pre-war years, the more so because the war was to cast such a dark shadow over the years to come. We had no inkling of that in 1936 and from a personal point of view couldn't see that Herr Hitler was intent on more than bringing a confidence back into a war ravaged Germany. Perhaps we were innocents but I think that most of us ordinary folk were in those days. It was hard enough to keep afloat let alone worry about the plight of nations.

Just past the Queen's Hall we could see the new, white painted swimming pool that had been widely advertised as the finest in the west but we turned about and made our way back, past the Beach Hotel and up the tree lined Avenue to the Regal Cinema to see what film was on during the week. The stills, displayed in glass cases on either side of the main entrance, were advertising Maurice Chevalier in The Merry Widow as the main feature with a travelogue about Norway in support. The film had been in Bristol the previous month and we hadn't bothered to go and see it then so we crossed that off the list. Across the road some notice boards were announcing tours by Scarlet Pimpernel motor-coaches to local beauty spots and resorts. Parked outside, apparently waiting to load passengers for an afternoon drive, was a huge shiny scarlet coach with its canvas roof folded back. Annie walked over and read its number, AYC 926 and said it was a Leyland Lion and we should all go for a ride into the countryside on this lion's back. We all agreed that we should add at least one of these tours to the plan. It was all quite exciting. There was so much to do. There were motor-car trips, boat trips, theatre visits, concerts, walks, steamer trips, cream teas, deck-chairs on the beach and of course lots of ice-cream cornets. Wonderful.

By tea-time, we were making our way back through the Blenheim Gardens towards Quay Street. Our plan was already taking shape and we felt as happy as we'd ever been. There was country dancing going on to a pair of fiddles under the trees as we walked through and a sprightly gentleman was warmly inviting folk to join in. The fiddles were being played by a very old lady and gentleman who were real entertainers of the old school. We stopped for a while. It all added to the enjoyment of the day.

After tea, not a cream one, at Stargroves we agreed on the evening's entertainment. Quite simple really. There was going to be quite a high tide at nine-o-clock and we thought that we'd walk right around the promenade, past the new pool and on along sandy Warren Road to Warren House and the beginning of the golf course. Then we'd turn around and walk back on the shingle by the beach huts and back to the promenade where perhaps we might watch the tide dashing over the sea wall. That was the plan.'

Jill smiled.

'I still love that. It's really spectacular sometimes isn't it?'

Angela nodded and continued.

'We didn't start off until eight and by then the tide was already far up and washing about among the flotsam under the wall in a froth. There was very little beach left and only the banks of shingle that lay piled against the stone groynes were still out of reach of the waves. As we walked along the front, there was again music from the Jubilee Gardens and lights in every room of the Metropole Hotel and the Esplanade buildings. Elsewhere the soft fingers of dusk were reaching into the darkening recesses between the hotels and houses rising black against a pale orange and azure sky. All the deck-chairs had been cleared away and stacked in a huge pile opposite the wooden stairs near the ice-cream and gift kiosk. Coloured lights were hanging in loops between the street lamps and there was an air of magic in the air. Beyond the toll-bar and Fortes Ice Cream Parlour, the road continued to the swimming pool where the glow within flung up the high diving boards in relief upon the darkening night. Beyond, the sea wall gave way to timber pilings nailed horizontally to posts driven into the shingle and the beach huts began. It was growing dimpsy and here, out of the lights, walking the sandy lane between the huts and the wide stretch of the marshes set with willow and tamarisk trees, it was quieter.

Over the sea to the east a large moon emerged from a band of hazy cloud and crept slowly up the sky, growing to a yellow maturity and dropping its cloak, dancing and glittering all down the broken ocean to our feet. And so we turned back to retrace our steps and climbed up to the shingle ridge to walk back along the top among the other folk that were watching the tide coming in. It was not quite high tide yet, perhaps another ten minutes or so, yet further along the front, plumes of water were jetting into the sky and we could hear shrieks of laughter as some spectators were getting very wet. Along the front the sea was the main attraction. A great tide, its crests rolling in like wind across a cornfield, was lurching up against the sea wall opposite the Queen's Hall and retreating as swiftly seawards. Then as the two crests met, the water leapt like a dancer leaving the spray to scatter down in a welter of sea drizzle. It was marvellous. We walked on fascinated and stood with dozens of others to wait for that special moment when the tide would reach its maximum height before relenting and slipping back exhausted into the Channel.'

Jill's eyes shone.

'The road was streaming, one or two unfortunate and perhaps unwise open motors had retreated to a dryer spot. Some sea-wrack and small pebbles lay scattered across the pavement. We were standing, admittedly quite foolishly, a little too close to the sea wall. We should have noticed the ground was wet but were too intent on gazing seawards to see a ton or so of white water rise forty feet into the air.

All at once a blue-clad young man with straw coloured hair snatched Annie's arm and propelled her out of harm's way. The sea flailed down and we were drenched. Annie turned alarmed, then relieved, burst into laughter.

"You saved me!"

Instantly I knew. In that salt-soaked frozen second it

happened for Annie. Like a bright snapshot the picture was pasted into our lives and something had changed for ever.

Perhaps it was her face as she turned, her mouth open and her eyes wide or perhaps it was the young man's arm still outstretched in mid air as he released her, safe from the descending weight of sandy water that even now was swirling down the grating.

That was the moment Annie fell in love and she knew it. The moment too for him when, transfixed, he found his future. I knew it because I had never found mine. No young man had ever looked at me like that and my heart had never leaped with the intoxicating delight that was gripping Annie's in that moment.

That second was the turning point in Annie's life and for her, and indeed for us, the holiday immediately became more significant. When the young man turned up again, hardly by accident, both mother and I knew we could tease her relentlessly without fear of retaliation. There was no opposition, or fears or jealousy. We were all delighted to be a part of Annie's happiness and found joy in encouraging every precious moment. Whether or not the attraction would survive and blossom into a future for them both was the question hanging in the air and I'm pleased to say that both mother and I truly hoped that it would.

We soon learned that the young man was David, David Pollard from Porlock Weir. He was, surprise, a sailor, Third Officer on the London registered cargo vessel Antares and presently on leave after bringing a cargo of Baltic softwood into Acorn Pond in Surrey Docks. He'd been at sea since he was fifteen and had already passed for First Mate. We felt that father would approve.

It would be unfair to gloss over the only family romance since father and mother met in Dunster at the turn of the century so I shall tell you what happened as the years unfolded. During that holiday he was never very far away and he joined us on all our chosen excursions becoming our funny, wise, sensitive and interesting companion. I think we all fell in love with him a little but it was Annie that grew and blossomed before us. She shone and we never saw her so happy.

Like that first meeting after which Mother and I dripped and squelched back to Stargroves, there were other cameos that survived and became family possessions. Tea at Horner Woods after the drive in Scarlet Pimpernel's 'Lion' and the climb up North Hill to St Michael's Well in the wall outside the cobbled gateway to St Michael's church. It was told us that if we made a wish in this one and dropped a pin in the pin-well in Pemswell Lane it would make our wish come true and so we had all solemnly stood by each well in turn knowing exactly what was in the hearts of David and Annie. Then there was the boat trip with Tom Rawle in the Margaret when Tom had said to David, "You sit with your back to the bows. That's the pointed end." And David, winking at us, had said nothing about spending his life in boats of all kinds!

Then, on the last day, having taken mother to catch the train for Watchet where she could spend some time with her friends, we set out for Dunkery Beacon. Mrs Harrison had kindly packed a picnic for us and we caught the Blue Motors Porlock Weir bus from outside the Beach Hotel and travelled to Allerford. David had taken the earlier bus from Porlock Weir and would wait for us to arrive at the corner by the fir trees.

It was one of those wide sky days of wind music and blown grasses and as we swept down the slope of Venniford from Headon Cross the whole of Dunkery Hill and Robin How lay sprawled under bright rafts of dazzling cloud that swam in great schools across the top of the world. The high moors, mottled with golden greens and sharp-etched bronzes danced and played under the swift cloud shadows from Luccombe Church to Horner Water. I'd forgotten how beautiful it was in the Vale.

David greeted us with a wave and we all walked back along the road towards Pile Mill where our ascent began. We talked slowly up the lane to St Leonards's Chapel where we rested a while in the ivy-clad ruins to gain our strength for the climb ahead. Deciding not to picnic until we had reached Webber's Post we climbed on up through the wood towards the hill gate. All the while the wind bowed through the trees like a great string orchestra, supporting the leafy light patterns and the shifting reflections of the filtered sunshine as it scattered from the bending treetops. I was happy to lead the way, just off the road, along spidery paths of leaf-mould crossed with bright tendrils of fern and clumps of sturdy whortleberry. Annie and David followed hand in hand and we wound our way upwards, over the ancient Celtic bank and ditch towards the edge of the Holy Hill itself.

Within the hour we arrived at the group of pine trees that marked Webber's Post and stood looking out over the deep wooded valley of the Horner Water. What magic was it that cements a time into ones mind for ever? Was it the sound of the wind out of an Exmoor sky as it blew in our ears, was it the earth itself with its resilient ling, heather and bright green whortleberry or was it an awareness of a sense of belonging to this sacred place? I put it down in the end to our happiness on that day, a delight in each other's company and a delight in the inspiring beauty around us. Whatever it was, I can see us all there now as I talk, despite the passage of the years.'

She blinked and smiled wryly.

'Well, we climbed Dunkery, right up to the cairn itself and sat awhile taking in the views that only poets could describe. We ate our picnic and drank a bottle of wine that David had brought with him. We must have stayed for some time as the sun had started its westward dip when we set off down the track to Dunkery Hill Gate and the road to Wheddon Cross where David said we could catch a bus for Minehead. He was right, for one was timetabled for five fifteen outside the Rest and be Thankful and we had just twenty minutes to wait. We travelled back through Dunster and arrived at Minehead in good time for the evening meal at Stargroves which David shared with us. Later that evening and before the last bus departed for the Weir, David and Annie sat on the sea wall talking and making plans. Mother was smiling and I felt we'd come to the end of a perfect day and a perfect holiday.

Two further things stuck in my memory about that first holiday. The first was the sight of Annie leaning again out of the train window but this time with the intent of keeping David in sight until he became a dot at the end of the platform. The second was the moment when we drew level with the train standing in the loop line at Kentsford and waved to the passengers who were bound for Minehead. I remember Annie smiling across at us and we knew what she meant. I think, in retrospect, that was the best holiday we ever had although we went on others. It's strange thinking back now but all the holidays and the years leading up the war seemed special but perhaps that was because in the dark times we added a golden frame to the photographs of freedom. Having said that, the years that led up to the outbreak of war were crowded with incidents, not all pleasant.'

CHAPTER SEVEN

With the holiday out of the way, life in the Cumberland Road house soon reverted to normal. Domino continued to ply regularly up the west coast some three hundred nautical miles to Belfast and on to Glasgow which meant that Captain Vickery could have time at home in between trips. He never said much about them but the truth was that regular sailings and contracts lacked the emotion that his previous precarious voyages had engendered. He often harked back to the days when Dancer would be reaching down past Lundy for Ireland on the chance of a freight for anywhere in the Kingdom. Although now, the galley cupboards were well stocked and he could retire most nights and leave the ship in the capable hands of the Chief Mate, it was somehow not the same as being master and owner of his own vessel. He was however happy enough to see his family settled and be able to come home regularly. There was also the occasional interesting diversion usually caused by some sailor or another getting himself into a scrape.

The most recent had been when berthed in Belfast and the crew had gone ashore; not everyone, as the Chief Engineer and the Captain had remained on board for a quiet drink and a chat. To be on the safe side, Captain Vickery had twice taken a turn or two around the deck to check the mooring lines and to see that all was secure. It wouldn't have been the first time that gear had mysteriously vanished over the side helped by some enterprising and impecunious sailor. All was in order and the quayside unusually quiet and so he returned to his cabin. The deck crowd came off around midnight and at about twelve thirty the Captain sent for the Bosun and ordered the gangway to be hoisted inboard and to secure for the night. He then turned in himself. There were the one or two stragglers in the morning but soon everyone was busy getting ready to sail. They were due out at ten for Glasgow and the crowd were involved in battening down, washing down and securing for sea.

Accordingly at ten they cast off and slipped, unnoticed down the Lough on their usual leg. It was a fine day and Captain Vickery stood out on the bridge wing with a cup of strong coffee watching the land slip away. They were well past Carrickfergus when the Bosun climbed up the ladder behind him.

'Cap'n, I thinks you ought to know, we've a stowaway on board.'

Immediately Captain Vickery thought of the many possibilities that this might mean.

'Lead on. Let's see what we've got.'

He had cause to be concerned. Once in Limerick his vessel had been commandeered and on two other occasions he'd come under fire from gunmen ashore. Although peaceful enough for years, Ireland, north or south, could be tricky. He wondered what kind of fugitive he would find and was already trying to decide what he would do if the stowaway became violent.

The Bosun led the way for'ard until they were both under the break of the fo'c's'le. Up here in the bows was the paint locker and a store. Well up against the for'ard bulkhead was a large drum filled with fish-oil which was used for the running gear. Behind the drum, sitting on a coil of rope was the slight figure of a dirty faced and rather unhappy young girl who was obviously feeling the effects of the ship's motion and perhaps the penalties of her previous night's consumption of drink. She looked a mess and more than sorry for herself. She smelled as if she'd been in the fish oil drum and her dress was streaked with the stuff as well as rust and dust.

There were lots of implications. Domino was due in Glasgow and her berth would be waiting so there was no turning back. He could hand her over to the authorities in Glasgow and let them sort it out. He was also aware that she'd surely be missed and enquiries made as to what vessels were in at the time. There were also parents involved who might be aware that their daughter spent evenings on the dock-side but would still be worried if she failed to return home after a few days. He made his decision and sent for the Chief Officer.

'We'll log this Chief, then tell Sparks to radio the agents in Belfast. They can inform whoever needs to know. We'll be back in Belfast by the end of the month and I'm sure that we can return the young lady in better condition than she is now. Make yourself responsible for seeing that she is cleaned up and has some fresh gear and then put her to work in the galley. Both my own daughters have served as cooks and deckhands and the experience will do her good. Tell the Bosun to sort out who was responsible and send them to me.'

As it turned out it wasn't the fault of any of the crew. Teresa had climbed aboard herself shortly before the gangway had been hoisted inboard for the night. She was trying to run away from a violent father who was making life hell for all the children. When the crew discovered the facts of the matter Teresa was well and truly looked after. From Captain to AB, many were fathers themselves and each tried to make her feel that she was worthy of their concern. As the days passed, she grew in confidence and started to smile. In Bristol she became a part of the Chief Officer's family and was quickly kitted out with new clothes from his daughter's chest. The Chief let it be known that should she continue to find life difficult at home she could come and help out at his mother's shop in Hotwells.

When again Domino tied up in her regular berth at Belfast, only the agent's representative was there to greet them. He had been to see the girl's family and reported that although the mother had been worried, the father had said that he had eight other brats to support and it was high time this one started to make her own way in the world and good riddance. The agent also said that he knew of a religious charity organisation that could find her accommodation until she found a job. After the gangway had been rigged, Teresa was invited to go ashore. The crew lined the side to watch her as she went slowly down. At the bottom, she paused then turned and ran back up again to the cheers of everyone on board. The Captain signed her on and she turned to in the galley. After several trips she did indeed start to work for the Chief's mother and was very happy to do so. The story of Domino's stowaway was told over and over and both Angela and Annie soon got to know her. In a way, she was adopted by all the crew and she never lacked for friends in Bristol.

Mrs Vickery loved to listen to the stories that her husband brought home after each trip and felt she knew the crew personally. She did in fact know the Chief's wife, Sarah and the Chief Engineer's wife Hilda and they both used to visit and talk about family affairs. Hilda was from Clevedon and Sarah was from an old Bristol family that had lived in Hotwells for generations. The sea-going community in those days was a close knit fellowship of like-minded folk who had traditions and values they were proud of. There was always a helping hand or a pound or two for a family that were finding things difficult for none were proud enough to forget the days after the war or the struggles of the early thirties.

It was Annie's turn to weather the next storm. Things had been going well at work and the hotel was as popular as ever. Mrs Paterson was well pleased with her and she had progressed through the full range of culinary expertise to the position of Assistant Cook with occasional responsibility for large parties or special groups. As the winter of 1937 turned into spring, Mrs Paterson let it be known that she was thinking of leaving the hotel and taking up a post as resident cook in a private house near Porlock. However what excited Annie was that Mrs Paterson had told her that she had spoken with the management and had recommended that she be considered for the position of Cook in Charge on her departure. Naturally, Annie was thrilled and made every effort to show that she was worthy of the position.

Everyone in the kitchen was fond of Annie for she was hard-working, fair-minded and straight in all her dealings with those she came into contact with. She also has a sense of humour which helped her deal with some of the potential explosions that could arise when speed or carelessness led to ruined dishes. To put it plainly, Annie was the popular choice to replace Mrs Paterson should she leave and it was clearly the best way of dealing with the situation. However, the management, which consisted of a husband and wife team, were of the opinion that the time had come for them to employ a Chef, someone who had worked in large hotels and preferably, had some kind of reputation.

Shortly before she left, Mrs Paterson was summoned to the office where the two managers shared a double desk. The wife began,

'Now, Mrs P, I know that you favour young Miss Vickery for the post but she is just that, young, and not really experienced enough to hold a senior post.'

'It's not my place to argue but for what it's worth, I'd say that Annie is the best you will do. She knows everything I do and gets on well with everyone. You need have no fear for the quality of food served in your hotel. In fact I'd say she will improve it.'

'It's our decision to employ a Chef, a man with experience in one of the big hotels. He'll be more expensive that Miss Vickery but will give the hotel the professional touch it perhaps lacks at the moment.'

Mrs Paterson tightened her lips.

'I think you're making a mistake. Annie is the right person for the job.'

'As we see it, we get the best of both worlds, Annie stays on as Assistant and the new Chef takes over the kitchen. That's our final word.'

It was Mrs Paterson's difficult task to acquaint Annie with the outcome of this meeting. She didn't enjoy it.

'I'm sorry Annie love, they're just too pig-headed to see or understand what I've tried to tell them. It looks like you're going to have a new boss.'

Annie's answer was a quick, cheerful smile,

'I suppose I'll get the opportunity to learn some fancy

dishes. Where's he coming from?'

'I don't know, one of the big London hotels I expect.'

Annie raised her eyebrows,

'We'll all have to get used to some class in here then.'

She hoped that she hadn't shown too much disappointment. She liked and trusted Mrs Paterson and was sorry that she was to leave.

'Still,' she mused, 'life must go on and I'm sure that we'll all get on well enough.'

As the weeks went by to the time when Mrs Paterson was due to leave, the kitchen crew became more and more apprehensive. All sorts of speculations were voiced. After all, they had been together for a number of years and were used to the way things were. Finally the day arrived and sherry was taken, words said and the traditional gift of a wooden spoon baked into a plum and apple pie was handed to a tearful Mrs Paterson and she walked out of their lives knowing she'd left a job well done.

The Chef was due to start on the first of September but before that day arrived all eyes were on Annie. It was Annie who ordered, Annie who worked out the menus, Annie who managed the large kitchen with a practised and confident air. They all worked well with her and for the two months that remained before the arrival of their new master, nothing happened that would have disappointed Mrs Paterson's predictions.

During the latter half of August, the Vickery family were again thinking of having a holiday. David would be docking with another load of Baltic deal and Angela would be able to leave Miss Peath John on her own for a week. Annie was a little worried about taking time off just before the arrival of the new Chef but was thrilled at the prospect of seeing David again. Mrs Vickery was looking forward to a break in Somerset too. There was never any doubt about where they would be going, only which hotel or boarding house. They thought at first that they'd go to Stargroves again but with a little more money put by they could all afford to stay in quite a nice hotel and have a bit of luxury. That appealed and so they booked into the Beaconwood Hotel at Minehead for the last week in August. David was due to arrive at any moment and had sent a cable to the effect that he would go straight home to Porlock Weir as soon as he was discharged.

And so it was that they all left for Temple Meads again but this time in Mr Marlow's big black Hudson Terraplane. It felt very grand to be sweeping up the station approach and then to have their luggage whisked away by the porter and placed in a strategic position on the platform ready for the express. The train journey was every bit as exciting as before. There was again the mesmerizing rhythm of the telegraph wires as they undulated past the carriage windows, sometimes high above the track and sometimes almost below it in their flying pursuit of a common distant destination. Then there was the change at Taunton to the Minehead train with all its tiny stations in between where standing flocks of rosebay willow herb crowded against piles of ancient sleepers and cattle pressed galvanised fencing. On down the line to familiar, workaday Watchet to stop with smiles at Kentsford before chuntering on to Blue Anchor Bay and open windows, beach huts and blown sand. Dunster then Minehead in sight at last as the last straight mile saw

North Hill grow from a hillock into a headland with St Michael's church and a dozen hotels basking in a westering sun. This time it was Mr Hobbs who collected them from the station yard in a huge, black, silent Buick with West of England cloth seats and purred them up the Avenue, up Martlet Road, right at The Cross and then the steep climb up Beaconwood Road to the hotel. It cost two shillings but was worth every penny. When they were greeted at the hotel as Captain Vickery's party, they felt quite important and knew that they had indeed arrived for a special holiday.

Early that evening, a telegram arrived for Miss Annie Vickery. It said,

'ARRIVING MINEHEAD STATION 2.15 PM TOMORROW STOP PLEASE MEET STOP LOVE DAVID'

Annie was hardly able to contain herself and went about the business of unpacking with an infectious grin on her face. Soon everyone was smiling.

After a excellent evening meal Mrs Vickery telephoned her friends in Watchet and settled down to a gin and tonic in the tastefully carpeted lounge overlooking Minehead Bay. The two girls went out to explore and discovering the top gate of the hotel grounds, wandered along the narrow pine-clad road to the top of the Zig-Zag where they looked out over the pier and harbour. The Emma Louise was in and one of Campbell's steamers had just left the end of the pier for the Welsh coast hazy on the horizon. It fell quiet and there was just a hint of a seaborne breeze as it vied with the heady scents of pine and bruised bracken.

The next day there was no holding Annie and her

mother suggested with a twinkle that she might like to go and meet David on her own. As her mother seemed happy enough to read and Angela wanted to go off somewhere else, Annie set off with a light heart to the station. It had been three months since their last meeting when David had visited Bristol. He was still on the Antares and liked it well enough although when he had his First Mate's ticket, he thought he might have a change and see if he could sail as Second Mate on a bigger ship. He'd written regularly ever since their first meeting and felt that Annie was a wonderful girl, not only practical and sensible but loving and kind. Kindness, he always thought, was the mark of the truly mature person and he'd noticed the many little acts of unconscious kindness that Annie left in her wake and it touched his heart. Kindness was the expression of love he knew and he felt himself honoured to know her.

As for Annie, she'd found her man and he was the summit of all she could ask for. He was straight, serious, resourceful and interesting. Like her father he was plain speaking and easily able to command, not through any exercise of power but by his obvious knowledge of the job in hand and his ability to encourage with a smile and a nod. She knew he'd be a good man in any crisis and she was happy to trust him.

Although she'd started out with half an hour in hand, it took her only five minutes to drop down the hill and reach the station. She was in good time to see the train as a puff of white smoke beyond Dunster and then to watch it as it grew from a black speck in a shimmering, unstable landscape to a reality as it passed the signal box. On and on it came until it met the platform and the distance between them could be measured in yards. Annie thought of the hundreds of miles that had separated them now being reduced to a few short feet and she felt her pulse quicken and a lump start to rise in her throat. In minutes they would be together again. She could hardly remember what it was like. The feel of his hands, the scent of his hair as he held her close. She trembled.

The train slowed to a hiss and a shudder. It was here, the doors were flung open and a mass of happy, chattering, cluttered holiday-makers crowded towards the barrier with tickets outstretched. She couldn't see him. It was almost a panic, she couldn't see him. Had he missed the train? The crowd herded past and melted into the station yard heading for taxis and cars. Within seconds they had gone. Still no David. Annie turned away and felt a wave of anxiety sweep over her. What should she do now? What if he hadn't been able to make it after all? Then she looked back. David was there, pulling an enormous parcel along on a trolley. He handed in his ticket.

'Had a devil of a job with this but I've carted it all the way from Kristinestad and I'm not going to give up on it now.'

He grinned,

'Hello my lovely.'

'It's grand to see you at last.'

'I can't wait for this holiday, I've been thinking about it since we left the Baltic.'

'What's in the parcel?'

'It's for father. He's a boat-builder and I found this fantastic wooden model brig in Riga and couldn't resist it. Weighs a ton!'

He ran his hands through his hair and adjusted his suitcase on the trolley.

'I'll leave it the luggage office and get Parcels to deliver it in the morning. Here, this is for you.'

He put his hand in his pocket and pulled out a mysterious lump wrapped in tissue.

'Go on, unwrap it.'

Annie gently unwrapped the gift to expose a piece of Baltic amber enclosing a perfectly preserved wasp.

'It will make a splendid pendant when cut and polished.'

'It's incredible. How did you find it?'

'The timber workers collect them and bring them down to the ships. Some of the sailors take amber to the shops in Britain and sell it for a good profit.'

'Oh, it's beautiful. I shall never sell it.'

David smiled.

'It's supposed to have magical and medicinal properties if you wear it next to the skin.'

'I shall, I shall. Thank you David.'

Somewhat tentatively and with a little hesitation Annie drew closer to him and he reached out for her and held her. They folded their arms about each other and felt content. There would be time for words later.

Like last year there were the highlights. One of them had been a trip on the Ravenswood down the coast to Ilfracombe. It had been a splendid day with just a gentle breeze. They had left Minehead Pier at ten in the morning without the need for coats. It was one of those sparkling, breath-taking mornings when the sea flashed a million mirrors and the land rose green and trembling into a flawless sky. They spent the whole of the outward trip on deck watching the familiar landscape slip by.

Grixy, Hennerscombe and the rusty fist of Hurlstone Point pressing into the sea off the Porlock Vale. Distant Porlock hidden among the trees and then little Porlock Weir crouched at the foot of the hill rising dusty brown and bramble clad to Whitstones under the flawless roof of the sky. Then on down the Channel with Ravenswood threshing the now translucent waters to a vibrant mash of boiling cream from her twin whirling water-wheels. From down in the engine room came the delicious sound of sturdy steam as the engines hissed and thrust in their regular heartbeat voicing the life force of the vessel. Next came Glenthorne, that amazing house that every mariner would like to own and then the little port of Lynmouth with Lynton hanging precariously above like icing atop a vast cake. And all the while, the great bulk of the high moor with its solitary combes pitching into the sea, its wooded slopes crowded with scrub-oak and dense coppices of beech and alder, flung its presence into their minds and spoke of age and power, of history and pride.

After they had picked up two or three boatloads of passengers from the sea off Lynmouth, they gathered speed for Lee Bay and it's tower, Coombe Martin and Ilfracombe and were soon in sight of Lantern Hill and the jetty.

Whether it was the beauty of the day, the landscape or the seascape or whether it was the nearness of loved ones and loved places or the magical combination of all these elements it would be hard to know. Suffice it to say that they combined to bring a joy and a delight that etched its way into their minds and left a legacy that would not be forgotten during their lifetimes. There are moments in a life that can do this and that shared voyage, although brief in terms of sea voyages, was something to grasp at in times when life was not so kind.

Ilfracombe was crowded with folk and there was hardly a place to sit let alone have a cup of tea. There was another Campbells steamer in from Cardiff and if you didn't know, you could tell from the accents as the passengers mingled with the holiday folk. At last they managed to squeeze into a harbour-side Café and order a light meal. While they waited, they talked, hands clasped over the table, about their jobs and ambitions for the future. The tea arrived and they were ready for it.

They didn't walk up to the town but took off their shoes and socks and splashed into the harbour among the moored boats and playing children. Later they just sat on the slipway and watched the seaside juggle its summer occupants with a practised ease. There was a photographer at work with a large plate camera, probably from one of the photographic firms that produced postcards. Next to him, obviously wise to a good vantage point, was an artist with watercolours. It was all brightly busy. The tide was creeping in and one by one the boats righted themselves and nudged and jostled into their high-water positions tugging at their lines and lending darting reflections to the water wrinkling under their hulls. One or two were preparing to leave on the evening tide and their owners were busy with bait and lines.

The trip back was, if possible, better than the outward leg for the sun was lowering over the stern causing the land to darken and the sea to shatter into a gently heaving lake of crushed crystal, through which the paddler's twin wakes scored a glistening shroud for the day. The pair of them sat aft of Ravenswood's single funnel and faced the glory all down the sun-path home to Minehead past each well known landmark until White Mark off Ossy Point where she turned in for the pier. It was almost dark when they walked up the pier and stopped for a hug in the midway shelter. Then Ravenswood rang down for speed and the echo of the repeater sounded across the water under the hill as did the thud and plash of the paddles as they bit into the evening flood. They thought that was probably the perfect day but the one that followed was the one they remembered when the time for remembering came.

The day dawned and promised fine. Annie was late getting up and Angela had to nudge her more than once before she surfaced. Mrs Vickery had struck up a friendship with another guest, a Mrs Atkins who was a retired headmistress. The two of them were off to Cleeve Abbey for the day leaving Angela to explore on her own. This suited her as she didn't really want to spend the day with her mother as well as the evenings and she didn't want to spoil Annie's fun either. In the end it proved a blessing as she was to meet a remarkable lady who was to alter the way she thought about life.

Angela's adventure began when she walked down the road to have a closer look at St Michael's church. She knew St Decuman's church at Watchet and most of the stories about it but not a lot about St Michael's. She was inside the building looking at the painted reredos nailed to the north wall when the lady came and stood beside her.

'You look serious. Do you believe it all?'

Angela jumped and looked at her. She was about eighty years old or more, slight, sharp and wiry with the most amazing eyes she'd ever seen.

'Do you believe it all?' She repeated.

'I was brought up to,' answered Angela.

'That's not what I asked.'

'Well, yes, I suppose I do,' said Angela looking again at her companion. The old lady nodded.

'I can see you've done no real thinking yet. Do you believe everything you're told or do you ever challenge things. I mean do you believe in the actual physical resurrection of Jesus?'

Angela thought back to her Sunday School and the many church services she had been to.

'The bible teaches us that Jesus rose on the third day.'

She went on.

'And do you believe that Jesus was a real flesh and blood person that walked this earth near two thousand years ago?'

'We've always been taught that.'

'Then you have been caught in the story, the literalist view. There are two ways of reading gospels you know, one for the folk who stay at the story level and one for those who question further. There are clues everywhere if you care to look for them. I was in Egypt in 1897 when they found the latest gospel fragment. It said "Lift the stone and there you will find me, cleave the wood and I am there." These are the instructions for the reader to look deeper, to look underneath if you like.'

Angela leaned back against a pew end and the lady continued.

'The gospels, and there were dozens of them, were stories that carried hidden truths about human nature and how to deal with the human predicament. In the accepted version we all treat as gospel truth, Jesus says, "Seek and ye shall find." Here is the clue again but the trouble is, nobody bothers and the function of the story is lost in the magic of the narrative.'

'But Jesus was a real person.'

'It doesn't matter whether he was or he wasn't. The story or myth carries the formula that the gospel writers wanted to convey. It was the early church leaders that weeded the garden of all that didn't fit in with a narrow band of what became orthodoxy. Before Nicea, many gospels were working all across the Mediterranean world. Afterwards, power and social control lay in the hands of the party and much was destroyed. One day, someone will dig up a gospel about a condemned and executed saviour who commanded his followers to partake of a ceremonial meal and who rose from the dead on the third day only it will be positively dated to a couple of hundred years before Jesus was supposed to have been born in Bethlehem.'

Angela sat down.

'It was a laudable attempt to freeze a dogma in the interests of all but all it did was to create an eloquent but clumsy monster that successive generations were left to puzzle over. Especially in these days when more folk are thinking for themselves as the Greeks were encouraged to do.'

'Do you believe in Jesus?' asked Angela.

'As a historical figure claiming to be the only son of God, no, but as a powerful mythic creation encapsulating essential truths about us complex humans, yes. Dionysus was another and Apollonius of Tyana followed close after him. Osiris predated them all but it is the same figure, the same basic message.'

'Why are you telling me all this?'

'Because although I won't live to see it, all this is changing and perhaps in your lifetime the people will no longer be lead by dogma but be free to work out the meaning of these ancient myths in their own lives as they were originally invited to do. Remember the key lies in looking underneath.'

She nodded and reached out and patted Angela's arm in a maternal fashion, then walked slowly and deliberately around the back of the church, up the main aisle and, without a wave, down the steps and out of the porch into the sunshine. Angela wasn't quite sure what to think about it all. True, she hadn't really thought about the gospel story, just believed it was all there as the vicar had told her. It certainly got her thinking. What was the purpose of the story in the first place and why had it dominated the western world with such power for so long. She began to wish the old lady hadn't said anything at all. It was more comfortable to go along with the story as she'd heard it. She was used to a real Jesus being born in a stable at Christmas.

Coming out into the world beyond the porch revealed a brilliant panorama of moors, trees and fields that surrounded the town on the landward side. Near at hand thatched cottages crowded down Church Steps and she could see over the tops of hundreds of roofs to where the town merged into the countryside below Hopcott Hill. It was a beautiful spot. She thought that she could do with a little bustle and noise and so set off for the town again wishing that she didn't have to start thinking but she knew that she would. She wondered who the lady was. She certainly spoke as if she was used to authority. Perhaps she had been a teacher or scholar.

Annie and David had arranged to meet by the war memorial underneath Elgin Towers at eleven. This would give David time to come into Minehead on the Blue Motors bus that got into the Parade at ten fifteen. He'd suggested looking into Boddy's to buy some cakes for a picnic on the way and Annie had thought that a bottle of wine might be a good idea.

He found her sitting on the little wooden bench under the wall surrounded by clumps of bright valerian and twists of ivy. She saw him as he strode up the hill towards her, a paper carrier in his hand and a big grin on his face. They both started to laugh, it was nothing funny, just sheer happiness as they came together at the start of their day. They turned up the road towards the church and passed under the wall by the top of Church Steps. There was nobody abroad and they walked in the middle of the road chatting and occasionally swinging about on each other's arms. As the road turned up to the left for Higher Moor Farm, they left the rough tarmac and pressed on up the stony path, past the quarry for Moor Break. Up here the ferns, man high, crowded across the path, flies whined around their heads and they hurried for the cool dark of the first pine trees and the soft needles underfoot. Up and up they went until they could see the moor horizon light and high beyond the pine crests above. Just as it was a shock to enter the dimmed, dry carpeted vault of whispering wood it was another to emerge into an explosion of greens where the heat reasserted itself and the light seemed more intense.

They'd decided on Selworthy Beacon and so after topping Moor Break, they set off along the rough stoned gravel track for the ruins of East Meyne Farm. Bratton Ball lay hazy on the left and two ancient barrows were still prominent enough to be noticed as they thrust their heads into the still moorland air. Up here, bracken had given way to clumps of brown, wind-blown grasses and patches of heather and ling interspersed with bushes of whortleberry. It was heavy going off the track and they found walking on the rough stones of the path hard enough. Not only the moor but the sea was at hand and they were always conscious that six hundred feet below, a blue-green Channel was washing into the massive sea-crafted boulders that littered the steep beaches out of sight beneath their feet in Grixy and Bramble Combe. Although it was not too hot, the journey was beginning to tell on both of them. For David because he was not used to a lot of walking and for Annie because she found the rough ground trying. They could see Selworthy Beacon ahead with its little cairn of stones but it was still probably half an hour away and so they decided to stop and look into David's paper carrier.

He'd brought two bottles of Sauternes, a medium sized pork pie and a pair of pasties. The pasties were from home and his mother had made them. They sank with relief into a grassy hollow and David took out his knife and cut the pie into halves. Then as Annie bit into her half, David opened the first bottle with the corkscrew attached to the knife.

'This is a shoreside knife. A seaman's knife doesn't come fitted with a corkscrew. A lot would like it to be but so far it hasn't happened.'

Annie smiled, 'You forgot something to drink the wine

out of. Mrs Paterson would have a fit if she saw me drinking from a bottle.'

'I shan't tell anyone.'

They soon revived and saving the pasties and the second bottle for later, pressed on up the gradual slope to the Beacon. Not as popular or as well visited as Dunkery Beacon it nevertheless had stunning views. There they bumped into a young couple and their three or four year old child who had climbed up from Selworthy village. The child, a girl, was sitting right on top of the stone pile. The man fished in his haversack and pulled out a leatherette-cased folding Kodak. He opened it and checked whether it had been wound on.

'Would you mind taking a picture of us all? It's been quite an achievement for little Hazel. She's walked the whole way up from the Porlock Road.'

David laughed,

'It's been quite an achievement for us too and we've taken time off for a picnic on the way.' He took the proffered camera and checked the focus for eight feet.

'Right, here we go.'

The family closed ranks with Hazel peeping over her Dad's shoulder. It was a happy snap and David thought it would turn out well.

'Would you like us to take a picture of you? If you give us your address we could send it on to you when we get the film developed.'

Annie smiled up at David and David responded,

'That's very kind of you.'

He gathered Annie under his arm and she put her arm about his waist. The man carefully wound the film on to the next number and squinted into the viewing prism.

'Ready?'

With more that a vestige of self-consciousness, they nodded, there was a click and the record was frozen on film for ever.

'Thanks, if you could send it to David Pollard, Porlock Weir, it should find me.'

They chatted on for a while, exchanging opinions of where to go to see the best of the area and where the tastiest cream teas were to be found. They all came up with Horner Woods but the lady thought that Cloutsham Farm was equally as good.

'If it's views you're after, you can't beat the one from the end of the hill here overlooking Porlock Bay. If you're local, you'll know it.'

David nodded,

'Yes, I know it. It's one of the best places for sunsets locally.'

He turned to Annie,

'Have you ever been along to the end here above Bossington Hill?'

Annie shook her head,

'No, this is as far as I've been along this range of hills.'

'You'll love it, it's probably the best view down the coast in the whole of Somerset and Devon.'

They thanked the couple, grinned at Hazel and with a wave, set off westward to the swell of Bossington Hill. They followed a rough path for a few hundred yards and then descended to the stony track that ran on to the end of the hill. Beyond them the ground started to fall away revealing the whole of the vale of Porlock stretched below, its fields reduced to a fine mosaic of yellows, browns and greens dotted with tiny trees like crumbs on a finely textured tablecloth. To their right, a sighing summer sea crawled unheard along the mile or so of brilliant limestone shingle that curved towards Gore Point and the tiny port of Porlock Weir tucked under the bulk of Exmoor rising over a thousand feet above.

'This was the view they were talking about,' indicated David. 'You can see Porlock Weir over there under the hill and if you look carefully you can see our house there at the end of the harbour.'

Annie shielded her eyes from the sun that had begun its slide to the west and was directly in her eyes.

'I can make out Porlock Weir but don't know where to look for your house. They all seem to be merged together.'

David stood behind her and placed his hands on her shoulders. 'Follow the shingle round and when you get to the little inlet look for a white painted house quite close to the sea.'

'I still can't see it, They all seem to be bunched up together.'

'Never mind, look on down the coast towards the Foreland. Can you see the little boat way out there, about half a mile out?'

'Just about. You've got good eyes.'

'That's Tommy Ley in the Mistletoe. He'll be out fishing off Glenthorne. Remember, we passed it yesterday on the Ravenswood.'

'Don't tell me you can see that from here. Nobody can see that well.'

David laughed.

'No, he told me he was going out this morning. I saw him getting her ready.'

Annie punched him playfully and ran off a few strides looking back over her shoulder. David laughed again.

'It's too hot to run after you. Let's stop here for a while and have the rest of the picnic.

They turned together and set off for the fringe of trees erupting from the tangled thickets of scrub oak and elder that clung to the side of the hill below them. Close to a steep bank and a stand of young fir was a square of fine, light coloured grass. They headed for it and were soon settled with the paper carrier spread between them and the pasties set out invitingly. David opened the wine.

'You'll get me all tiddly.'

'Not a chance with all this walking and climbing about,' returned David, taking a long draught. 'See what you think of mother's pasty.'

'We used to make these at home. Learned how when we went with father in Dancer to Cornwall.'

Annie bit into the crust. It was full and sharp with herbs.

'Does it pass?' quizzed David.

'Lovely!'

They set to and tucked in, waving away the occasional fly and picking up the inevitable bits that were the penalty of eating a fresh, well-filled oggie. Notwithstanding Annie's apparent reluctance, the wine also quickly vanished and rather than feeling tiddly, she found it refreshing. Despite chattering almost non-stop since they set out, they both recognised the ease with which they had slipped through the hours. They were well matched, equally used to hard work and unspoiled. They both appreciated and valued the gift of such a day and were grateful.

As if prompted by the same muse, they both fell silent for a minute or two. David folded the carrier neatly and purposefully buried the bottles, marking the spot with a pile of stones which he gathered from beneath the bank. Annie sat quietly and followed his movements with wide eyes. They both started to speak.

'Annie?'

'I'm sorry, after you.'

David sat down suddenly, clasping his knees to himself.

'It's been super hasn't it?'

Annie agreed, silently inclining her head but still looking full at him.

'I didn't think I would find this hard but this is the serious bit, I think I've got to the stage when I realise that you are the centre of all my thinking. I go to sleep thinking of you and you are still there when I wake up. Every moment I am away from you I count the hours and minutes until I can be with you again. We seem so complete when we are together I find it very difficult to be parted from you. If this is called love, then I'm telling you that I am in love with you and would like to spend my life with you.'

'Oh, David.'

'I don't want to push myself into your life if you don't feel ready but if your feelings are the same for me could we tell the world that we are walking out together and have an understanding?'

Annie held on to the moment, still consuming him with her gaze. She'd wanted so very much to hear him say something like this, anything at all would have done but his actual words would remain with her for always.

Somehow he'd said all there was to say and far more eloquently than she could have done. Precious seconds slipped by, the trees froze, the sea ceased to move and the moors stood in silent witness to the moment.

David sat there, his head held by the question he'd posed. Then Annie reached out both hands to him.

'I thought that yesterday was the most beautiful day of my life but today is certainly the most special. Oh yes, dear, dear David, the answer is yes. Let's tell everyone our news. I know my family will be so happy for us.'

All at once they became aware of their surroundings. The place was a chapel to their declaration. The trees were the vaulted pillars and the brown, bent grass tussocks a patterned carpet beneath their feet. The moorscent became their incense and all the world was holy. Taking her by the hand, he led her around the sacred spot.

'This will always be our special place. Look about and remember. This is our hill and this is our view and the sea that stretches out past the Foreland is our sea. All this is our legacy, our dowry, all we need to have to believe in a future where we can build and grow and delight in all that life has for us.'

Annie dared to believe it and in that moment knew she had made the decision of a lifetime. She would belong to this man and he would belong to her. Slowly, gently and with a trembling sensitivity, she reached up and kissed him. In that same moment David understood the depth and power of the gift he had been given and vowed never to do anything that might harm or destroy it.

They stood for a while as the day burned out over the

gathered folds of ocean flung far below, the light started to die and the first shadows began to creep under the dusty bent branches and probing meshed fingers of woodland just over the bank.

'We should be getting back,' said David, casting a concerned eye around the empty moor. 'I think we ought to take a quicker route and drop down to Selworthy church and on down to the Porlock Road for a bus.'

Annie agreed. It was beginning to get a little colder as a sea breeze replaced the warmer air that had been rising from the hills all day. They set off and soon found the path that wound down between the hunched hill shoulders, past a small larch plantation and into the moving darkness of the trees that crowded above Selworthy. It was even darker by the time they skirted the village green and followed the steep lane down to the main road below. The first bus that rumbled out of the night, its yellow lights thrusting a pool of scrambled tarmac before it was heading for Porlock and the Weir. It slowed to a stop and the conductor leaned out.

'Allerford, Horner turn an' Porlock village. This is the last one.' Then he added, 'Unless you waits for us to turn round at the Weir an' come back. That'll be in about half an hour.'

David pulled Annie after him.

'Come on Annie, we'll go to my house. You can phone the hotel from there. Two to the Weir please.'

Annie didn't argue. She was tired, happy and only too pleased to sit down. She was with David. That was sufficient.

With a clunk, the bus slipped into gear, the engine asserted itself and the conductor clipped their tickets. They were on their way.

CHAPTER EIGHT

As before, the holiday fled the way of days and was soon swallowed up by memories. There were more special moments to remember for all of them. For Mrs Vickery it was the peace of sitting in the gracious lounge of the Beaconwood Hotel and allowing herself the luxury of recalling her younger days. For Angela it was the push she needed to begin to think about her role in life and what she found of eternal value and for Annie and David it was the heady recollections of beginning their journey together.

Mr Hobbs had taken them back to the station. David had another four days and planned to visit Bristol before going on to London and Surrey Docks where Antares would be waiting. It wasn't a case of not wanting to go on with their lives but priorities had shifted and David was thinking of changing his ship so that he could be closer at hand and home more often. Now that her children were more settled Mrs Vickery wondered if the time was approaching when she and her husband might think of retiring and maybe, just maybe go back to their beloved West Somerset. It was a case of the holiday stirring up the pot and giving rise to many possibilities and options. As it was, fate took a hand and events dictated the outcomes.

It started with Annie returning to the hotel. From the moment she walked through the door she sensed the tension. The staff still missed Mrs Paterson of course but they'd had a temporary cook to fill in while Annie was on holiday and all had, apparently, gone according to plan. They seemed happy to have Annie back and the first day went smoothly enough. On the second day one of the assistants, a promising young girl whom Annie always found conscientious, mentioned that during her absence on holiday the female management had been down and told the kitchen staff that Miss Vickery was not to be regarded as in charge of the kitchen and that a new structure would be published as soon as the new chef arrived. This was nothing new to Annie and she assured the staff that all would be well and that she was sure that they could all work together satisfactorily.

Another week went by and Annie soon had everyone working with a cheerful enthusiasm. There were lots of jokes, quips and stories that had them all flying through the routine and several encouraging compliments relayed back from the dining room soon assured Annie that her staff were working at their best. She didn't think that the arrival of the new chef would alter the situation and there was always the possibility that he might make things better.

The long awaited day arrived soon enough and one morning at eleven, work stopped in the kitchen to welcome the female management accompanied by a short, balding middle aged man of about forty years of age. He carried an air of self-importance that seemed to go down well with the female management but failed to impress those studying him more closely as he walked in.

'This, ladies is Monsieur Jacques. He comes from one of the leading restaurants in Paris and before that he was at The Strand Palace Hotel in London.'

She beamed.

'Monsieur Jacques will be giving us a French menu

and turning this kitchen around from the old ways to a bright and, shall we say, a 'chic' future.'

Monsieur Jacques already seemed to be preoccupied with the way the kitchen was laid out and was casting a critical eye over the equipment he could see arranged in racks or hanging from the wall hooks. All was well scrubbed and gleaming and fell easily to hand when needed. The staff just hoped that 'turning things around' didn't mean too much interference in the way things were done.

'Monsieur Jacques will be starting work here tomorrow ladies. Miss Vickery will be responsible for showing him where everything is.'

Female management then left the kitchen followed by the new chef. There were no smiles or words, not even 'I'm very happy to be here and I look forward to working with you all.' It was all very formal and did nothing to allay the fears of the staff.

The next morning at eight, Monsieur Jacques complete with check trousers, white jacket and tall hat entered his new domain. After a tour of the kitchen and scullery, still-room and larders he asked for the menus and recipes. They were all surprised to discover that he was not French at all. He was from Ramsgate and had spent his working life in hotels and guest-houses all over London and the south east coast. His last job in Paris hadn't lasted long apparently and he soon told everyone that he was pleased to be back in England.

The menus in French appeared to be a success. The cooking didn't change much, just the addition of some new sauces and the way in which the meals were presented. However, it wasn't very long before his little habits started to affect the kitchen. Unknown to the management he stopped the beer allowance for staff but continued with the tradition, taking up the ladies portions for himself and starting to make inroads into his salary by ordering brandy 'on the slate' from the pot boy. By the late afternoon he was, to put it mildly, in his cups and swerved about the kitchen leaving a trail of minor damage in his wake. When sober he seemed plausible enough and had obviously managed to pull the wool over the eyes of the management but here in the kitchen he was becoming a liability. Annie thought that at one time he might have been a good chef for in the early days there had been glimpses of excellence that showed flair and imagination. She might have felt sorry for him had he not been condescending and hurtful to the staff. Others were blamed for his mistakes and the still room assistant who had been making splendid sandwiches for a decade, was blamed for sending up some dirty orders. It transpired that Monsieur Jacques had tipped the sandwich mix onto the floor and put it back without saying anything. Of course she should have noticed something was amiss but as she had just finished making up the bowl she assumed that all was well.

Things went from bad to worse until in November Annie was confronted with an ultimatum from the rest of the staff.

'Look Annie,' they said, 'someone's got to tell them about this and we think it ought to be you. We trust you and are happy to go on working with you but if this situation continues, we shall start to think of leaving.'

Annie was still hopeful that things might improve though she doubted whether Monsieur Jacques could be cured of his problem. The very next night they were busy with the dinners and Monsieur was flitting ineffectively about the kitchen putting his nose into everything and often taking charge of tasks already allocated to others. The fact that the kitchen worked as well as it did was down to teamwork and the efforts of all the staff to make the best of a bad job.

On this occasion, Monsieur pulled a shoulder of lamb out of the gas oven spilling a stream of fat across the tiled floor. He carried it unsteadily to the central table and put it down with a crash. Concerned that it might roll from the table Annie left her task and made hurriedly for the table. As she did so, her feet slipped from under her and she went down heavily on one arm, hitting her head a crack on the side of the stove. The last thing she remembered was the sudden pain in her wrist as she fell.

Several of the staff rushed forward to discover Annie lying awkwardly with a nasty gash on the side of her head. She was unconscious. Carefully they lifted her, paddling uncertainly in the spilled fat, and carried her to the still-room where they laid her across three chairs and sent for help. Someone placed a tea towel over her head wound and supported her damaged arm across her chest. It was half an hour before the doctor arrived and advised that Annie be taken to the hospital so that her head wound could be looked at. He added that he thought that her wrist was broken.

The drama was broken by the bell ringing to indicate first orders were on the way and so the staff fell to with a will, and being short handed, made every effort to get things back on schedule. After dinner, the management sent for Monsieur Jacques to discover what had happened and Monsieur, not too drunk to think up an answer that would explain the situation to his advantage, said, 'I'm afraid it was her own silly fault. She took the lamb from the oven without using a suitable glove, burnt her fingers, spilled the fat on the floor and slipped in it. I managed to rescue the joint and get it to the table but Miss Vickery had fallen badly and I failed to catch her. I must say that lately I have found her most unhelpful and not at all the skilled cook she is cracked up to be. This is not the first incident that I have had to speak to her about.'

Female management nodded sagely and thanked Monsieur for his trouble.

'We think that under the circumstances and taking into consideration the length of time that Miss Vickery will be absent with her injuries, we will be terminating her employment here.'

Monsieur Jacques smirked.

'Perhaps, as you are in charge of the kitchen staff now, you will go and see Miss Vickery and convey our decision to her. When she comes out of hospital, that is.'

Monsieur Jacques grinned inwardly. Not only had he managed to get rid of Miss Vickery who was in every way a much better cook than he would ever be but he had covered his tracks and palmed off all the recent inadequacies of the kitchen onto her shoulders.

'Yes, of course, in a week or two. I should be pleased to assist in any way I can.'

He steadied himself against the table with his ample belly. The effort was beginning to tell.

'I'll be getting back to the kitchen then. Lots to do. I'm preparing some special dishes for tomorrow evening.'

The sweat was beginning to roll down Monsieur's forehead as he pushed himself away from the desk and walked as steadily as he could from the office. The interview seemed to have gone well but he dreaded having to tell Annie that her job had been taken from her and yet a part of him was glad that the skids had been placed under her feet.

'Literally,' he smiled crookedly as he carefully negotiated the stairs down to the kitchen.

It was the second day before Annie came to in the hospital. Her mother was beside the bed.

'Oh Annie, love, I'm so relieved.'

She looked at the pale face, mostly bandage, lying before her. Annie attempted a smile.

'I had a bad fall. My, my head's awfully sore.'

She attempted to raise her hand to her head and discovered her arm was strapped across her chest.

'You've a badly broken wrist my love and you've suffered concussion but the doctor says that you'll make a full recovery. The wrist's been set and your head stitched and at the end of the week, if the sister thinks you can walk well enough, you can come home and start to get better.'

Annie tried the smile again.

'I'm sure I'll be fine after a rest. What did they say at work?'

'The manager said that his wife was looking into the accident and that the new chef would be coming to see you when you were feeling a bit better.'

'I can't really remember what happened before the fall or what job I was working on. I think it was just before dinner. I went down with such a bang. How did I hurt my head?'

'The manager said your head struck the oven top. That's where the blood was found.'

Annie slowly and painfully shook her head.

'I just can't remember.'

Mrs Vickery laid her hand gently on her daughter's arm.

'Don't worry about it now. Just rest and you'll be home soon enough. We can talk then.'

Annie went home at the week-end. The Sister had told her that if she felt dizzy, she should sit down and rest for a while. The turban of bandages came off too and was replaced with a dressing held down by two plasters. As the days passed she began to feel stronger and to worry about her job at the hotel. At the end of the second week she still hadn't heard anything from them and wondered if she ought to arrange for a taxi to take her into the city. Her mother thought otherwise.

'You're not going up there. It's obvious to anyone that you still need to rest and there's no way you could do a full day's work with your arm still strapped up. Just accept that it will be some weeks before you are fit for anything.'

Annie knew this was right but it still worried her that no-one had contacted her from the hotel.

Monsieur Jacques was worrying too. He knew that the time was ripe for his visit. In fact he'd already told the management that he'd been and that Miss Vickery had accepted the decision as the right way forward. He was proud of that phrase. It sounded as if he'd had a sensible discussion and the outcome had been agreed. In fact it was a phrase that had once been used to him when he

had been asked to leave in the interests of the establish-
ment. He ought to go soon or Miss Vickery would contact the hotel and then the truth might come out. A little
more truth than he could do with. Accordingly he set
aside an afternoon for the visit and in due course, found
himself on the doorstep at Cumberland Road. Annie answered the door.

'Monsieur Jacques!'

At last, a visit from the hotel. Annie pushed open the
door with her shoulder and invited him in.

'I was wondering when the hotel would call. How is
everything?'

Monsieur Jacques managed a sick grin.

'Just fine, everyone is asking about you and they all
hope that you'll make a speedy recovery. I've brought
you these.'

He thrust out a small, tired bunch of anemones wrapped
in a wet piece of green paper. He took a deep breath and
thought he'd better get on with it.

'While you've been away, there's been decisions made
about the management of the kitchen. I'm in charge you
know.'

'Of course,' replied Annie. 'Have you managed to find
a temporary replacement while I'm away?'

Monsieur coughed.

'It's my duty to tell you that it is the management's
decision that your position is closed and we won't be
replacing you.'

'But I'll be fit for work shortly and surely I still have
my job at the hotel.'

'The management has asked me to tell you that your
services are no longer required. You will be paid until

you are fit to resume work and the hotel will, of course, give you a reference.'

'How has this decision been made? I've been with the hotel all my working life. I thought they valued me.'

'I'm afraid the truth of it may hurt,' said Monsieur Jacques beginning to enjoy the situation.

'I understand the hotel sees the accident as very much your own fault and cannot run the risk of any further lapses of concentration in the kitchen. It can be a dangerous place for those that are careless.'

'So I am dismissed?'

'I'm afraid so.'

Annie sat down, the breath quite taken away from her. True, she couldn't remember just what had happened in that last fateful moment. Perhaps she had fainted or perhaps she had suffered a momentary blackout and fallen against the oven. She took a deep breath.

'Thank you Monsieur Jacques. Do you think the hotel will want me to get in touch with them before I apply for another post?'

'I'm sure that won't be necessary. I'll make sure that your references are sent to this address.'

Annie was very shocked. That she had been the cause of the accident in the first place and that she might have been the means of danger to others was hard to accept. If only she could remember just what had happened.

Monsieur started to leave. Annie, confused, followed him to the door.

'I'm so very sorry. I had no idea that I was the problem. It was my own fault then?'

'I'm afraid so,' intoned Monsieur, 'the hotel takes the view that you could pose a danger to others and that it might be in your interests to reconsider your choice of job.'

This last sentence was another that had been addressed to him on more than one occasion. He felt it suited the moment rather well.

'Goodbye then Miss Vickery.'

'Thank you, goodbye.'

As the door shut upon Monsieur Jacques so it shut upon Annie's career at the hotel. It was a blow she hadn't reckoned with. Suddenly she felt weak and found herself shivering. She sat down and started to worry. She'd never had a lapse of concentration before. What had happened that had caused her accident and, apparently, been the cause of some concern. And why didn't they want to see her? It must have been serious. Her head started to ache again and she felt miserable. If only David could be home but he was at sea and not expected for three weeks yet.

When her mother found her sobbing, she knew that her Annie had touched rock bottom and needed some positive support.

'I'll cable the ship and inform David. I know he'll want to be here as soon as he is able.'

Annie looked up through the tears.

'I'm sorry, it's all been a bit much. The hotel doesn't want me any more and....and my David seems so far away. I wish I felt better than I do.'

Her mother smiled.

'Just concentrate on getting better. Don't worry about the job. Things have a habit of working out for the best. You'll see.'

In her heart, she doubted whether things would heal

quite as quickly or that Annie would be fit enough to handle heavy pans for some time. Relationships at the hotel had been far from satisfactory since that new chef had arrived and if the management had any sense they would look a little closer into the way the kitchen was being run. She'd heard rumours and of course, Annie had let several things drop about the way the staff were feeling. Whatever the immediate outcomes, she thought that Annie was well out of it and when she was fitter, she'd tell her so.

Sparks handed the cablegram to David on the bridge of Antares six hours off Gdansk. When the Chief came up to relieve him he went below to determine the quickest way he could get back to the United Kingdom. Sparks came up with the answer. Train to Berlin and on via Hanover to Rotterdam. He should be home within forty-eight hours. The skipper was adamant he should go.

'We shall be three days in Goteborg and another three or perhaps four in Hamburg. Be a good fortnight before we can run up the London River. You go today as soon as we tie up. I can sub you all you'll need. You'll also need a special pass from the company agent. They're getting very tight on security in Germany these days. And your discharge book or a passport. I'll stamp up a document from the ship's office too. That might prevent any delays.'

Accordingly, as soon as the ship was secured and cleared, David was on his way down the gangway with a canvas grip. He was wearing uniform, rare for a ship's officer ashore but the skipper had advised it on account of the growing suspicion that the German police and internal security organisations seemed to have of civilian movements in and out of Germany.

'You're not Jewish are you?' he enquired, 'because if you are I ought not to let you go. For some strange reason, they're likely to detain all Jews for questioning whatever nationality. As a British passport holder they'd have to let you go but they could hold you up for days if they wanted.'

David had assured him that he was Church of England upon which the captain had offered him one last piece of advice.

'Whatever you do, don't argue the toss with anyone. The present regime doesn't have a sense of humour.'

David had promised to be careful. As far as he was concerned all he wanted to do was to reach home as quickly as possible.

The rail journey to Berlin was uneventful. No-one bothered him and he was able to spend the hours looking out of the window or dozing to the rhythm of the rails as they sang him ever closer to his Annie. The massive station at Berlin was different. Here he had to change trains and book a seat for Rotterdam via Hanover. His German was dreadful and limited to what he had been able to pick up from his brother officers in ports around the Baltic so he soon found himself in touch with officialdom. Luckily he discovered a ticket clerk who spoke fluent English.

'Why are you leaving Germany when you have just entered it?'

David explained that he was off a ship and travelling home for compassionate reasons.

'Are you meeting with anyone in Berlin?'

David assured him he was not, just passing through.

'What identification documents are you carrying?'

David showed him the papers from the shipping agent and the document prepared by the captain.

'Pollard is a Jewish name. Yes? You are perhaps making contact with a Jewish family here?'

David assured the clerk again that he was merely a British ship's officer crossing Europe to get home as quickly as possible. The clerk looked at him over the top of his oval spectacles.

'You speak very good English.'

'I am English. My papers tell you this.'

'Perhaps. I must confer with my colleagues.'

He beckoned and two National Police with the longest bayonets that David had ever seen strolled over and looked at him intently for what seemed an age. Then one of them spoke.

'Reisepass! Papers!'

David handed them over for the second time, his eyes reaching beyond the two policemen to a frightened man being held in a nasty arm lock by another officer. The man seemed terrified. David thought that he'd better try a little harder to convince this pair that he was genuine.

'Look,' he urged, 'I'm off a British ship called the Antares. She's a regular trader to the Baltic and we often call at Hamburg on the way home. I've never had any trouble with the police in Hamburg.'

'Have you ever helped any Jewish people to leave on your ship? Ever taken Jewish passengers out of Germany?

'Of course not,' replied David.

'You've never helped people like him?

The policeman spat towards the terrified man.

'No.'

David looked again at the man. His face bore the marks of being hit, and hard. He feared for him and wished that he were in a position to do something about it but knew that he was powerless.

The policemen handed David back his documents.

'The clerk will help you plan your journey. You must understand we have many enemies of the Reich. Filth like that,' he spat again, 'must be dealt with.'

David found himself feeling a bit weak about the knees. He had no idea that things were as bad as this. The skipper obviously knew which was why he had prepared the additional documents. On previous trips he'd never wandered far from the ship and most of the contacts he had made were with other seafarers who were decent enough chaps.

'You may continue with your journey.'

David nodded and went back to the ticket desk. A further glance about him confirmed the place was teeming with uniforms. Even the youngsters were dressed in uniform and there were some very impressive folk about. The naval ones he recognised of course. They were little different from his own but there were several regimental outfits he'd never seen before. The whole nation seemed to be on the move and they all looked as if they were marching to the same band. Glancing up at the huge red banner surmounted with a black swastika that was undulating slowly above his head he felt again the unease he had just experienced. This nation was moving for a purpose and it wasn't peaceful.

Finally, with a ticket and a rubber stamped endorsement on each of his documents, he was directed to the right platform to wait for the express to Hanover. Here there were more military personnel but among them some familiar blue uniformed figures belonging to the Kriegsmarine. One of them raised a thumb and smiled. David felt a little more at ease. Settled into a compartment the German sailor smiled again and offered David a tot from his flask.

'Hans Feldmann, Engineer Officer,' he grinned, holding out his hand.

'David Pollard, Second Mate.'

The other seamen smiled and nodded to David. Hans continued.

'I saw you with the Schupos just now. Don't worry. Those bastards bother everyone. They are after those who oppose the State. Terrorists and the like. Honest sailors have nothing to worry about. Going home?'

He proffered the flask again.

'Yes, from the Baltic to Britain to see my girl who has been injured in an accident.'

'I'm sorry to hear it. We too have been in the Baltic on a training exercise. On unterseebooten. How do you say, submarines. We here are all from Hanover. Next week we report to Wilhelmshaven for duty on a front-line boat.'

David looked at the smart Naval uniforms and nodded.

'I'm just an old fashioned sailor, cargo here and cargo there and home whenever possible. You speak good English.'

'Yes, before I join the Navy I was Third Engineer on a British ship, the Wanderer out of Avonmouth.'

'I know her.'

There were never the national barriers among seamen.

They were well used to depending on each other in all conditions across the oceans of the world. Dutch, German, British, Scandinavian, it made little difference where one came from, they were all brothers under the skin and more likely to trust each other than the landsman who knew little of the ways of the sea.

'Are you going to the Holland Hook for the ferry? You will need to change trains at Hanover. We will see you right at Hanover. It is a very big bahnhof, very busy, more like one of your football stadiums.'

David thanked him. They seemed a good crowd and the time flew by as they sped across the open countryside past vast fields, sleepy farms, small towns and miles of open forest. One of the other officers pulled out his wallet and extracted a well thumbed pack of glossy photographs. A smiling family looked shyly at the camera, their Daddy proudly in uniform and two young girls by his side. His wife was pretty and had fair curly hair.

'My wife Paula and my children, Margot and Frauke,' he said with a smile.

'You have a lovely family.'

'I go to see them before we go to Wilhelmshaven.'

'Ich habe Durst!' Hans thrust out the flask again and soon they were all enjoying the comradeship that bound all sailors the world over. The flask was followed by a bottle and then by a couple of tasty giant sausages as everyone shared what they had. David relaxed. He was among friends and soon forgot the aggressive police at Berlin. At Hanover, his friends were as good as their word and they ushered him across to the right platform and past the demands for his Reisepass. He finally boarded his train amid further toasts, slaps on the back and hearty handshakes. Hans, very much the spokesman, thrust a ball of paper into David's top pocket and looked him in the eye.

'God speed my friend. Give our love to your girl.'

David gripped his hand again. He'd valued their friendship on his journey across a strange land. He was quite happy at sea wherever he was but they had instinctively known of his unease and shared their resources with him unstintingly.

'Good-bye Hans. Best of luck on your new ship! Sorry, submarine.'

He walked down the train. It was not as crowded as the Berlin train and there were fewer uniforms. He wondered if there would be another fuss at the Dutch border but the wine, schnapps and sausage had rendered him sleepy and he decided to worry about that when he got there. Just before he fell asleep he wondered what it was that Hans had pushed into his pocket. He twisted his wrist up to fish it out. It was a crumpled bank-note for one hundred Deutschmarks.

CHAPTER NINE

It was a very tired David that left Temple Meads station some thirty hours later. The crossing had been rough, not that it had worried David but berthing had been delayed and he had missed his connection. The train from London had been crowded and he'd had to stand for a part of the journey. He caught a bus to the Centre and dropped off on the corner of Baldwin Street. He thought he'd buy some chocolates at the little shop opposite the picture house and call at the Post Office before walking down the Narrow Quay to Prince Street Bridge and over to Cumberland Road. Despite his tiredness and apprehension at what he might find at the end of his journey he felt elated and thrilled at the prospect of being able to show his love and concern. Annie was such a treasure, such a loving, generous girl he hated to think of her being hurt in any way.

'A bit like a school-boy,' he thought, 'I can't wait to see her reaction as I walk in through the door!' He chuckled to himself. If the telegram he'd sent brought good news he'd be able to provide the perfect solution to her problems. He crossed the bridge seconds before it swung open to allow a tug to pull a salt-streaked rusty freighter slowly through the gap. The basin was crowded. A ragged line of vessels lay in various stages of unloading all down the dock. An endless train of lorries growled past him as he pressed on past the last warehouse and turned into Cumberland Road. With the house now in sight, he quickened his pace and was soon standing before the door.

Annie was sitting at the kitchen table when the knock came. She had that thought which had often surfaced lately that it would be her David but quickly squashed it because of its sheer impossibility, he was weeks away somewhere in the Baltic. Her mother, engrossed in turning a pan of sizzling tomatoes, sang out,

'You go dear.'

Annie heaved a sigh. It would not be her David. It would most likely be the breadman or some sailor looking for lodgings close to the docks. Her wrist ached and although her head had cleared she still felt far from able to cope with anything but the simplest routine. She wondered when things would start to improve and she could think of work again.

The knock came again. She grasped the heavy brass doorknob, twisted it and the door swung open. A figure in uniform clutching a large ten shilling tin of Mackintosh's Double Centre Chocolate Toffee Assortment stood there smiling at her. His eyes were tired but wide. A grip lay on the doorstep.

'Ooh, David!' She stared at him.

'David! It's David. How on earth...?'

'Hello Annie.'

For what seemed a minute Annie stood there grinning at him, her face alive with delight. She caught her injured wrist and folded both hands beneath her chin. Her feelings were right. It was David.

'Is it really you or do I have to pinch myself and risk waking up?'

'It's me alright. Oh, Annie I've thought of this moment, thought of it all across Europe. Can I come in?'

Annie shyly pulled him in with her good hand. He

looked at her, hair falling over the jagged tear now heal-
ing on the side of her head and her injured arm held close
to her breast. He bent to fold her against him, feeling the
tenderness and love burst from his heart and found himself hugging the tin of toffees.

'For you.'

He stepped forward and put them on the little side table then turning, took her gently in his arms and pressed
kiss after kiss upon her lips until she gasped for air. She
coloured and clung to him.

'Oh, David, my David, you're really here.'

'Yes, it's really me.'

'How?'

'Your mother sent me a cable.'

'She knew?'

'Oh yes, I've been on my way for two days.'

'I dreamed you were but dismissed it as silly. Somehow I knew you were coming. Strange isn't it, almost as
if we were part of the same person. I can't describe it
but, believe me, I knew you were coming.'

David shook his head and laughed.

'You've got psychic powers then. I hardly knew myself whether I'd make it through Germany without being
locked up. The country is swarming with police. I was
stopped and questioned twice. On the Dutch border they
wanted to know if I was bringing money out for anyone.
I ask you? A sailor with money! I told them I had only
the cash in my pockets and that I was going home to my
girl. They asked if I had been approached by any Jewish
families to smuggle cash or valuables out of Germany. I
tell you, they are security mad. As if they were under
threat or something. If it were not for meeting up with

some sailor friends I think I might have been delayed a lot longer.'

'Never mind, you're here now.'

'And a relief to be back in a sensible country with good old British bobbies. No long bayonets here, thank God.'

He looked at Annie again. The journey was behind him now and he could concentrate on helping this wonderful girl to get fully better.

'Annie, my love, I'm here for you now. I'll look after you.'

'Looks like you could do with some looking after. How does eggs, bacon and tomatoes sound David?'

Mrs Vickery smiled over Annie's shoulder.

'Come on, you two, come through to the kitchen and I'll put the kettle on.'

'I could murder a cup of tea,' grinned David.

They trooped through to the comfortable kitchen, David guiding Annie before him with a gentle hand on her shoulder. The smell of bacon and hot toast awaited them and David felt the tension of the journey begin to fall away from him He was here and he could begin to help make things better.

Between mouthfuls he again relived the trip across country and by way of answers to their many questions tried to describe the crowded snapshots of the adventure. At the same time he was anxious to discover just how Annie had come to be injured and what had happened at the hotel. He was aghast at finding that Annie had lost her job and was all for leaving the table there and then to go and sort it out. It didn't seem to add up. Mrs Vickery wisely interrupted.

'I think that things are best left as they are. From what

Annie has been telling me it can't be long before there's a real bust-up in that kitchen and I feel that Annie's well out of it. If an injustice has been done, it will soon come to light. I would feel happier if we all left the matter behind us.'

David fell silent and Annie nodded. It didn't always pay to jump too quickly. In their hearts, the three of them felt that what was important was that Annie should get better before she started to worry about any further jobs. A loud knock on the door snapped them out of their silence.

'Your turn Mother,' smiled Annie.

Mrs Vickery pushed back her chair and left the two of them gazing at each other across the table. She was back in a trice.

'Telegram for Mr David Pollard. Someone's quick off the mark!'

She handed the envelope to David. With a half smile he tore it open and read out the contents.

'DELIGHTED TO WELCOME YOU BOTH STOP EVERYTHING AWAITS YOUR ARRIVAL STOP MOTHER'

'I think that I might have the perfect solution.' He beamed at Annie. 'How would you fancy a little holiday by the seaside...in that cottage you said you couldn't make out...remember?'

Mrs Vickery put her head on one side.

'Oh, Annie, how lovely.'

Annie started to cry. It wasn't her injuries, it wasn't even the moment, it was the thought that someone had travelled half way across Europe to be with her and had then gone to the trouble to set up the perfect way for her to convalesce in such lovely surroundings. It began to dawn on her just how much this man loved her.

'That would be wonderful David, just wonderful.'

'Then it's settled. Tomorrow we shall set off for Porlock Weir and aim to be there by tea-time. I know that mother is looking forward to having you stay. She's always wanted a daughter but always had a house full of menfolk.'

Annie bit her bottom lip and blinked back the tears. Her mother handed her a handkerchief from up her sleeve and they both switched on a shaky smile for each other. She heaved a sigh and turned her eyes towards her David. She was convinced that her heart had moved, so great was the feeling that her stirred within her.

'I don't know what to say. It's such a lovely idea. Oh, thank-you, thank-you David.'

She reached out to him and he stretched out his hands across the table to grasp hers.

'We can spend as long as you like. I intend to take some leave before thinking about another ship. I have a little money put by. I'm sure that we could both do with some time apart from the world.'

Mrs Vickery crossed the kitchen and stood behind her daughter. She looked across at David.

'I think I know what's best for Annie and that's why I cabled you. I know you'll look after her.'

'I will Mrs Vickery, I will.'

'Now, I think we all deserve a glass of sherry. Annie, fetch the bottle and David will reach down the glasses.'

Annie's eyes twinkled with what could have been the residue of her tears or a little mischief.

'Let's have some of father's special Madeira. You

know, the Malmsey.'

Her mother smiled. 'As it's a very special occasion.'

The bottle was duly brought and the glasses placed neatly on the table. Annie poured a liberal measure into each glass.

'To a perfect holiday.'

'To a lovely man.'

'To you both.'

The next day dawned fine and blue. David had been awakened before six by the squeal and chatter of the little steam engines that shuttled busily to and fro along the crowded dockside behind the house. He'd made some decisions in the early morning and thought that under the circumstances, although perhaps a little impetuous, they were the right ones for the occasion. Long before breakfast, he slipped quietly out of the house leaving a note on the kitchen table.

At eight, Mrs Vickery came down followed shortly by Annie. Soon, the smell of breakfast filled the kitchen and Annie thought she would wake David with a cup of tea. She was halfway out of the kitchen when her mother called her back.

'There's a note here signed David.'

She pushed the folded note across the table and Annie sat down.

'Just slipped out for an hour or two. Some business to see to. See you shortly. Start packing. Love David.'

Annie took a sip of the tea.

'I wonder what he's up to?'

'There must be quite a bit to see to,' commented her mother. 'He's only been in the country for a few hours and there will be the shipping line to talk to and probably the bank and then the arrangements for today. He's hardly got any luggage with him and I expect he'll want to buy some personal things.'

Annie nodded.

'I'll get some of my things together.'

'Have your breakfast first and then I'll help you.'

By ten thirty Annie was packed, ready and anxious and had stationed herself in the front room behind the curtains so that she could observe the road.

'What it is to be in love,' her mother smiled in a sing-song voice. Annie blushed.

'I know it's childish but I want to catch sight of him as he comes back.'

She suddenly thought of her sister.

'You'll tell Angela.'

'You try to stop me. We'll be talking about this for days. She'll be over today I expect.

'Tell her thanks for all she has done to help.'

'Of course dear. You just concentrate on getting thoroughly better. You'll keep in touch won't you?'

'I will.'

At eleven, Annie was persuaded to leave her post for another cup of tea. Just as she left the window and crossed to the door there came a tap and the door opened.

'There, I think we're all set.'

He grinned, and the smile became infectious.

'We're going in style.'

He steadied Annie by the arm and led her to the open door. Parked neatly at the curb was a shiny dark green tourer with its hood folded back.

'Your carriage awaits.'

Annie laughed out loud.

'I didn't know you could drive a car.'

'Oh yes, a couple of years now but it wasn't worth getting a car because I was always at sea and it would have been left at Porlock for months on end without any attention.'

'What make is it?'

'It's a Morris Eight. I'm told they are very reliable. It's not new, a few years old actually but it's not been very far. Belonged to a chap in Clifton who has bought a bigger car. I saw it in the garage window. Looked perfect for touring Exmoor and if it rains we can put the hood up. It's got side screens too.'

'Oh David, I love it. Can I give it a name?'

David smiled.

'You think of one while I go and say good-bye to your mother and put your bags in.'

Annie ran her fingers along the bonnet and up the chrome of the windscreen. She looked up.

'It's lovely David. Can we call her Greensleeves? After the song.'

'Right you are, Greensleeves she will be. If you'd like to get in, I'll make sure we've got everything.'

David fussed around for a while, checking that the luggage was on board and that the several parcels he had purchased were secure behind the front seats. Satisfied, he climbed into the driver's seat and started the engine.

'All set?'

Annie looked up at her mother and sideways at David. Both were smiling.

'Aye aye Cap'n!'

'Then off we go. 'Bye Mrs Vickery, I'll look after her.'

"'Bye mother!'

'Goodbye Annie, take things easy.'

'I'll write.'

With a wave, David slowly moved away from the house and drove carefully down Cumberland Road. Mrs Vickery waved them into the distance until she lost sight of them as they rounded the bend before turning left for Bedminster Down.

The little car coped easily with the hill and was soon running along the ridge of the Down with the city spread out below them. Far in the shimmering, sparkling distance, the suspension bridge seemed closer than it was and ships in the Basin became unreal toys glinting in the morning sun. Soon they had left the city behind and were motoring out into the Somerset countryside with the winding road ahead and the lively chatter of the engine to pull them along. David seemed relaxed and Annie felt safe in his hands.

'Look under the dashboard Annie,' he indicated, 'you'll see some bars of Kit Kat. Break one up for yourself and feed me with the other.'

Annie did so.

'There's all sorts down here. Cadbury's and Rowntree's Aero bars!'

David grinned.

'Let's start with the Kit Kats. We've a long way to go!'

'You're spoiling me.'

'That's the idea. We'll stop after Bridgwater and have a little picnic. Then we'll motor on via Watchet and Blue Anchor so you can see your old haunts. Mother isn't expecting us until tea-time.'

'You are spoiling me.'

The sun shone and the way beckoned. Everything was looking full and summery. Cows lay dreaming, up to their necks in lush grasses. Orchards, jewelled with fruit, crowded ancient farms and whitewashed cottages and everywhere the hedges were full of flowers. The road was clear almost all the way to Bridgwater when they slowed to follow an enormous lorry towing a trailer. Bridgwater seemed crowded with folk and Annie noticed that the tide was up as they crossed the bridge.

It seemed only minutes before David swung Greensleeves off the road and parked under the shade of some trees. The road had been climbing and winding for some time as it skirted the Quantocks and David had counted on finding the spot in the woods just before Holford free of traffic. It was and they had the place to themselves except for the occasional car passing, scuffing on the rough gravel. For a moment they savoured the peace. Dappled woodland bent down to the roadway and bracken was twisted and woven among the grasses that swept up the hill. Birds sang and there was the hum of flies from between the textured trunks where the sun splashed through velvet shadow.

'It's lovely.'

'We often stopped here when I was a child. Mum would open the thermos and I would go exploring in the woods. It's not too far now. We can turn off for Watchet at St Audries. Just a few miles.'

'How's Greensleeves?'

'I was thinking that. I'll just see if she wants a drink.'

David climbed out and checked the radiator.

'All OK. She's a good girl.'

Annie laughed.

'I'll bet you haven't got a thermos this time.'

'No, but I have got a bottle of wine and two glasses, and a couple of pasties. Won't be as good as mother's but they look fine enough.'

'You've really planned this haven't you?'

'This is our time Annie. I want us to remember this in future times when things might not be as perfect.'

Annie looked at him shyly.

'It's all special with you. Thank you for coming home as you did and for thinking of all these things.'

David put his arm about her shoulders.

'I love you Annie.'

It was a memorable moment. The wine, the sunshine, the leafy security of the trees, listless in the summer warmth claimed both their hearts and they wrote it in the book of their lives. All too soon they decided to move on and having packed up, they started Greensleeves and nosed their way back onto the highway. There had been little traffic while they had been parked and they saw even less as they dropped down through Kilve and on to St Audries.

Watchet slept easily in the late afternoon sun. It seemed smaller and David parked for a while at the end of the Esplanade overlooking the harbour. A coaster lay under the Eastern Breakwater and a few boats dipped and bobbed at their moorings.

'Just over there is where father used to keep his schooner Dancer. We all went to sea on it you know.'

David nodded.

'I think that qualifies us both as sailors.'

It all seemed so familiar to Annie, as if she'd never

been away. She took her mind's eye along the Esplanade and up Swain Street to the junction with Anchor Street. It was like being a child again as if she could just walk home and find tea waiting for her. And yet here she was with her man and she was never so happy.

'Oh look David, there's Captain Bob Chidgey. He was captain of the Louise when I was a little girl. Father used to meet up with him in harbours all over the place.'

'They were grand old sailormen. We shan't see their like again. They used to navigate the Bristol Channel by eye you know. Knew every rock and current. My father still tells stories about them.'

Annie agreed.

'Father used to estimate the time he'd arrive off Watchet when leaving the Bar and he'd be right to the minute. He could tell where he was on the darkest night by a sounding.'

They sat for a while feeling the warmth on their shoulders. Gulls shrilled and screamed abusively and a lone fisherman wound in his line from the rail.

'It hasn't changed much,' decided Annie.

'Let's hope it never does. It's part of our heritage,' added David seriously.

They moved on their way, through busy Swain Street and left into Market Street. Annie saw several other folk she knew but they didn't see her sitting in the car as it drove past. Greensleeves whined her way up the steep slope of Cleeve Hill and was soon flying along the old ridge road at a good pace. Next came the descent to sea level at Blue Anchor and they dropped down past the long line of beech trees atop blown clusters of tossing willow herb and splashes of bright valerian. Far beyond them, a long line of sharp-edged cumulus, white against the green, grey shifting waters of the Bristol Channel, lifted above the blue distant line of Wales. These were the colours of home for both of them. Here were tall bleached grasses, bronze cast bracken and the pale kisses of golden gorse, alive the whole season through. Here too, the trailing wild honeysuckle, lone, bent crabs and miles of wind sculptured beech hedge, secret with nuts and sharp-eyed life. Or to climb beyond the field line knee-deep in pillows of bright ling and wine-dark heathers where the ageless, ancient moorland reigned before plunging hundreds of feet into dark combes etched deeply with incisive pine and clutching scrub oak. There was always a magic here, a magic known only to those who were privileged to hold the key.

They motored happily on passing Minehead under Hopcott and were soon on the Porlock Road climbing out past Bratton. Ahead of them, the sun was dipping down the sky and had lost much of its strength. They topped the rise at Headon Cross and beyond them the steep purple of Dunkery Hill was painted on the late, yellow afternoon haze, its beacon indistinct in the thick, boiling air that trembled up the sky. The cumulus had retreated before them, collapsing to lie trailing over the Chains and the whole vale of Porlock lay before them on a canvas of barley browns, russetts, ochres and the pale golden legacy of harvest. Trees in their thousands marched to a silent sea where, timidly, few stood their ground against the bright highway of salt stones that guarded the sea gate of the valley.

They drove in silence past Holnicote, Pile Mill and Allerford under great thrown branches, over stone bridges and past impenetrable hedgerows until descending swiftly through a leafy tunnel into Doverhay. Suddenly they were in Porlock. After the heady companionship of the day the very stones of the village seemed to cry reality. A tractor was easing past a Blue Motors coach and a crowd outside Capes shop were giving loud instructions to the driver of an ancient Sunbeam tourer stuck in the way. David reversed back to the turning for Doverhay and waited for the result. After what seemed an age, the coach swept by en-route for Minehead.

'They've been to Lynmouth and back via Oare. Have you ever been on that trip?'

Annie nodded. 'Yes, on our first holiday. Loved every minute!'

'There's so much to see along this coast. I'll take you over to Culbone in a day or two.'

'That would be lovely.'

They successfully drove through Porlock with no sign of the tractor or the Sunbeam. David looked across at Annie.

'It's all wonderful isn't it? No matter where I go in the world there's nowhere quite like this. It's sheer magic, like a huge secret garden and we have the password. A wise lady once said, "Thank God, for a lifetime, I am England." I know what she meant. It's like being joined to the soul of the country, knowing you are a part of it and all it has and can be. I sometimes play Vaughan Williams' Lark Ascending on the gramophone. It seems to sum up all I feel about this lovely part of Somerset. Do you know what I mean?'

Annie's answering squeeze told him she did.

'Feeling as I do, I often wonder if we've been here

before and walked these hills, fished these streams and cut hay in the sea meadows there.'

Annie joined in quietly.

'I love the peace that has settled here. I get the feeling that no war has torn these hills and only honest endeavour has enriched the villages and towns.'

The last mile to Porlock Weir dropped under high hedges flecked with stands of stiff sorrel, lacy cow parsley and the ruddy fruit of the dog rose. A liberal coinage of dandelion mingled among the insistently nodding verge grasses as Greensleeves pressed on her way along the narrow, sticky tar and gravel roadway to West Porlock and the Weir. A moor-scented land breeze wind-sweetened by a thousand thousand acres of high heather moorland sank through the trees above the road and lent a wine like quality to the air that was both intoxicating and exhilarating. Then the sea burst into view and they bumped along the uneven beach road past Oyster Perch toward the cluster of white-washed cottages half drowned in hydrangeas and hollyhocks.

Annie knew that the end of her journey was only seconds away and felt just a bit nervous. David sensed as much and rested his hand on her arm.

'They'll love you every bit as much as I do. Just remember you're here to get well. Let other folk fuss about for a change and concentrate on getting better.'

For Annie the journey had flown by and she felt that she had come to know even more about the sensitive man that sat beside her. He was such a joy. That he shared her depth of feeling for beauty and magic was almost too good to be true. Her arm hadn't hurt over much and her head was still clear which boded well for the days ahead.

They slowed to a crawl and soon turned off to park on the old fish market above the shingle opposite the Cottage Hotel. David pulled the brake on.

'There, home at last.'

Annie stretched.

'Lovely.'

Collecting the bags, David lead the way to the white painted cottage. His mother, wearing a patterned pinafore, stood smiling at the door.

'Welcome both of you, 'specially to you my dear. I hope you'll be very happy with us.'

'I'm sure I will, thank-you,' smiled Annie, her nervousness already flowing away. Mrs Pollard knew exactly what it was like to be in Annie's shoes. She stepped forward and put her arm about her.

'Come in my dear, I'll show you your room. David will bring your things up. Did you have a good journey?'

'Yes Mrs Pollard, it was lovely. David is a careful driver and we made splendid time. I thoroughly enjoyed it. It's a super little car.'

'Very smart I'm sure. Look, please call me Lizzie. We don't stand on ceremony here. You'll soon meet everyone else in the Weir. A bit like one big family. We all know each other very well. I'll tell you who to look out for. Nothing serious you understand but Mr Pugsley for instance will try to pull your leg or play tricks on you. It's just his way. Oh, and Bernard at the Ship will want to meet you. He was a friend of your Dad's when they were youngsters.'

'We'll keep you busy,' laughed David at the door with the bags.

Annie felt among family. Everyone seemed happy to welcome her into the community. She relaxed and smiled.

'Thank-you Lizzie. Thanks for everything David. I know I'll be happy here.

'That's the idea,' smiled Lizzie. 'You're home now.'

CHAPTER TEN

The summer gradually matured into autumn and the westerlies strengthened bringing grey seas and paler blues beyond the Gore. The lane to Worthy heard the chuckle and thrill of the robin as the other birds fell silent and the first yellow leaves bent their faces to a reluctant sun. For Annie, it was still summer, the fullness of her heart told her it was so and on their many walks they had shared a bounty that many had found before them. She'd written home of course and received letters back from her mother and Angela. All had urged her to stay until she felt thoroughly rested and fit to take up her life again. It was the case, however, that she had been able to cope well enough after a fortnight and was now feeling a bit of a fraud for staying on and taking advantage of everyone's care.

She'd become David's inseparable companion and friend. They had been out with Captain Ley in the Mistletoe, walked the steep crumbling hillside to Culbone and climbed up from Porlock to Hawkcombe. They'd ranged over Doverhay and up to the Nutscale valley where, they understood there were plans to build a dam. They had watched the red deer moving through the slanting shadows of young rowan as they fed and wandered the valley floors. They'd seen clever badger and nimble fox wander and dart across pale carpets of pine-needles tufted with thin grass and hidden from the world by close families of silent conifers. Then, as day had followed day, the pair of them exulting in the joy that comes from the heart, found all their experiences heightened to a degree they hardly knew existed. Life was full and life was a joy.

At the beginning of October, Mrs Pollard decided that it was time for the youngsters to come down to earth and start to pick up the threads of life again. She didn't say as much but asked the odd question, dropped the hint and made a few suggestions that prompted David to start thinking of the future. She was much reassured when David announced that he was thinking of driving Annie back to Bristol as soon as it could be arranged. As for himself, he thought he might try for a berth on board a coaster which would mean he could be home more regularly.

'Annie's father is the skipper of a coaster running in and out of Bristol and that seems to be the best solution for them. I'm not suggesting that he find a berth for me, I'm sure he already has a Mate but I might find something similar in the London area. I know one or two shipping firms that operate out of the London River and now I have the car, it won't be half the problem it was to travel across the country.'

His mother nodded.

'You might try Avonmouth. One or two of the local lads have been able to get jobs up there.'

'Yes, I'll aim to do that but I'm due to sit for my Master's ticket at the next session in December and so would find it more practical to stay in the area for the time being. I shall need tuition and some help.'

'What are Annie's plans?'

'Well, she's hoping she can find a position as a cook somewhere in the Bristol area so she can live at home.'

'I know it's difficult to make plans at this stage but if

you'd like to think of coming here for Christmas both of you, we'd love to see you.'

'I hope that will be possible,' said David, 'it's very thoughtful of you to suggest it, however, we shall have to see how things work out. I may be at sea and Annie might be in the throes of cooking a Christmas dinner for fifty.'

It rained on the day they set off for Bristol. Greensleeves had her hood up and the side-screens fitted. The plan was to drop Annie off at Cumberland Road and then press on for London where David could look for a position which would enable him to earn some money and prepare for the exam. The journey was one that spelled separation and uncertainty and that, coupled with the memories of the last few weeks, made for long periods of silence as they splashed their way back up the A39 and the A38 to the city. It didn't take them long. They didn't stop and they were soon parked in Cumberland Road where it was still raining. David carried her bags to the front door.

'I'm not finding this very easy so I'll say my good-byes here and get on my way. I'll be in touch within a day or two as soon as I get settled. I hope you find something suitable. 'Bye my love.'

He bent and kissed her gently and with a lump in his throat, turned on his heels and almost ran to the car. Annie stood there and didn't know whether it was the tears or the rain that blurred the image of Greensleeves as she turned the corner. She knew that the holiday couldn't have lasted for ever but it was hard to accept that she had to move on. She opened the door and called out.

'Hello, I'm back.'

'Oh, Annie you do look well.'

Annie grinned ruefully.

'I've got to admit I didn't want to come back.'

'That's always the way. How's the wrist?'

'Pretty good now, just a bit of a twinge when I lift things but almost as good as new.'

'You'll have to think of somewhere to work.'

'I know. I'll look at the paper tonight.'

Annie soon felt a bit better. She could talk to her mother and knew that any advice that was given would be carefully thought through.

'You go on up love, I've got your old room ready for you. Your father will be coming home tonight. He's got three days before he needs to think of sailing.'

'How is father?'

'Well enough, although he's been complaining about getting out of breath lately. I expect it's his age. He should be retiring soon.'

Annie thought it would be nice to sit down with them both and to share her holiday with them.

David's drive across country towards London was miserable. He kept looking at the empty seat beside him and wishing they hadn't had to part.

'Still,' he thought, ' I've got to move on and find a decent job if I'm to provide a home for both of us.'

He was tired when he finally turned into Rotherhithe Street. He'd been lost twice and both times been confused by the miles of high brick, crowded terraces and busy warehouse yards that backed on to the narrow maze of streets and alleys sprawled against the docks. He followed the bend in the river and was soon in sight of St

Mary's church and the Ship Inn where he and his friends had often stayed when they were in dock. It was friendly and clean and unless there'd been a ship in today, there would be a bed and a pint waiting for him. He pulled into the small yard and eased himself stiffly out of the driving seat.

All was well and the landlord, Mike Prescott, suggested he might like to put his car in the double lock-up across the road from the pub.

'How long will you be staying?'

'Just a day or two. I'm looking for a ship.'

'Might be able help you there, Skipper of the Jasper was in here today. He's looking for a Mate. They run up the east coast out of the Pool an' sometimes over to Denmark.'

'I could be interested.'

'Well you'd better look smart. I told a couple of the lads about it earlier today. Jasper is one of the Gemstone lot. They have their offices in Hays Lane. Nice little boats, always very smart.'

'Thanks, I'll nip over now. Let you know how things go.'

'Right you are, see you later.'

David thought the idea over as he drove back to Jamaica Road and on up to Hays Lane. The job sounded ideal. With a bit of luck he could be home every fortnight or so. The offices were down by the river close to Hays Wharf and he found them easily enough. A model of a small three-island tramp was displayed in the window and there were several posters advertising the Gemstone Line on a board outside the double doors. David had never heard of them but that was not unusual as there were dozens of small companies operating out of London with two or three vessels and he couldn't be expected to know of them all. The offices were busy and David waited in a small queue at the desk. Most of the customers were concerned with shipping manufactured goods to Leith and it sounded to David as if there was a regular 'packet' to Scotland.

When his turn came, he explained that he was seeking a berth as Mate while waiting to sit for his Master's ticket at the end of the year. The clerk rang a bell and a smartly dressed silver haired gentleman stepped out of the rear office.

'Name's MacDonald, Manager, We need a qualified Mate for the Jasper. Sail on Wednesday from the Pool.'

'I have my ticket. I'm sitting for Master at the next examinations.'

'Last ship?'

'Antares, Surrey Docks, to the Baltic.'

'I know her. Can you get your dunnage on board by Tuesday and be ready to square away Wednesday morning?'

'I can.'

'Then they'll see to your papers and book here in the office. You can sign on now.'

He tipped his head to one side.

'Any questions?'

David thought for a moment. He hadn't asked about pay or how long the vessel was likely to be away. It wasn't 'foreign' so not likely to be longer than a week or so. He answered smartly.

'No Sir.'

'Right,' concluded Mr MacDonald, 'interview completed in five minutes. Very efficient. I'll contact the skipper for you. Just report on Tuesday.'

David thanked him. The clerk pushed the papers across the counter and David signed on. He couldn't remember anything happening with such speed before and felt just a little alarmed about the whole business. He thought he'd just drop down to the Pool and have a look for himself what the Jasper was like.

He had a pleasant surprise. She was moored outboard of the Emerald at a little wharf below Hays. Both vessels were as smart as paint and looked well cared for. The hatches were open and the for'ard derricks busy unloading what looked like canned goods.

'Well,' thought David, 'I'd better let Annie and mother know what the score is and then start to get my gear together.'

Back at the Ship, Mike clapped him on the back.

'Well done Dave old chap, I told him I'd find him a good 'un.'

David laughed.

'A bit like being shanghaied modern fashion. What do you get out of it?'

'A pint if you're any good!'

'As long as I'm not drugged and shipped out down your back stairs I'll double that.'

David went up to his room and wrote some letters and then went out to post them and put the car away. Mike had said he could keep the car in the lock-up for five shillings a week which David thought was fair. With all settled he went down to the bar for a snack and a pint.

The Jasper was a real find. Her skipper was a jovial character who had been on minesweeping trawlers during the Great War and had been blown up twice. Nothing seemed to daunt or haze him and he ruled the Jasper with a practised and avuncular air causing everything to be done with the minimum of fuss.

'Once I see you can do the job son, I'll leave you to it and if you want a hand with your exam' navigation or stowage or whatever, I'll test you.'

David soon found his way around. She was a well-run ship with no evidence of scrimping. There were no cases of lifeboats painted into their chocks or tackles clogged with varnish. Above all she was a happy ship which counted for much. Most of the crew signed on again and again, a sure sign that all was well. He soon found out that she made a regular and perhaps boring pattern of trips down the London River and up for Hull, Newcastle, Leith and sometimes Copenhagen. She was seldom away for more than a month which suited David well enough in his present circumstances.

Annie hadn't fared as well. She'd read the Evening Post and searched the Employment columns but had failed to find any positions as cook. There were washers-up and still-room hands but it would be a shame not to find a job where she could start again where she had left off. The letter from David had cheered her up. She would see him in a few weeks and it was good news about the job. She thought she'd better make some enquiries in the city.

Accordingly, the next day she set out to walk across the bridge and on up into the Centre to see what jobs might be advertised outside doors and in windows. Someone mentioned to her that there was a job going at the Mauritania in Park Street but when she enquired she found that it had been taken only that morning. Not to be put off, she walked up Park Street and right into Park Row, then down Christmas Steps and back into the Centre before walking the length of Baldwin Street, High Street, Broad Street and back into the Centre again via Quay Street. Nothing, absolutely nothing. Annie thought that perhaps she should try shops instead but she'd seen no vacancies on her way around. It was all most unsettling.

Feeling weary, she crossed to a wooden seat close by a pair of telephone boxes at the bottom of Colston Street and sat down. Suddenly she felt quite faint and putting her head down, rested her head on her arms.

'Are you all right Miss?'

It sounded a kindly voice. Annie looked up, still feeling a bit dizzy and saw a sailor dressed in square rig standing close by, his head on one side.

'Not meanin' to interfere Miss, but you was lookin' a bit under the weather.'

Annie took a deep breath and looked at him. He was an older man than she'd thought at first. She glanced at the uniform. He had three gold badges on his arm denoting over twelve year's service and the anchor told her he was a 'killick' or leading hand. Coming from a seafaring family, she could recognise most uniforms.

'I've been out round the city looking for work. Not found any and I guess I've overdone it a bit.'

'I've a girl about your age. She works in an office. She's a typist.'

Annie tried a smile.

'I'm a cook but earlier this year I had an accident and lost my job. Now I'm trying to find another one but there doesn't seem to be anything about.'

The sailor pursed his lips and nodded.

'I know 'ow it can be. Yet things 'ave a way of comin' right side up in the end. You see, you'll find somethin' soon enough. Somethin' that's good for you.'

Annie wondered if he'd prove right. She hoped so. With a wave, he moved on and Annie sat for a while thinking about the problem. Perhaps her mother or Angela would know of something. She hadn't bothered to ask. She sighed and started for home. She took the walk home slowly and arrived not a little weary just as her mother was putting the kettle on.

'Any luck?'

'Afraid not.'

'You look all in.'

'I am. I felt a bit wobbly just now.'

'Sit you down, I'm just going to brew up. Where did you try?'

'All over. Hotels, restaurants, pubs, just missed one at the Mauritania. Then I thought of shops...'

'But you're not keen?'

'Not really. Have you any ideas?'

'Well, it's funny you should ask. If you'd got fixed up I wouldn't have mentioned it but as things are I have heard of something that might tide you over for a month or two.'

Annie drank her tea thirstily and sat back.

'Go on.'

'There's a family just up the road here. The father is the captain of one of the Bristol Steam Navigation boats. They've recently added to their family, a little boy and the mother has had the fever very badly and needs some practical help in the house. You know, cooking, shopping and looking after the children. They are quite desperate to find the right kind of help and were asking around locally. I saw her sister only this morning and she said that it might suit Angela but I said she was already working. So if you fancy some home cooking instead, it might do for a while. They're a lovely family.'

'How many children?'

'Two girls and the baby. The girls are managing at the moment, but they should be at school.'

Annie remembered what the sailor had said to her and wondered if this was what she ought to be doing. It would certainly be good for her and helpful for the future.

'I'll walk up in a minute. What number is it?'

'It's four houses up with a blue front door. Big brass dolphin knocker.'

Annie finished a second cup of tea and then got to her feet.

'Thanks, I'll go and find out what I can do.'

'They'll want to pay you properly.'

It took only a minute to walk the few yards up the road. She knocked on the door. A pretty girl with fair hair answered. She looked about eleven years of age. Annie introduced herself. The girl was Georgina and her sister Louisa was in the kitchen feeding Thomas.

'Mother's awake now, she's been resting all afternoon. Would you like to see her?'

Annie took to them immediately and was made very welcome. Arrangements were swiftly made and Annie agreed to move in and take over. It was all done with a minimum of fuss and Annie spent an hour with Mrs Elliot going over all the details. She was much relieved.

'You can't believe how grateful I am. The children have tried to manage but they find it such a struggle. They can get back to school now. I should be on my feet in a month or so. The doctor says I am over the worst.'

Annie felt glad she was able to help. In fact it might work out better than she had hoped for if she had obtained a cooking job in one of the hotels or restaurants there would be no chance whatsoever of getting some free time at Christmas. Back at home, she told her mother of the outcome.

'I'm so pleased love, You'll be fine there and I know Mrs Elliot will be very relieved.'

She was indeed and Annie proved to be a blessing. She soon came to love the children; confident Georgina, clever Louisa and ever smiling Thomas and they all worked together like a team. Annie tried out all sorts of dishes and started to teach Georgina. Louisa was keen on art and soon had Annie cutting stencils out to make anchor designs for Thomas' bedroom. The time flew by and Mrs Elliot was becoming stronger by the week.

Letters from David reassured Annie that he had found a good ship and was making progress towards his next examination. He was still hoping that he would be able to get home for Christmas and as things looked, he thought that they should be back for Christmas Eve.

October turned into November and both David and Annie found themselves working hard but enjoyably. They both had dreams now and sensed there was an almost tangible future within their grasp. David found the short sea runs gave him little time for brooding, no sooner had they battened down than they were preparing the derricks for unloading again. He soon discovered that the tradition the line enjoyed for smartness meant taking every spare moment for chipping, painting and maintenance even if that was done in a choppy nor'easter or in the short seas off the Humber. Nevertheless, he was happy and true to his word, the skipper left him alone to run the ship. The skipper also sharpened David up considerably where theory was concerned and guided him through some probable questions he might come across in his forthcoming examination.

Annie worked long hours but they fled by. She cooked, washed, shopped, cleaned and nursed all of which she reckoned were laying the foundations of the life she hoped she and David would one day enjoy. December rushed onwards and soon there were only days left before arrangements needed to be made for their promised Christmas together at the Weir. David was due to dock on the 22nd and Annie arranged to exchange her place for Mrs Elliot's sister and husband who would make up the Christmas party when Captain Elliot docked for leave himself. Mrs Elliot was much improved and had discussed the possibility that Annie leave her in the New Year.

The Jasper, true to predictions, nosed her way up Limehouse Reach during the forenoon of the 22nd and secured alongside Number Four berth, Matson's Wharf ready for discharge the following morning. After checking the moorings, David went below to the skipper's cabin.

'All secure, ship's been cleared, the deck crowd are going ashore and the ship-watcher is on board.'

'You go yourself David, You needn't report until the 29th. We're not due to sail until the afternoon of the 30th.

I wouldn't be surprised if we were delayed until the New Year. Shoreside labour could well be thin on the ground at this time of year. Ring the office on the 29th. Oh, and good luck with the exam. It's tomorrow isn't it?'

David thanked him and confirmed the exam date. The skipper grinned.

'Bloody good job we got in today then!'

'True, while the others have been at the cramming school for last week.'

'You're more than ready, you'll see.'

David pulled a face.

'Hope so.'

Within minutes he was on his way through the crowded streets heading for the Ship and looking forward to getting Greensleeves out of dock.

The examination for Master was a very serious affair. The dozen or so other candidates he met with all seemed equally nervous. The day passed incredibly slowly and after the written paper it seemed an age before he was called for his individual questions. Luckily they covered situations he had encountered and he was able to give straightforward answers. Then it was a case of waiting again. It was a tense waiting room that watched the clerk walk out with results typed on a sheet of yellow paper. He pinned it to a board. As soon as the door was shut, everyone rushed forward to crowd around it and David started to read the list from the bottom up. When half-way up the list he still hadn't found his name, a dryness filled his mouth but then, three from the top, he saw it. He'd passed. The relief was wonderful. He could now sail as mate on a big ship or look forward to having a command of his own. With a light heart, he left the building and set off for Rotherhithe. It was entirely his fault in thinking that he could motor across to Bristol the same day that caused the accident. He'd collected Greensleeves and filled up with ROP petrol at the pumps in Lower Road when she coughed and stopped right in the path of an oncoming bus. There was a bang and Greensleeves' starboard wing was bent into the wheel. A couple of passengers levered it free of the tyre but it still scraped and the wheel was out of true causing the car to limp along in an alarming fashion. There was nothing to do but to return slowly to the Ship and to take stock of the damage.

'I've got to get away tomorrow. It's really urgent!'

Mike thought for a moment.

'There's a firm of coach-builders in East Street, off the Old Kent Road behind the Engine Repair Sheds. They're absolutely brilliant at all accident damage. Ask for Brian or Ollie and say I sent you. If you're desperate, they might even do it for you now and you could pick the car up tomorrow.'

'Thanks a million Mike. I'll get it there straight away. Could you ring them for me and say I'm on the way?'

'Cost you a couple of pints!'

David eased slowly into the courtyard of the garage, the engine still gasping. Brian walked out to meet him and smiled at the damage.

'We'll knock out the wing and paint it for you. I think we can find another wheel. The tyre's OK. You can pick it up first thing tomorrow. She'll be as good as new.'

Accordingly, shortly after first light, David was there to see Greensleeves polished and gleaming on the forecourt. There was no trace of the accident whatsoever.

Ollie stood by the car.

'What do you think of that?'

'It's little short of brilliant, You can't tell it was ever bent.'

'Of course not.'

'How much do I owe you?'

'Fifteen shillings.'

David walked over to the office. The main garage was filled with vehicles of all types and ages from Daimlers to Austins. All were awaiting work.

'You look pretty busy.'

'We are,' replied Brian, handing David his change, 'As the number of motors increase, we get busier and busier. By the way I suggest you drain off that ROP and fill up with Esso. You'll have a better journey. She's set up for a higher octane petrol than ROP.'

'I will, thanks.'

David did as he was advised and set off finally for Bristol having made all the necessary telephone calls the night before. He'd arranged to collect Annie at Cumberland Road in the afternoon and then to drive on down to the Weir. It was a long journey but he knew the roads and hoped to be home some time during the evening.

Greensleeves sang along with no hint of trouble and it seemed only a minute or two before David was entering the outskirts of Kingswood and on through St George. The weather was dull and overcast but his spirits were high. He'd passed for Master and in a very short while he'd be holding Annie in his arms. Annie meanwhile was at the window. No comments from her mother could deter her and as soon as the familiar shape of Greensleeves drew up outside she was out of the door like a shot and into David's arms almost before he had a chance to take a step.

'Oh my love, oh, how I've missed you!'

'Annie!'

They stood entwined until, dizzy, they almost fell over.

'Hey, steady on, you'll have us over.'

David rocked backwards and found the side of the car.

'Have you got your gear ready?'

'Ready and waiting for hours but mother says you've got to come in for a while and have a cup of tea before we go.'

David nodded and accepting her hand was pulled into the house for another welcome. Sitting round the kitchen table it was hard to believe that so many weeks and miles had passed since they were last sitting there. Mrs Vickery had made some cakes and soon had tea ready but Annie and David were all eyes and smiles and the tea went down unnoticed. Of course they had to be off but not before Mrs Vickery had pressed a parcel into David's hands.

'To hand round at Christmas.'

David had almost forgotten. Under the dashboard he had a present for Annie's folk and he dashed out to get it. Mrs Vickery put her arm around Annie.

'Have a truly wonderful time love. We shall be thinking of you.'

'I know I shall. Thanks for everything.'

David rushed in, deposited a small bright parcel on the table and with a wave swept Annie out of the house.

On the way down, it was all ideas and plans and for the first time they started to think seriously about a wedding. Annie favoured the spring and David agreed that a

March or April date might better coincide with his plans to find a home port nearer to where they planned to live. Bristol or Avonmouth were the first choices although David thought that he ought to stay with the Gemstone Line for a little longer as they had only just appointed him. They talked over the possibility that Britain might be involved in a war or that serious fighting might break out in Europe and David be called up or be away for long periods. David reassured Annie that Chamberlain was for peace and would do anything to keep Britain out of another war. Certainly Germany seemed very aggressive but not towards Britain. David also pointed out that Britain had the Royal Navy and that Hitler would never dare to face up to that despite his brand new battle cruisers.

'Things might look a bit unsteady Annie, but after Germany has settled its border problems I think Europe will settle down to a long period of peace. The lessons of the Great War are still fresh in too many minds.'

Porlock Weir looked very Christmassy with coloured lights in many windows. The Anchor Hotel was ablaze with electric light and there was a tree set up within that gleamed out through the windows, red yellow and green. There were visitors about and a dozen or so cars parked facing the shingle on the old fish market. A quiet tide lapped the pale grey stones and a heavy moon heaved itself above the dark trees behind Beelzebub Terrace. The sky was clearing and the last torn shreds of cloud were moving slowly inland. It promised to be a fine Christmas.

That evening above two dozen folk crowded into the little bar at the Ship. The lucky ones found a seat but most were happy to hang from the straps that were fixed to the low beamed ceiling. Bernard Perkins was in fine form with a smile from ear to ear and a joke for everyone. The fire crackled, the beer flowed and friends were just pleased to share in the occasion. Annie tried some Arnold and Hancock's Home Brewed despite Jim Pulsford's attempts to make her drink cider. David was soon talking about vessels with his father and Captain Tom Ley. Stories abounded and Annie was hugely amused at some of the naughtier ones. One in particular stuck in her mind as it surely showed that truth could be more entertaining than fiction. It was young Ben Norman from Watchet who told it and soon everyone in the bar was chuckling at it.

Apparently Ben used to sail with Captain Nathan Poole of the ketch Independence and one day they was going into Lydney when they came up with several Appledore and Bideford vessels. 'Cap'n Nathan was at the tiller an' I was up for'ard waiting to catch the heaving line. As we drew level with these vessels it was obvious they had some sort of joke as they shouted, "Tell Auntie I see'd 'ee!" Other vessels brought similar shouts, "Tell Auntie I see'd 'ee." So I went back to Cap'n Nathan and said, "What are they shouting about? What are they saying?" He said, "Don't take any notice o' they. They be mazed!" He looked most embarrassed at the incident and wouldn't tell me. The only other crew member was his son and he said, "Don't 'ee ask father about that. Leave it!" I was much puzzled about it and in fact was puzzled for years. A long time later a little Appledore vessel came into Watchet. Tom Ley here was Harbourmaster at the time and as the vessel made fast, one of the crew looked up and called out, "Tell Auntie I see'd 'ee!" Tom Ley answered, "An' give 'ee some 'teddies'!" I spoke to Tom Ley afterwards and asked him what it was all about.'

Tom laughed and took up the story. 'This Captain Nathan used to trade up to the Welsh Back taking cargoes of potatoes. Now Captain was a very religious man and a strict teetotaller and used to advise everyone to avoid the 'devil drink'. "I got good reason to tell 'ee this, 'cos my own father was found dead in Swansea Dock from falling overboard." Anyway, on this occasion his vessel was at the Welsh Back and the crew were aboard. "Aren't you lads going ashore?" He asked them. "No, Cap'n, we 'aven't got any money for a drink." So Captain Nathan gave them both a shilling and told them to have a drink on him. Now this was very unusual as the Captain normally warned his crew about the dangers of going into pubs. "This is funny," they said, "Cap'n telling us to go up the pub." So after a pint, they decided to go back to see what the Captain was up to. Crossing the jetty, they jumped down on deck with a clatter whereupon a very brightly attired and painted young lady stepped up from the cabin followed by Captain Nathan looking very embarrassed. As the young lady stepped ashore, Captain, he said, "Well, tell Auntie I see'd 'ee an' give 'ee a few teddies." This was picked up by the crew and spread round every vessel in the Bristol Channel. Captain Nathan never lived it down.'

As story followed story, the night drew on and it seemed only a matter of minutes before Bernard was ringing the bell to announce time. Tomorrow was Christmas Day and everyone had a thousand things still to do before thinking of bed. As the crowded room gradually cleared with many a cheery 'Happy Christmas' Annie glanced around the cosy bar. An oil painting of the Flying Foam opposite her was surely by the Watchet artist Captain Chidgey and there was a splendid painting by the door of ketches under the harbour wall at Minehead. It was a super little bar, no wonder it was so popular. David's laugh brought her back to present company and she finished her glass and smiled up at him. He was a real man among men and she felt proud to be his girl.

It was only a matter of yards across the road to the cottage. The night had cleared and the Nash light winked out its regular warning from the other side of the Channel. Across the bay the reaching hand of Hurlstone Point rested on a placid sea and a star or two shivered uncertainly on the surface. Arms linked, they crossed the road and waited for David's father to catch them up.

CHAPTER ELEVEN

Christmas morning was not quite what Annie expected. After a family breakfast and the exchange of presents, Lizzie excused herself and went into the kitchen to prepare the vegetables and start to make up the stuffing for the turkey. David was talking to his father about boats when there came a knock at the door. It was the landlord of the Anchor Hotel.

'I hope I've got this right but is Miss Vickery staying here?'

'Who wants to know?' replied David.

'It's the Anchor. We've got a bit of a problem. We're full up with guests for Christmas and the chef has just walked out, left, gone. Mr Perkins at the Ship can't spare anyone and everyone else has their own dinner to prepare. Mr Perkins said that Miss Vickery was a qualified cook. I'm afraid I'm asking a big favour. Could Miss Vickery come over and save the day? We'd pay her well of course.'

Annie went to the door.

'Please Miss!'

Annie looked back into the room and Lizzie came out of the kitchen. She smiled and shook her head.

'Go on Annie, you'll have to go.' 'What about our meal together? It's my first with you all.'

'I know my love, but there'll be other times. Do you think you can handle it?'

Annie spoke up.

'Is all the shopping done?'

'It is Miss.'

'And how many guests are we cooking for?'

'Thirty eight Miss.'

'I should be able to manage that well enough. Best get over there then.'

She looked ruefully at David who smiled back. 'Go on sweetheart, you go over and sort them out. As mother said last time you were here, we all help each other out when we can.'

With a last look over her shoulder, Annie crossed over the road to the Anchor. She found a clean, well-ordered kitchen and all the facilities necessary to cook a good meal. Why on earth the chef had left she couldn't imagine. The assistant was a young girl who seemed willing enough and so they set to. The menu was the traditional one but Annie thought that she'd add one or two little items of her own as well as tweak the sauces up a little. She had to admit, after the first hour of getting into her stride in a strange kitchen, that she was enjoying herself. It was good to be back.

She soon found chef's problem. Struggling to open a large drawer in the base of the dresser she discovered a cache of empty gin bottles. No doubt he was another Monsieur Jacques. The Anchor was probably well rid of him. She made a note to ask whether or not he'd paid for them all. She suspected that he hadn't.

The meal was served on time and to much acclaim. Annie had to admit that apart from slightly overheating the bread sauce, all had gone very well. She was disappointed to have missed the family meal but had to confess that hers was very tasty. When all was cleared away and the washing up well under way, the landlord came into the kitchen.

'I do congratulate you Miss Vickery. That was superb. Every bit as good as the chef could have done. Better in fact.'

Annie couldn't resist it.

'I was trained in one of the best hotels in Bristol. I would expect it to be good.'

'Some of our guests will be staying over the New Year. You wouldn't care to stay on yourself? We'd be happy to pay you the same rate as the chef.'

'Obviously I'll have to talk it over with the family but if they have no objections I could stay on for a while or at least until my plans change or you find yourself a permanent cook.'

The landlord heaved a sigh of relief.

'You'll never know how much we all owe you. There's staff accommodation available should you want it. Perhaps you'll let me know what you decide.'

Annie nodded.

'I'll let you know later this afternoon.'

Annie wondered what this latest development would bring and how it would be received. She'd talk it through with David and then see how the family felt. If it came to staying on for a while, she had the opportunity of taking the staff accommodation which would lessen the burden on Lizzie. She couldn't expect Lizzie to put her up indefinitely nor would she feel comfortable in doing so.

She had the chance to talk to David later in the day. They'd made their excuses and slipped out for a walk around the Dock and across the Marsh Field. The evening was still. A placid tide, brim full, sucked the cold stones beyond the Gore. The Dock was full and Mr Donati's

Kingfisher rode high against the wall. There were lights aboard two of the yachts and they could hear laughter from one of them. They paused by the gate at the top of the path and looked back.

'I hope this place never changes. I'd hate to see it spoiled.'

Annie slipped her arm around David.

'I don't think it ever will, no matter what happens on the continent. It will never be touched by aggression or conflict. Mr Chamberlain will see to that.'

'I hope you're right. It's too precious to let go.'

'And we'll always come back here, even when we're old.'

'Yes my love, we'll always come back and it will always be the same.'

Annie shared her thoughts about the possible job at the Anchor and to her surprise David thought it a wonderful idea.

'I'd know you were safe here among friends and family and if there ever was any kind of trouble, you'd be far away from docks and factories where there might be bombing. I haven't said anything before but they are setting up ambulance and first aid posts in the docks just in case anything goes wrong. These are troubled times and perhaps we ought to be careful. I'll send you the Boots guide to Air Raid Precautions so you can be prepared just in case.'

And so it was that Annie stayed on at the Weir when David went back to join his ship. She thought it best if she moved into the Anchor and after a week or so, had the kitchen running smoothly with a well-tried menu operating to everyone's satisfaction. David was true to his word and posted on the Boots guide. She didn't think for one moment that the Germans would want to bomb Porlock but she read it anyway.

Over the next few weeks she tidied and organised the kitchen discovering, among other things, several more caches of bottles. She shuddered as she remembered the episode that had put her in hospital. In a flash, it came back to her. She had been going to help the drunken chef when she'd slipped. Why hadn't she been able to remember that before? Strange how fate steered one along the pathways of life. She was almost glad of the accident now for here she was in a lovely place and with a splendid job just as that sailor had said.

David had suffered some leg-pulling on his return to the Jasper. The skipper, for one, had left a note for him addressed to Captain Pollard instructing him not to sail without him. Once at sea, several of the ship's officers gathered in the captain's cabin for a drink and congratulated him on his success.

'You won't be long on board this old barge then David.'

'I think I will actually,' replied David, 'I hope to get married in the spring and staying on here will allow me to get home more regularly. Perhaps I'll look out for a ship out of Avonmouth afterwards.'

'Or Cardiff or Milford, if you want to ship out of the Bristol Channel,' added the skipper. 'They run tankers out of Milford for the West Indies. That's a lovely trip and not too long away from home.'

David made a note of that, however he was aware of most of the shipping movements in the Bristol Channel and thought he'd have a closer look when the time came. It depended where they decided to live. If Annie thought she'd like to stay on at the Weir for a while, they could make that their base. Driving up to Avonmouth would be no problem. He wasn't very keen on living near the docks for if the balloon were to go up, the docks would surely be in the front line.

He hadn't mentioned to Annie that he'd been to see the Rector Mr Stanley Larrett about the possibility of getting married at Porlock in March or April. The Rector had explained that if they were both on the Roll, there should be no problem. He felt quite excited at the prospect of walking out of St Dubricius' church with Annie on his arm.

January and February of 1939 passed slowly for both of them. David broached the possibility of a spring wedding on his next leave and they both started to make preparations. Both sets of parents seemed delighted at the prospect and began to put things aside that might come in for the young couple. They decided that they would try to find a place in Porlock rather than take up the offer of a room with Lizzie. It would give them somewhere to put their things without imposing on the generosity of parents. And, of course, a measure of privacy which was at the top of their list.

David would be home for a few days a fortnight before the wedding was set due to a short trip when the Jasper was only going to Leith and back. As this would be the last opportunity for them to look after the final details, they planned each day with studied care, writing daily with ideas and suggestions. There was a bundle of letters waiting at Leith and an equally large bundle at London but David shuffled them into order and soon picked out the essentials. There was a best man to find, a dress to be made and a place where they could entertain their guests after the ceremony. There were the thousand and one little things that usually got left until the last minute but with only days to prepare, they managed to make an excellent job of it all. David's old school-friend John Pugsley was pressed into service as best man, the dress was ordered from Miss Alice Pittaway of Watchet and the reception was offered by Bernard Perkins at the Ship.

Unknown to the pair of them David's father had been busy making a dining room table and four chairs from a well seasoned bundle of mahogany that had been washed up on Bossington Beach in the early twenties. Annie's father had bought them a Cossor five-valve superhet radio which he had seen in Kille's shop in Parks Street, Minehead on his visit to Porlock before the wedding. Lizzie had made the cake and Annie's mother had provided a complete range of kitchen equipment from Tarrs of Minehead. Knowing of the difficulties that the young folk had in terms of available time, the older generation made it their business to see that all the details were followed up and there would be no hiccups on the day. If the happy fellowship that existed on those three days leave was anything to go by, the marriage promised to be a real success. Everyone worked with a will and by the end of the second day Lizzie declared that all was ready.

That third day belonged to David and Annie. In a fortnight they would be wed. There could be few folk in the land who were as happy. After lunch had been cleared away at the Anchor, Annie was free until five and the pair of them dropped into the Ship for a word with

Bernard.

'You leave it all to me my dears,' he smiled. 'You work hard enough I know. It's all been arranged. After the ceremony you and your friends all come here to me. It's all been taken care of. Matter of fact, the Anchor offered to help as well seein' as you works there but as a friend of the family I insisted that I had you here. There now, if there is anything that you want especially just let me know.'

The Anchor had offered as soon as they knew that Annie intended to get married but they weren't offended when Annie thanked them and said that Bernard Perkins was an old friend of her father's and he'd wanted to help. One of the difficulties was who to invite for the family friends were in Watchet, Bristol, Minehead and Porlock and it was a long way for some to travel. In the end they thought it best if they issued an open invitation and an offer of accommodation for those who would find it difficult to travel both ways on the same day. They didn't expect huge numbers but reckoned that about thirty folk would attend on the day. David would post the cards on his way back.

Bidding a cheery farewell to Bernard, they crossed the Dock gates and walked out past Turkey cottages to the ridge of shingle that swept on to the Gore. It was a cold day but a bright sun was constantly challenging the long battalions of cloud that swept up from below the Foreland. David pulled up the collar of his coat and hugged Annie tight. At their side, the Channel, green and grey with a thousand blown tufts of angry spindrift, splashed against the mottled pebbles and they turned and dropped into the Marsh Field for shelter. It felt quieter here out of the wind. Following the fence at the top of the dock they walked in silence towards the path that led on to Worthy.

'Here's a story Annie,' David pointed. 'Just there, do you see those three large stones?'

Annie nodded.

'Well, they are supposed to mark the graves of three seafarers washed ashore here a couple of hundred years ago. They were buried here because their religion was unknown and it was thought improper to bury them in a Christian churchyard.'

'Is there any actual record of it anywhere?'

'No, it's just an old tradition in the village. Most of the poor fellows that were washed up along this part of the coast were buried in Porlock churchyard but this story might be a very old one from before records were kept.'

Annie shivered.

'It's not very cheerful. Let's talk about something else. Are you sure that we've remembered everything for the wedding?'

'It's a bit late now if we haven't. The next time we meet, we'll have only a matter of hours before the service.'

Annie looked up at him. He looked so confident and reassuring that her trust in him was complete.

'Are you a bit nervous?'

David stopped and turned, grasping her by the shoulders.

'More certain than nervous, certain that I've found the one and only girl for me.'

Annie put her head against his chest.

'I'll always love you David.'

They walked slowly on to meet the road at Worthy and then turned for the village. Their conversation ranged from the practicalities of finding the right place to live to the serious matters in the news. Czechoslovakia had been taken by the Germans and there seemed no end to Hitler's ambition. Annie was still convinced that Mr Chamberlain would never let Britain enter another conflict but David had seen the preparations being put in hand and was not so certain. It was rumoured in London that conscription for men over the age of twenty was in the pipeline and several factories had been turned over to arms production.

'I hope you're right Annie, but if we ever do take on Adolf Hitler it will be a long hard battle and one we might not easily win.'

The day of the wedding dawned fine and fresh with a stiff westerly lifting the wave crests against far Hurlstone Point under swift cloud shadows. Annie had been given five days and she had used the first of them anxiously checking and re-checking that everything was indeed ready for the day. Lizzie had been a tower of strength and together with her mother, who had travelled down from Bristol, they exuded confidence and support, encouraging Annie to take a walk and relax. David had docked the night before and had driven straight down arriving at two in the morning. He was up again at the crack of dawn pressing his uniform and ironing his shirt.

Annie had particularly wanted to drive from the church in Greensleeves. It was pointed out to her that she could have Mr Hobbs' Buick if she liked but she'd felt that Greensleeves was special and nothing else would be as perfect so David's next job was to clean and polish it and find some ribbons. She was, however, happy to go to the church in a big motor and so it was that Mr Bryant's Austin was hired for the occasion.

The wedding was arranged for twelve o' clock and everyone had been invited to return to the Ship for two. Annie had made a lot of the dishes herself and Lizzie and her mother had made it their business to set everything up and decorate the room.

The day passed in a blur for both of them. It was strange how when they both wanted to savour each precious moment, the time shrank away and left only isolated glimpses of the occasion fixed in their minds. For David it was the dramatic way in which, as they emerged from the church porch, the sky cleared and the sun streamed out causing him to blink in wonder both at the freshness of the world and at the brightness of his bride, clad as she was in dazzling white satin, her veil blowing against the ancient mottled stones of the porch arch. For Annie it was piling into Greensleeves, all dress and excitement as they sped through the village past open-mouthed onlookers and on down to the Weir. Then the loving smiles of the guests as she and David pressed the knife into the cake, looking at each other as they did so. They seemed surrounded by love and felt it. David's father took a photograph at the church and another of the whole party outside the Ship in the little courtyard. They hardly noticed the food but everyone said how lovely it was or the speeches which seemed to have everyone in stitches. It was Annie's father who rounded off the day with a surprise that neither of them had anticipated. Raising his hand, he asked for silence.

'Now we are all one family here I know that we all wish David and Annie every success on the voyage they are about to take together. No father could wish for a finer son and daughter and so to set them off on the right foot, my wife and I would like to give the bride and groom this small token of our love.'

Amid further grins and good wishes he stepped forward and handed David an envelope. Everyone else apparently knew all about it but when David opened the envelope he found a reservation for two days at the Lyn Valley Hotel, Lynmouth with dinner and champagne.

'We'd have made it longer but we know that your leave is short. Enjoy yourselves!'

Bernard chipped in.

'Now you'll have to see if that car of yours will climb Porlock Hill.'

It will, if I don't put any more cheap petrol in it!' David laughed.

He'd been telling Bernard about his adventures motoring to and from London.

So it was that they spent two gloriously happy days at Lynmouth. They walked and climbed and scrambled down to Watersmeet and up to the Valley of Rocks and ended each day tired, fulfilled and exhilarated by the wonder of it all. On the first night it was hard to believe that all the fuss was over and they were on their own. They stood on the little harbour arm under the tower and watched as the gulls tumbled and glided, their plaintive cries answered again and again from the hill above. Now, apart from the world, they felt somehow insulated from it and from all the problems there were waiting in the wings. What was it Angela had said?

'Remember, we're more than sisters, we're friends and if ever you need me, you know where to find me.'

Sitting with his back to the harbour wall, they noticed a man close to them. He'd lost his right arm and was awkwardly throwing pieces of stale bread to the gulls with a badly injured left. Annie shuddered.

'Oh look at that poor man,' she whispered.' I do feel so sorry for him. I wonder who looks after him?'

David looked.

'I expect he has family.'

Annie went on.

'I mean, what work could he do with his problems?'

David took her arm and eased her back along the harbour.

'We shouldn't stare. He probably feels self conscious enough as it is.'

It was the only discordant note in the holiday and David became aware that in some inexplicable way this chance meeting had struck a rock somewhere under the surface. He couldn't pinpoint it but put it down to the severity of her accident which probably had a long term effect on her. She was still looking back at the poor chap as they left the harbour.

The following day was one to remember. After scrambling about the Valley of Rocks they walked on down to Lee Bay and despite the coldness of the sea paddled out among the rocks and finished with a drink from the little stream that dropped out of the low cliffs. Visitors were sparse as the holiday season had not really started. There were still primroses bunched in the hedgerows and tattered ranks of blown daffodils clustered under the bare cottage trees. Despite the sun, the wind was still tugging the skirts of winter and spring seemed elusive. It was not so in their hearts for they were full of that magic that springs from the earth. For all that glorious day, they were of the earth, of the sky and a vibrant part of life itself and when the evening came with its dusty orange pastel sky streaked by grey fingers they knew it sealed their future together and they were happy.

Far too soon, they had to think of heading back, first to Porlock Weir to leave Annie and to say their good-byes, then on to London and to sea again. It was another clear bright morning as they set off up Countisbury Hill and across the moor. They took the toll road down just to see Hurlstone Point through the pine trees and to drive along the Worthy road where they had often lingered. With one exception, all the guests had now departed and the Weir seemed very quiet. Angela had stayed behind and after David had walked Annie across to the Anchor she enquired whether there was a possibility of a lift to Bristol. Good naturedly, David agreed despite the slightly longer route than planned but had to admit that he was intrigued to discover the reason why Angela had not gone back with her mother after the wedding. Angela, David had decided, was a dark horse. She kept her council and was a good deal wiser than she appeared.

They were hardly past the Allerford turn when Angela twisted sideways in her seat and looked across at David. What he saw was a serious pair of eyes.

'We haven't had much time to get to know each other and we haven't much time now so I'll get to the point. Annie and I are pretty close and so I'm very pleased that she has found a good friend and partner. I also know that there is going to be a war, probably a long and nasty one.'

David interrupted.

'No, don't stop me, I know what is going on, in the aircraft industry and in the shipyards. Also I talk to folk in the city. Despite the efforts of a few politicians, this country is on course for a collision with Hitler and when that happens, our major cities will be prime targets. So I'm glad that Annie's out of Bristol and I hope that mother will also follow and go back to Watchet. I want you to promise me that you'll do everything in your power to keep Annie at the Weir until things are better again.'

David bit his lip and rested his hand on the gear-stick.

'I agree, there may well be a war and yes, I am aware of the preparations being made. I'm sailing out of London regularly remember. And yes, I'm pleased that Annie is near family at the Weir. Cumberland Road is too near the docks for anyone's safety if they are bombed.'

'Obviously, if the worst happens, you will be involved at sea in the same way that father was during the Great War. You won't be able to get home regularly and you may well be away for long periods. I want you to know that I will always look out for Annie. I've told her that she can always rely on me in any crisis and I want you to know that in the uncertain times that might be ahead, I will look after Annie should she ever need me.'

'Thanks for being so frank. I've already asked my parents to do much the same thing and I know that they love her as a daughter. It is a pity that my job often takes me away for long periods but the only solution to that lies in getting a shore job or a dock job and as I've just passed for master, I don't think that that is a sensible option if I'm to be a good provider. I was thinking of looking closer to home and sailing out of Bristol,

Avonmouth or Cardiff which would allow me to get back to Porlock more easily.'

Angela began to feel a bit more settled.

'I'm staying in Bristol whatever happens. I'll show you the house. The lady I look after will also stay.'

They motored back through Bridgwater where again, the tide was well up and running swiftly under the bridge in a rich, brown flood. A ketch was moored alongside the wall just below and the lads were unloading her. David nodded at her.

'Not many of those around nowadays. We still see a number of barges on the London River but not as many as the old days.'

Angela turned her mouth down.

'It's an antiquated way of life and it can't compete with the modern motor-coaster. Let's face it, who'd want to stand in the open for hour upon hour in all weathers when they could be steering the vessel from inside a comfortable wheel-house. And look at cargo handling, modern methods can turn a vessel round in half the time it took us to do it with a shovel. I know, I've done it.'

David looked across at Annie's sister. She was obviously nobody's fool. Quick, practical and alert, she impressed him with her grasp of current issues. He felt relieved that she would be there in the background to watch over Annie.

It didn't seem long before the suspension bridge could be seen as they crossed Bedminster Down and dropped down to the Basin. He'd nearly turned for Cumberland Road when Angela prompted him to continue.

'Under the bridge and right up Bridge Valley Road. Straight on and I'll tell you when to stop.'

They passed the Zoo and wound up towards the water tower. Close to the imposing block of Belgrave Terrace Angela asked him to stop.

'See that house there,' she indicated. 'That is where I'll be if ever I'm needed. Annie knows where it is too.'

She thanked him and taking her bag, she crossed the road and waved from the pavement.

'Good luck and have a safe trip.'

David glanced again at the elegant house set back from the road then pulled away and turned at the crossroads, down through Redland and Montpelier to Lawrence Hill and the road for London.

CHAPTER TWELVE

The summer of 1939 was glorious. Jasper plied up and down the coast in blue seas and under bluer skies. On board it was shirt-sleeve order though among the crew there wasn't a shirt to be seen all the day long. David was well on top of all the jobs that needed to be done and it was a very smart ship that berthed at the end of a run. There was no mention of war on board and it so came as a shock when in June, Johnny Roberts the Bo'sun was called up as a Special Class Reservist and had to leave the ship. Apparently all the old destroyer men were wanted and several old ships were to be re-commissioned. Johnny was sent to HMS Versatile, but kept in touch, after which those on board the Jasper were more aware of the build-up that was quietly going on.

David managed to get home in June and July for a few days. As at sea, the weather was perfect and he and Annie managed to squeeze a few picnics and walks into their days. Annie had been kept busy at the Anchor and they were very pleased with all that she did. They had asked her to stay on for the season and had offered her an increase in wages which she felt was generous as she was enjoying every minute of it. She now had two assistants which made life easier. Both were local girls who were looking towards cooking as a profession and so were keen to learn. There was also a happy atmosphere in the kitchen which went a long way to make things work well. David again mentioned the possibility of switching from London to a port nearer home so that the travelling could be cut down. Annie thought that they might like to look at the possibility of Bristol and perhaps getting a flat or a rented property there but David felt that the present situation was probably the best for the immediate future or until he'd actually changed jobs.

'If anything looks likely, I'll let you know and we can take it from there. At the moment I think that you are best off here and I come down to you whenever I can.'

August brought a rare trip over to Denmark and across to Sweden before crossing back to Leith and so it was that David was not back in the United Kingdom until the very end of the month. Within hours of securing he was in Greensleeves and driving across country with the hood down. He'd mentioned to the skipper that he was thinking of doing only one or two more trips before changing to Avonmouth as a home port. The skipper was encouraging.

'I can see your reasons but should you want to stay on with the line, I understand that there might be a captaincy available soon. The manager asked me to sound you out about the possibility of taking on the Emerald in the New Year.'

David had been flattered of course but it hadn't deterred him from wanting to be closer to Annie and have the opportunity to get to her side within an hour or so rather than drive all across the country. They had agreed on two more trips and the Jasper would be sailing again on 4th September. So, by mid October at the latest, he would be seeking a berth from Avonmouth and hopefully on one of the newer tankers that made short deep-sea trips to the Gulf.

In West Somerset summer was still in spate. As he drove through Taunton and out into the country under

Crowcombe, he became aware of the Quantocks ablaze with purple, the hedges afire with willow-herb and plum-sized rose hips and the fields sprawled naked and bronzed among still trees. It was a view that made him proud to belong here and he enjoyed again the thrill of being alive and a part of it all. It was late afternoon when he drove through Porlock and down to the Weir. There were quite a few holiday-makers about on the shingle and on the far side of the Dock. The tide had passed half flood and a couple of yachts were waiting to enter. He'd been all over the world but there were few places he'd trade for this unique spot. The sun had now lost its power and the shadows were lengthening but there was still that lingering, shimmering golden magic in the air that held the dusk at bay and seemed to tarry for full flood when the tide would cease its striving and slide back into the darkening depths of the Bristol Channel. He loved the Weir and the folk who lived here. He trusted that Annie did too.

Leaving Greensleeves on the fish dock he went around to the back door of the Anchor and tip-toed in. Annie was preparing the vegetables for dinner her hair tied up under a white square. She caught sight of him out of the corner of her eye and squealed with delight. He swung her around and kissed her.

'Stop it David. I'm working!'

'If I book in for dinner will you serve me personally?'

'Of course not you naughty man. Get out of my kitchen, you're putting me off!'

'Then I'll see you at home when you've finished.'

'Try to stop me!' Grinned Annie.

It was always a honeymoon whenever they were together. It had become a bit of a joke. Most people only had one honeymoon but they shared one every time David came on leave. They'd only been married for a few months but it seemed to get better as time passed by. They both had difficulty in waiting for dinner to finish.

It darkened, leaving only memories of the day and the cottage walls still warm to the touch. The sea vanished and the hill leaned closer as the familiar pattern of summer stars slanted up the sky. Annie came across as soon as she could and the pair of them set off walking slowly along the chezil only feet above a placid waveless sea.

Neither of them actually heard Mr Chamberlain's wireless broadcast. They'd been well up the Dock with David's father looking at a damaged and apparently abandoned carvel built motor-boat with a view to taking on the repairs. They heard the news as they walked back. It was Sid Stenner who lived close by the gates who stopped them.

'Now young David, when you sails again you'll be on a war footin'. The news 'ave jus' come over. We're at war with Germany.'

Annie held tight to David's arm.

'It's official then? I'd hoped the Government would do everything to keep us clear of a war.'

'Aye, but it's this Polish business, the Germans are goin' through 'em like a knife through butter.'

'So we're signing up against them then?'

' That's about it young David. Just like in the Great War.'

David turned to Annie.

'There now, there's every good reason for you to stay put here away from any trouble spots. I should be based at Avonmouth soon and will be better placed to get home.'

'Do you think that Germany will attack us next?'

'Could be, we'll have to wait and see. They've got a huge air force and some pretty powerful ships.'

'Ah,' retorted Sid, 'but not as good as our Royal Navy. We'll soon have 'em locked up in port jus' like we did afore.'

David was recalled by telephone later in the day and by six-o-clock was on his way back to London. Annie went back to work with a heavy heart worrying whether David was driving into a battle zone. He telephoned at ten and apparently all was quiet.

David soon learned that all shipping out of London was to be organised on a convoy basis with escorts provided by a destroyer flotilla based at Harwich. In fact the Versatile could be one of them. Mines were to be laid immediately and it would be a case of single-file up the coast as far as Flamborough Head. The escorts would be coming as far as Rosyth which would mean Naval cover for the whole of the trip to Leith. There were the inevitable crew changes as several officers and hands transferred to the services as 'hostilities only' personnel. All RNR officers were to report at once and there were openings for navigating officers to apply for RNVR commisions. The lights went out all down the river and there was talk of having a gun mounted on the stern of all the fleet's ships in the near future.

There were twenty ships in David's first convoy escorted by several trawlers plus the Bulldog and the Versatile. They left the Pool with a Tannoy system blaring out 'Hearts of Oak' and proceeded at eight knots in single file to Harwich where they were joined by another elderly destroyer of Great War vintage. Up from Harwich, the speed was increased to ten knots and the rest of the trip passed uneventfully with no attacks made. There was not a glimpse of aircraft or submarines and it was the same on the way back.

On the next trip there were twelve ships, eight of them colliers. Versatile was escort and there were no incidents unless the sighting of three German E Boats could be counted. As they were making over a minefield at an estimated twenty knots, they were left well alone.

Early in October David had his first experience of war. The Jasper was well back in a very mixed convoy of freighters and colliers when out of a cloudless sky three bombers came in very low on the starboard bow. The one in the centre let loose a bomb while the other two opened fire with machine guns. The bomb missed but the machine gun bullets scythed across the Jasper smashing the bridge windows and splintering the decking on the starboard bridge wing. Two other vessels were hit but there were no casualties. Just off Ravenscar the weather started to break up with a fresh easterly wind sweeping in from the North Sea. It quickly grew colder and the sea rose to a sullen swell. At dusk the Versatile was detached to search the corridor for survivors following an attack on a south-bound convoy three days previously. Two ships had been bombed in the area and one had subsequently sunk. She rejoined during the forenoon and the convoy sailed on with the increasingly bad weather preventing any further attacks. It was almost as bad on the return from Leith with the weather on the port quarter causing the Jasper to roll and pitch through the giant seas in a sickening cork-screw manner.

Johnny Roberts managed to get a 'short week-end' and came up to the Pool to see his old shipmates. They had managed to find some survivors but it was a very chancy business.

'I dunno how we found 'em. It was sheer luck. They was almost invisible between the swells. There was six of 'em, no shoes, freezin' cold. They was cryin' when we picked 'em up. They'd been three days adrift and had turned over twice. When we got 'em inboard we was goin' to feed 'em but the Doc', he says, "Turn 'em in and let them get warm first." So we gave 'em some milk and turned 'em in. They was able to feed in the mornin', seemed right as rain. Bloody lucky they was, the only ones out of thirty six.'

Versatile had other problems that were not seen as very helpful when Johnny explained them.

'When they bloody planes attacked us off Flamborough we thought we'd get off a couple of shots at 'em. That's when we discovered we couldn't bring the guns to bear. The loading trays were hitting the deck. We'd no high-angle guns. Fact is, where enemy aircraft are concerned, we're bloody useless. Only got twin Lewis' an' a 'pom-pom'.'

Johnny went on.

'Lt. Cdr. Palmer, the skipper, says we've got a big job on next week. Takin' a large convoy to Bristol to tranship into the big boys for foreign. All classified but I 'spect you'll hear about it soon enough.'

David did. The next morning they were unloaded and by the afternoon reloaded with military stores for tran-shipment at Avonmouth. There were to be thirty six ships from a few hundred tons up to two thousand tonners escorted by four destroyers and three trawlers. David would be sailing as master of the Jasper for this trip on the understanding that he would be leaving her at Avonmouth where a new captain would be taking over.

He was sorry in a way that he was leaving the Jasper. She was a good ship and he liked her qualities. The Gemstone Line was also a good company to work for. It was small but efficient and treated its people well. However, it was time to move on and if a berth out of Avonmouth meant being closer to Annie then that was the right move to make.

They sailed on a Friday which should have resulted in some superstitious grumbling but with a war on, it was not even mentioned. One by one, from wharves, docks and moorings the ships slipped and proceeded slowly down the Thames. Off Harwich, the familiar lean grey shapes of Bulldog and Versatile took up their stations and together with the armed trawlers with their conspicuous four inch guns mounted on their fore-decks, the long strung-out convoy set off at eight knots for the North Foreland.

They had just sighted Margate when the port look-out yelled out.

'Aircraft, dozens of 'em, high off the port beam!'

David brought his glasses to bear and saw a formation of twin-engined bombers heading right for them. Above them were a large number of fighter aircraft. In what seemed seconds, they dropped out of the sky with engines screaming. It appeared as if all the bombs were dropped together. There was an enormous detonation as hundreds of tons of water were thrust into the air. Bulldog completely vanished and David reckoned she was a goner but moments later she re-appeared with the water streaming from her. The next few minutes were chaos with every machine gun in the little fleet hammering away and the planes roaring down the line with guns blazing. Then the Royal Air Force arrived and the fight swept into the sky with planes wheeling and circling each other. David tried to follow what was happening as several aircraft spiralled into the sea and the fight drifted away to the eastward. Bright sparkles from the wings told him the battle was still going on but the outcome seemed to be that the attack on the convoy had failed and the enemy chased away. Looking back across the line of ships he could see no stragglers or casualties as the escorts took up their places and they continued on course for the English Channel.

Off Start Point there was a U Boat scare as one of the merchant ships signalled they had spotted a periscope. Versatile went to investigate but the sighting wasn't confirmed. The convoy plotted a course north about Lundy Island and picked up another trawler escort out of Belfast before leaving the two biggest vessels in Cardiff Roads to await the outward convoy. The rest passed Flatholm safely and were soon in sight of Avonmouth with Portishead Radio confirming their arrival.

Jasper was eased into King Edward Dock and moored alongside the Manchester Progress by the tug Ino. Before the evening was out the Dock was crowded with vessels and work had commenced transferring cargo into the larger ships. The warships had also berthed at Avonmouth and set about re-oiling ready for the return trip to Harwich. Johnny managed to slip on board for a while and brought news of the engagement off Margate.

Apparently it was the biggest raid on shipping so far with over thirty bombers and sixty fighters taking part. Enemy losses had been calculated at twenty-three whilst the Royal Air Force had lost seven. There were no hits on any ships though Bulldog had been well shaken up with several plates sprung and hardly any glass surviving.

David stopped on board that night and had a few drinks with the lads. He was due to leave her during the forenoon and the next skipper would be joining before the watch was over. A part of him was sad to be leaving but it was good to be back in a Bristol Channel port. It had all been very familiar to him as he ran up the coast with all the well-known landmarks slipping by. He'd started his sea career here shipping out of Cardiff on a Pen boat.

It wasn't difficult to find a tanker berth. In fact the pool were looking for a master and mate, a chief engineer and a second plus two dozen hands to go down to Truro and bring back the Inverdargle for cleaning and commissioning. Two other Inver tankers were to be fetched in the next fortnight from where they had been lying idle in the King Harry Passage. They were brand new vessels and had never carried a cargo. The White Star liner Laurentic was also due to be brought back from there and re-commissioned as a merchant-cruiser.

There was no time for leave. David as Chief Officer and his new skipper George Martin from Bideford were issued with travel warrants and found themselves on their way to Truro before noon. Details of their ship were sparse. Apparently she had only recently been built in Belfast and due to the recession had been laid up pending movement in the oil trade. She was a motor ship, which meant a much cleaner life for the 'black gang' and had superior accommodation for the crew aft in cabins rather than the old fashioned fo'c's'le. They reckoned that despite being new, she'd need some licking into shape after being neglected in the Passage for a twelve-month.

Truro was busy and a berth for the night was a first priority and so they booked in at the Red Lion and went straight to the dining room for a meal. Enquiries soon revealed that the rest of the makeshift crew would arrive the following day. Captain Martin hoped that the Chief Engineer would be someone who was familiar with Kincaid engines and that there would be enough engine-room crew to get power on. Half a dozen on deck would be quite enough but he knew from experience that starting a big motor from cold was a complex task. They also learned that the three tankers had been in the care of a ship-keeper and that he would be available to take them on board by launch when they were ready. David thought that he'd need to go over her pretty thoroughly before sending for the tug that would take them back down the river to Falmouth for fuelling. His fears were again provoked when they met the ship-keeper the following afternoon.

'I'm afraid you'll find a few bits missin' here and there. I can't be everywhere at once and there's bin a few lads aboard over the year. It's bin a bit better since the River Patrol was started up but you'll 'ave to look-see if there's anythin' vital missin'.'

George shot a look at David and David lifted his eyes. They left the Feock shore by launch shortly before three-o-clock and were soon alongside the black painted hull of the Inverdargle. She was riding light with minimum ballast and the hull was streaked with weed and rust as was the massive mooring chain that held her to the buoy. Towering above, the once white superstructure told of her idleness and the lack of an efficient crew. Even the gang-way, let down from the starboard side midships, was green with weed and neglect.

They climbed in silence up to the deck and waited for the others to join them. The skipper nodded to the Chief.

'You'd better take your lads below and see what needs to be done. It looks as if we've got our work cut out up here. I suggest we meet up on deck here just before the First Watch and then we can assess whether we stay on board or go ashore.'

He beckoned to David.

'Take a couple of the lads and start for'ard. See if we've got the necessaries to move her and berth her. I'll have a look on the bridge and check out the compass, telegraph and instruments if they haven't walked!'

The next couple of hours proved the Inverdargle was in fair shape despite needing chipping and painting over-all. The ship-keeper was right. Two mooring ropes had vanished as had the ship's bell, the Pyrene fire extin-guishers and the port midship lifeboat. Just how some-one had managed to steal one of the ship's boats without the ship-keeper being aware of it was hard to understand. Down below, things were a bit better. There was nothing significant missing but without power for heating and lighting it would be uncomfortable to stay on board and so they decided to go ashore and signal the tug for the following day.

Breaking her free of her moorings needed a sledgehammer but a line was aboard the tug by midday and she was pulled slowly stern first down the river. With her four hundred and sixty foot length, she made a clumsy tow and a second tug joined in the task under the bow. At Falmouth she was boarded by a veritable army of 'dockyard-mateys' who soon made short work of cleaning her up and re-painting her a uniform grey. The only colour on board then was the red, green, yellow and blue of the valve wheels that sprouted from the well decks. There were other vessels being fitted out at the same time and the noise was terrific with hammering and rivetting, cutting and welding all going on at the same time. There was a CAM-ship nearing completion and it was rumoured that she would be escorting the next Atlantic convoy. David watched as the Hurricane fighter was craned on board and poised delicately at the rear of the catapult. The name Empire Dell was painted out but could still be seen in raised letters around her stern. On the fifth day the Inverdargle was deemed ready for sea, the missing lifeboat was replaced and all the electrical and mechanical machinery overhauled. The last thing to come on board was the ship's bell which had not been pinched but removed and packed in grease for safety.

With her engine turning over and all generators working, she proceeded to Carrick Roads where she hove to and dropped anchor to await another tanker. Both were due to sail for Avonmouth with an armed trawler escort from Belfast. David felt a bit frustrated. He had been unable to get ashore whilst in Falmouth and he was stuck again here not knowing when they would be on the move. Rumour had it that they would be in Avonmouth within the week as the tanks needed preparing before the next convoy was due to sail. It was strange how the bits of information that drifted in via the escorts or dockyard workers proved fairly accurate. The skipper had to wait for his orders to proceed or be summoned to a conference before it was official.

The weather was definitely turning colder when three days later the Inverdargle and the San Antonio were ordered to sail for Avonmouth. Two Cardiff freighters joined them off Rosemullion Head and the little convoy set of for the Bristol Channel and the familiar pattern of bearings and lights that would herald home waters. Off the Longships, an angry, grey sea backed by a blustering westerly wind dropped the tiny escort from view between the crests as they turned. The Inverdargle and her sister tanker, riding light, pitched and yawed before settling down to a steady roll. Autumn was turning into winter.

David telephoned Annie from Avonmouth telling her that he would be getting a few days leave. Inverdargle was to have her tanks cleaned before sailing to pick up oil. David had queried whether it was to be heavy oil or aviation spirit. The difference was crucial. If it was heavy oil then a torpedo might only cause a nasty leak but if it was aviation spirit, the smallest spark could produce an inferno. To avoid such an accident, the crew were issued with boots with wooden peg soles and all the deck tools were made from non-ferrous metal. The destination of the forthcoming convoy was still secret but the 'buzz' was that it would be either Staten Island, New York or Aruba in the Dutch West Indies. He told Annie that he would be joining an Atlantic convoy but the port of call was still classified. He'd also puzzled why the tanks needed cleaning when the vessel was new but was told that the tanks and valves were tested as a matter of routine. There was the possibility also that they might be fitted with a gun.

A few days leave was a welcome relief and David ordered a taxi to take him to Temple Meads. Greensleeves was still in London and he didn't want to waste time going to fetch her. Bristol to Taunton was a fast journey and the branch line to Minehead only took an hour after which he could take a Blue Motors coach from outside the Beach Hotel.

The sea-front at Minehead was deserted. There were a few minutes before the bus for Porlock and he walked over to the sea wall by the trees. Inevitably there were changes. All the slipways had a number of conical concrete mountains built on them and the whole foreshore was planted with hundreds of posts. Opposite the Bungalow Café a concrete machine-gun emplacement was disguised with a coat of paint and a shingle roof and there was another just past the wooden steps down to the beach. The harbour looked different too. There were buildings on it that probably housed a gun. It was the same everywhere he went. It was all air-raid shelters, sand-bags, water tanks and pill-boxes built wherever they could provide the maximum support for a community at war. He remembered that Annie had said that no-one would want to invade West Somerset but he had heard several quite serious comments indicating that it was quite a probability that an invasion might involve cutting off the south-west peninsula by a simultaneous attack on the English and Bristol Channel coasts. As he turned away from the empty beach the bus swung into the station yard and as he seemed to be the only passenger he doubled across the bottom of the Avenue and climbed aboard.

Being with Annie and being again at home was a tonic despite seeing yet another pill-box perched on the shingle ridge behind the harbour. It was as if his little haven had been infected by the war. Even here there were one or two uniforms about even if they were only Home Guard. Annie had been busy as the Anchor moved towards the Christmas break. There had been several visitors despite the war and the darker nights. Back at the beginning of the month there had been some sort of conference with representatives from Whitehall as well as senior military figures. They'd spent most of the time talking over maps of the area and seemed to be talking mainly about North Hill and Bossington Beach. Annie wondered if it might have been to plan some further defensive measures along the coast. She had been curious but had been deterred by a large military man with a red arm-band and a heavy pistol strapped to his belt standing outside the room when she took the coffee in.

David had explained that it was like that everywhere and the authorities were very concerned about security.

'There might be spies about who could pass on information to the enemy.'

'But you know everyone here, a spy would stand out like a brussels sprout in a trifle.'

'I think they need to impress everyone that there's a war on and we're all a part of it. Getting in and out of docks and dockyards is quite a business. Everyone is carefully looked at.'

He went over the possible timetable for the next few weeks and explained to Annie that he was on stand-by for the next convoy out of the Bristol Channel. Allowing for time to queue up for oil wherever they were going he estimated that he would miss Christmas and not be back in the United Kingdom until mid January at the earliest. Annie was disappointed but resigned to the fact that the war would be making decisions for them at least until it was all over.

Despite having only a few days, there were some blissful times when they felt really close to one another, by the fireside in the cottage and surrounded by friends in the Ship with Bernard smiling along behind the little bar. Several times the talk returned to the lovely summer that had blazed all along the coast with so much laughter and happiness, made all the more poignant by the onset of the war There was a great deal of love and generosity in the village and both of them realised the wealth that surrounded them. It was a wrench to be going back but David knew there was a job to be done and that it was his way of making a contribution to the war effort. The one thing that hurt above all else was to see Annie biting back the tears as the bus drew away from the Weir and pulled around the bend beyond Mizpah.

CHAPTER THIRTEEN

One by one the vessels slipped out of Avonmouth, dark shadows on a winter sea. As they proceeded to lie up in Barry Roads, David counted four tankers, two Grange boats, two Fyffes and half a dozen smaller freighters. Apparently this was only a part of the convoy as a similar number was to join from Liverpool. The next day they were joined by a CAM-ship and three corvettes and at noon were signalled to proceed to rendezvous with the Liverpool section off the Smalls. The weather could best be described as murky with a short choppy sea slapping the hulls as they built up to eight knots past the Gower indistinct through the fine driven drizzle. David squinted through the salt stained glass and checked his course and station some two cables from the tanker in front. There were no lights showing which made for difficult station keeping. He would have to keep alert.

They met up with the Liverpool vessels some five miles off the Smalls. There were several more tankers, four big square bulk cargo ships and an armed merchant cruiser plus a number of smaller three-island tramps. Heading almost due west, they formed three lines and commenced to zig-zag at a uniform nine knots out into the Atlantic.

As soon as he could, George informed the crew that they were heading for Sandy Hook where the tankers would be diverted southwards to the Dutch West Indies for loading. Following that they would be returning up the east-coast of America for Halifax and joining a convoy for the UK. Barring any accidents he estimated that they should be back in home waters by the end of January.

The first two days saw the tail end of a bullying gale that had its beginnings off Iceland. The glass started to rise on the third day and by the afternoon patches of wild blue could be glimpsed between the horizontal layers of low streaming cloud. It was good news for the little corvettes which had been dwarfed by the huge rollers and had inevitably suffered damage. One in particular, David thought she was the Myosotis, had no boats left at all. As the day progressed, the seas went down and the danger from U-boats increased.

At dusk they spotted an aircraft which crossed the path of the convoy heading north-west. The CAM-ship Hurricane remained on its perch and so they assumed that it was friendly. The weather continued to improve and as night fell they settled to a more comfortable routine. Inverdargle was the second ship on the port leg of the convoy with the CAM-ship ahead of them. George had mentioned that they were well placed to see the Hurricane 'bang-off' if it had to. In that eventuality they were now well out of range of any possibility that the pilot could land safely and he would have to ditch as close as he dared to one of the corvettes and hope to be picked up. Not a job that anyone on board felt a vocation for.

They had just changed a zig for a zag and were nearing the end of the middle watch when it happened. A great tearing whoomph detonated ahead of them followed by a second sharper explosion etched in fire. George brought his glasses to bear on the ship ahead and shouted.

'Hard a' port. Full ahead!'

They passed her on the starboard bow with smoke billowing from a ragged hole below the boiler room. The second torpedo had opened up her number one and two tanks and she was settling fast by the stern, the Hurricane drooping precariously from its mountings. David could see the crew trying to lower the port midship boat but they seemed to be having difficulties and several figures were leaping over the side. Within minutes the escort was on the scene and all gun crews closed up for action. As the outer line of the convoy struggled to form up again the escort dropped several patterns of depth charges before leaving to search for survivors. The last David saw of the CAM-ship was the dark lifting form of her tilting bow topped by a pall of blacker smoke as she dropped away in the night. The next day the aircraft returned and circled just out of range. She was obviously not friendly.

The rest of the voyage passed without incident though why the U-boat failed to press home any more attacks was a mystery. Perhaps she'd run out of torpedoes or been scared off by the escorts. Certainly, the corvettes failed to find any trace of her. Off Sandy Hook the convoy split up and the majority headed in for New York. Inverdargle and the other tankers turned southwards for warmer climes and started to relax a little. Across here, the war seemed far away and the clusters of lights ashore told of a peacetime regime. As the days passed the temperatures rose and they soon changed into tropical rig. David felt slightly guilty at being out here under warm skies whilst those in Britain shivered in the cold drabness of the first winter of the war.

They dropped down through the Florida Strait and the

Windward Passage in unbelievable blue seas. The sun seemed kindly and there was that warm breeze caused by the motion of the ship. If they were not on a war mission it could have been a cruise. The little island of Aruba in the Dutch West Indies lay off the Gulf of Venezuela and was an established oil port. There, the Inverdargle took on her cargo of 12,554 tons of aviation spirit and then withdrew to lie off. One by one, the other tankers lay alongside as the giant hoses pumped the vital cargo aboard. In five days, the little fleet had loaded and was ready for the return leg. David and George managed to get ashore for a brief spell in one of the ship's boats. They brought back enough oranges for the whole crew.

Aviation spirit had the lowest flash-point of all the oil fuels and was the one cargo that all tanker men had the healthiest respect for. The slightest spark could mean disaster. There was no need for George to spell it out and everyone knew that the voyage back to the United Kingdom could be a very dangerous affair.

Halifax, Nova Scotia, proved a cold miserable place after the bamboo groves and tropical palms of Aruba and David, in common with the rest of the crew, had the greatest difficulty in adjusting to it.

George went ashore for the convoy conference and returned with a pack of orders and signals. He explained how they would be having air cover for the first six hundred miles by Hudsons and then further cover by Flying Fortresses which was reassuring. Apparently the danger area was the middle section where the aircraft could not operate. In place of shore support, the convoy would be accompanied by a 'Mac-ship' carrying three Swordfish torpedo aircraft. In addition to the corvettes, two Canadian destroyers would be coming over as well. George went on.

'All our cargoes are desperately needed back at home and it is our responsibility to get them there. The Convoy Commodore asked us all to be especially careful about smoke. It could well give us away to the enemy. If we spot a submarine, we are to open fire, our splashes will guide the escorts and, of course, we might even hit it.'

David didn't rate Halifax highly. He hadn't been there before and didn't feel the urge to return. Over the next week, the convoy slowly built up with fuel, ammunition, stores, food and crated aircraft being the major components. Since their arrival it hadn't stopped raining and all the activities went on under a perpetual blanket of grey. It was a case of grey ships on a grey sea under a streaming grey sky. Apart from the trip down to Aruba, it was a grey war and its grimness began to make itself felt. The tankers had been lying off but were now split up and directed to their lines. This time Inverdargle was well back in the second line with a large grain carrier ahead of her.

They left Halifax in pouring rain on 5th January and immediately started the familiar zig-zags with extra lookouts posted to watch for vessels slipping out of station. The night watches were the worst when visibility was poor and concentration likely to slip. The Inverdargle, steady with a full cargo, thrust her way through the heavy seas at a regular nine knots and the crew settled down to the daily routines set before them. The escorts thrashed up and down the lines with their signal lamps clattering against the occasional light and the even more threatening smoke and the 'Mac-ship' ploughed resolutely along in their midst with the three Swordfish lashed down on deck, the angle of which prevented their taking off.

If the weather was rough, it was kind to them in that it prevented any enemy attacks. After the rain came a great blustering gale which pressed them eastwards over mile-long breaking crests of wind-torn water flecked with blown spume. The heavily laden convoy took it all in its stride, wallowing boldly up to each peak and slipping down with a shudder and a crash of smashed ocean. There was a grandeur about the elements and another majesty in seeing the vast fleet pressing its way determinedly to its goal. With his glasses David could see dozens of vessels rising and falling about him like some giant orchestra bent on delivering a great shouting symphony of steel and sea.

While off watch, David had thoughts of home and Annie. Christmas had come and gone, for them a non event as few of them managed to get ashore and had to make do with a few drinks on board as there were no pubs or places where one could buy or consume alcohol. He'd managed to pick up a present or two on one of his rare runs ashore but even this was a difficult exercise as nobody had any confidence in British money thinking that the British were doomed. He had to go to the Dockyard to exchange pounds for dollars. He hoped that it wouldn't be long before he could be back at the Weir again. Strange, how one could conjure a picture of home so detailed that it was almost a reality.

Some two hundred miles off Valentia Island the gale blew itself out, the sea went down and the stars appeared flying through the tattered remnants of the day. It was still cold in fact the temperature had dropped several degrees causing the Skipper to comment that if it continued to drop they would be chipping ice by morning. At two bells of the morning watch it passed freezing and the rails and ladders took on a ghostly hue. A vast quiet descended on the ocean contrasting markedly with the continuous roar of the last few days. If he went out on to the bridge wing, David could only hear the swish of the vessel's passage as she folded the water away from her forefoot. At times he was unaware of the other ships and felt a strange isolation as if the Inverdargle was the only ship on the Atlantic.

It was a pale sun that pushed up from the ocean's rim but it brought no comfort or warmth with its wan splash of orange colour against the grey frosted steel of the bridge. The skipper came up and nodded.

'Thought so, we might see some snow before we dock.'

The Second Mate chipped in.

'Will that keep the U-boats down?'

The skipper looked grim.

'I shouldn't think so. Visibility will be excellent until it actually snows and in this calm they'll be able to see us miles away.'

They were almost in sight of Ireland when the first ship exploded. It was likely a tanker as the column of smoke that started its climb into the still air was dense black. They could see no ship at the base of it and could only assume that it was a vessel on the far side of the convoy. The next was a little closer, perhaps half a mile on the starboard bow and another huge cloud of smoke burst skywards. A Swordfish left the deck of the 'Mac-ship' and commenced circling the convoy and all the guns crews stood to. Then firing commenced on the far side and the focus of the action seemed to be some miles away on the starboard beam.

David knew it was a U-boat out there somewhere but where was the problem. The escorts had 'Asdic' but as far as David had been able to gather from the corvette's officers it was a pretty inaccurate science in practice. It was one thing to prove able to detect a tame sub' in quiet home waters but quite another to find an operational U-boat bent on eluding an armed escort. The U-boat was a formidable opponent and if it came to a fight David didn't reckon their four-inch gun would have much effect. As the skipper said grimly.

'More for morale than for battle.'

They passed under Ireland and the convoy split with ships heading for Liverpool and Cardiff, Bristol, Newport and Avonmouth. The destroyer escorts left for Liverpool with two of the corvettes leaving the Inverdargle and four other tankers in the care of an armed trawler from Belfast. Whilst the freighters headed for Barry Roads in the care of the third corvette, the small oil convoy set off in single file for Lundy. Once inside Lundy David was home. It was all familiar from Hartland to the Foreland and from Worms Head to Lavernock Point. He was home.

It was a good job for Annie that her Christmas was busy. They'd had forty guests at the Anchor and the Ship had been full as well. She'd busied herself with every aspect of the kitchen until the girls had wearied of her and complained. Annie had apologised although they knew full well the reason. She was missing David terribly. Lizzie was in the same boat and together they tried to work out just when they would hear from David that he had docked.

David's father was positive as was Bernard and the two of them were constantly encouraging and supportive. News of the war was always the most important of the day and the Weir was deserted at the end of the day as everyone gathered around their wireless sets to listen to the latest reports. The Royal Navy's victory over the Graf Spee on the 17th December had heartened them all especially after the loss of the Courageous and the Royal Oak. That the Royal Navy was still the most formidable in the world meant that the merchant ships would be well looked after wherever they were.

On January 2nd Annie received some bad news. Domino, diverted to London to load aircraft parts for Bristol, had been strafed by two raiders off Ramsgate and father had been injured. The ship had limped into Folkestone and repairs put in hand but father had been taken off the ship and after treatment had returned to Bristol by train. Apparently a bullet had passed right through his shoulder breaking his collar-bone. He was more angry than ill and after the initial shock had asked to return to the ship but a wise superintendent had decreed that he take survivors leave and had insisted that he remain on the sick list until they were satisfied he was fit enough for command. Mrs Vickery had other plans for the family and sent for Annie.

And so it was that Annie travelled back to Cumberland Road and found the whole family in residence. Father, pale and looking a lot older than she remembered him, was sitting in the high-backed kitchen chair with his arm bound up in a sling. Mother was full of warmth and good humour but Annie could see right through her act whilst Angela had taken the situation well in hand and was steering each exchange with a compassion and strength that was as comforting to Annie as it was to her father and mother.

It needed only Annie to agree to the plan they had already thrashed out. Father would retire and leave the sea. He could see the good sense in it as he had been far from well since before the outbreak of war. It was only his stubborn nature that had held him and now that he had the support of his family and had been told his course, he was resigned to it and accepted it. Next, they would return to Watchet and if failing to sell the house by virtue of its position right next to the docks, rent one until the situation improved. Towards this end the following week, if father was up to it, they would travel down and see if there were any likely properties.

Angela had hoped and prayed that all this would come about. With her mother and father safe from danger she would have a great weight lifted from her shoulders. It needed Annie to add her thoughts and help to push things along. Annie was pleased to and so it was settled and the special bottle brought out to seal the decision.

On the 15th January Captain and Mrs William Vickery signed an agreement to rent a house on the Doniford Road, Watchet and duly sent for their things. Annie went with Angela up to Upper Belgrave Road to stay for a day or two before travelling back to the Weir. Miss Peath John was delighted to have her, the more so when Annie declared that she would cook some of her special dishes. She telephoned the Anchor and Lizzie and planned to be back at the Weir by the 20th.

It was good to be with Angela again even if only for a short time. Angela had grown a lot, in maturity and understanding. It was very apparent to Annie as she talked things through with her and listened to her advice. Angela had, quite simply, become wise and was well worth listening to. Annie thought that it might have grown from the friendship with Miss Peath John but Angela let slip a few pointers that led elsewhere.

Angela's present poise and confidence had in fact stemmed from that chance meeting in St Michael's church several years ago. It had challenged her just as the lady had hoped it would. Not content to let questions lie unanswered, Angela had puzzled and pondered until she found her feet on the road. The journey started, she read and read and read. Then she began to attend lectures at the university, slipping quietly in at the back when no-one was looking. After two years of patient learning and some well engineered chance meetings with lecturers and professors she finally grasped the form and basis of the question. It literally blew her mind; clear of all the clutter and baggage that had collected in the name of religion down the ages. It emancipated her and enabled her. It gave her a freedom and the vision to create her own contemporary drama and to discover herself as a whole human being with the power to help others. It engendered compassion and that great legacy of love, kindness which is the badge of all who have found the track. She would never try to change anyone's views for each child was at a different stage of awareness. It also brought Angela humbleness and a sensitivity that was visible to those who sought her out as she found herself ready to play out her role in the lottery of life. She had chosen a selfless path and in losing herself, had gained knowledge and the responsibility that went with it. Right now, she needed to settle her family and see them safely through the present conflict.

CHAPTER FOURTEEN

The night of the 15th January was dark and bitingly cold with snow flurries and the occasional white squall. It had promised snow for some days and here it was at last now flailing down in a tattered curtain and now streaming in an almost horizontal blizzard as the bitter wind rose and fell. Earlier the weather had been bad as the remnants of a full Atlantic gale had flogged itself out on the rocks and coves of West Devon. At least now the seas had dropped and the surface was less angry. Kapitan-Leutnant Dreski brought the U 33 to the surface at 0230 to check conditions. It had been steadier below but regular checks were essential to keep the North Devon Foreland abeam and to check for shipping running south-about Lundy Island. The convoys and the escorts all hugged the Welsh coast for Barry roads but several vessels, which had been proceeding independently, had thought they could slip up the North Devon and Somerset coast for Avonmouth and Bristol. Hans Dreski had sunk a 3000 ton freighter on the 5th. He'd been given no limit to his patrol other than to keep within his operational box allocated by OKM. This included the whole of the Bristol Channel which were waters he knew fairly well from before the war. U 33 was a fine boat. Built at Keil in 1936 she was a Type VII A with a speed of sixteen to seventeen knots on the surface, quite fast enough to catch the swiftest merchantman and escape the smaller escorts. Hans knew because he'd outrun one of the Royal Navy's new corvettes and found her gunnery pretty ineffective.

This was his second patrol in these waters and it suited him well. A few years earlier he had spent the summer months in North Devon and had thought the coastline particularly beautiful. He'd visited Lundy Island on a paddle steamer from Ilfracombe and had been fascinated by its history and its ancient castle. Only a couple of weeks ago at the outset of his present patrol the sun burst out and the skies cleared and he had surfaced off Shutter Point and cruised along the western shore, past Dead Cow Point and on up to the Hen and Chickens off the North West Point. It had been a rare day out of the war, a day in which he could be a sailor again and feel the keen wind and watch the hull surge through the transparent green water. On that occasion he'd thought of his Chief Engineer who never got the chance to see much of the outside world and passed word for him to come up. He seemed to remember that Obertechnichermaat Feldmann had also been here before and had sailed out of Avonmouth on a British ship.

Hans Feldmann climbed up the steep ladder and blinked into the bright light. The steep slabbed and cracked cliffs of Lundy swung past the starboard side and the scream of herring gulls bounced from a sparkling sea. He pulled his collar tighter and grinned at his skipper.

'Schöne tag!'

'Sehr kalt! Es is wärm unter!'

Gesehn, über, das islet Lundy. Ich habe eine tag urlaub; zun schlepperschiffe im 1936 - schöne tag! Ich niemals ganz wir zuruck hier im eine stahl racktiggernhundes!'

Kaleu Dreski slapped the steel bridge rail.

'Dieses kriegschiffe ist so schöne - aber techniker

vorhühl. Ganz wir gehn!'

Obertech Feldmann agreed, they were marvels of modern engineering and very well put together. He was, however not particularly happy at sending other fine ships to the bottom and wondered how he would feel if, for instance, he was to discover that they had sunk his old ship, the Wanderer. It wasn't so bad in a non-combatant role down below but he'd hate to actually fire the torpedoes. Raising a finger in salute, he pointed below and climbed back down the ladder. The Fähnrich, bridge watchkeeper, watched him return below before resuming a careful lookout for aircraft or other surface craft.

Tonight was a far different state of affairs. It was exceptionally cold for the time of year and the persistent snow flurries brought visibility down below five thousand metres. All his bearings had to be visual for there was no chance of a shot under the present cloud blanket. He didn't want to be caught on shore. It was all rocky here. He'd be opened up like a can of sardines. The four of them kept alert despite the discomfort. They'd all twisted towels about their necks under their weather gear but it wasn't enough to stop the icy water from getting through. All were clipped into their safety harnesses and it was as well they were for despite their forward motion, the U 33 reeled and bucked under the fierce squalls. Then, waterfalls engulfed them and streamed through the bridge gratings leaving them frozen, soaked and gasping.

It was Fähnrich Preyer who saw it first. Low in the water and punching her way through the darkness, a long, indistinct form took shape to the west of them. Increasing revolutions, Kaleu Dreski moved ahead to gain sea room and the best opportunity for a kill. It was a ship alright, and likely a big one though he couldn't make out from his present range whether she was a tanker or an ore ship.

Extending the distance between them he raced along the Exmoor coast some five thousand metres off shore and turned into a projected attack position. He estimated the vessel, whatever she was, should be within attack range before the hour was out. Sure enough, she appeared right where he expected even if a little closer inshore than normal in such conditions. There didn't appear to be an escort.

'Achtung! Kampfestationen!

Links ruddern grosse. Steur ein-neun-nul!'

The crew moved with practiced ease to their stations and U 33 started to swing into her attack position. Down below, the red night vision lights illuminated everyone with a dull red glow. Leutnant Geldmann, on the attack plot, sang out.

'Feinde linie! Kömpasse rote nul-acht-fünf. Ganz zehnknötten. Viertausendmetre auf! Grieffen unter funfmetre, los!'

Kaleu Dreski acknowledged and prepared to leave the bridge.

Slamming down the hatch, those above brought the usual shower of ocean with them as they dropped down the ladder and discarded their topside gear.

'Perisköppen unt!

Links zehn.

Mittlezum.

Hälten! Feur zum dreitausand!'

'Es ist eine ölenschiffe. Steuren zum mittleschiffehaüsen.

Feur wenn sie zum haben!'
'Jawohl, Herr Kaleu!'
'Zum steuren, Vor-vor-vor!'
'Feur! Feur!'
'Los! Los!'

Two torpedoes spat from U 33's bows. She rocked back momentarily then steadied as the familiar hiss of released air announced their departure. There was a pause that seemed for ever.

The explosion was massive. A sheet of bright yellow flame leaped into the night followed immediately by the shock wave that came as a thump that could be detected equally below as above the surface. The whole forward section of the tanker was torn open like a flower and the rest of the ship was a blazing inferno from stem to stern. There was no chance that anyone could have survived but Hans surfaced nevertheless and cautiously motored back to see if he could render any assistance. No boats had got away and a lake of blazing fuel was growing by the minute. Smoke like a giant tree was growing into the night and realising that the Royal Navy would soon be on its way, he ordered a course to take them back to Lundy and the next target.

David heaved a sigh of relief. It was his watch and he was almost in sight of home. Despite the darkness he could make out the bulk of Exmoor slipping by on the starboard beam. Shortly after they'd been joined by the trawler, Inverdargle had suffered engine trouble and signalled XYZ denoting that they needed to stop for repairs. It wasn't serious but the main shaft needed to be stopped for a while. The trawler had proceeded with the other tankers and George felt that he would be able to catch them up before Portishead if he piled on the revolutions. The repairs had only taken just over an hour and she was on her way again. David had his Bristol Channel tide tables in his cabin and reckoned they could take advantage of the flood to pass in closer to the Foreland, past Hurlstone Point, across Bridgwater Bay and into the mouth of the Severn south of the Holmes. He'd also thought that this course would take him right across Porlock Bay, the closest he'd been to Annie for some time.

'We might even beat the others in!'

From the Foreland up to Glenthorne it snowed in fits and starts, the blown squalls plastering the bridge with white. Inside, it was warm enough and there was hot cocoa to help. Just as they were passing the house, looking even more remote without the usual lights showing, David rang down for one zero zero revolutions in order to slow down for passing the Weir. No-one would see them, it was far too early for that, but he might just catch a glimpse of the cottages huddled under the hill and feel he really was home at last. Twisting the ends of his muffler about his neck he pulled on his reefer, jammed his cap on his head and slid open the starboard bridge door.

'Just having a look-see. Keep her on course to clear the point.'

The starboard bridge lookout who had been looking out just inside the door slipped out with him and trained his glasses along the shore.

'Pretty bleak Chief.'

'Not when you get to know it, you should see it in summer.'

'You lives near here don't 'ee?'

'Just around the next shingle point.'

David squinted ahead past the white clad bulk of Worthy and the indistinct finger of the Gore pushing out into the flood. As he did so, a snow front pushed in and the view vanished into a swirling pattern of whirling white in which nothing was real.

The enormous detonation defied description and plucked both figures from the bridge with an obscene ease. The Inverdargle split apart with her for'ard tanks thrusting fire into the winter air. A huge cloak of black smoke tumbled into the frozen sky and mounted higher and higher until it cleared the snow clouds and pushed into the very atmosphere itself. Tons of petrol ran blazing across the surface of the sea and formed an impenetrable barrier to any who would dare to come closer to the grotesque floating pyre that had been the Inverdargle. No human could survive in such a conflagration.

By seven thirty, the column of dense black smoke had reached four thousand feet into the cold Exmoor morning. Visible far inland it had become a trailing extension to the ragged edges of the departing snowstorm. In Porlock it had snowed for much of the long January night and a pale yellow dawn had only reluctantly pressed itself against the persistent squalls that still raced up from beyond the Foreland. The column, drawing strength from the inferno at its base, began to flatten out against ragged patches of lighter sky high above Glenthorne to the west of Porlock Weir.

As light strengthened and folk began to stir the first muffled figures began to move in Porlock's streets. It was the children on their way to school who first realised it was a huge fire and that the flames were coming from a large black-hulled vessel half awash down beyond the Gore. She was listing to port and the sea was ablaze all around her. There were no boats in sight and it didn't look as if any of the crew could have escaped. As they watched from the end of the village, planes could be seen circling the area and they could make out the shape of a warship on its way from across the Channel.

Within the hour, quite a crowd had assembled beyond the school but after exchanging concern they realised that there was nothing they could do and the children went into the school leaving the adults to attest that this was the nearest the war had come to Porlock and that it was a pretty terrible thing happening right in front of their eyes.

'Must have bin' an oil-tanker.'

'One o' they bloody submarines!'

'Our lads 'll 'ave 'un.'

'Oh I 'ope so. That were a British ship out there an' I 'spect all the poor buggers are either drownded or burnt up.'

'The Navy's out there now. Look.'

'Ar, but I reckons that submarine is miles away by now.'

'Hope none of our local lads were on it. There's several at sea from Minehead and the Weir.'

Down at the Weir an equally concerned crowd had assembled on the shingle west of the harbour. Sid Stenner, the village's Naval veteran, was among them and folk were taking him seriously.

'Jus' the same as the first lot, they bloody U-boats are murder. You never knows when they'll strike. One moment your sailin' along an' the next, BANG an' you're lucky to find yourself alive.'

Lizzie was quiet. She knew that David was due any day now and she hadn't heard from him that he'd docked. It couldn't be him. Surely it couldn't be him out there in that burning thing. She clenched her teeth and turned for home willing as hard as she was able that it could not possibly be her lad out there burning and dying within a few hundred yards of his home. She was not alone in her anguish. There were other mothers and wives whose sons and husbands were also expected in home waters about now. She noticed Elsie from across in the terrace was crying.

Following a radio message, the Belfast based armed trawler Tango crossed the Channel and arrived off Glenthorne at 0835 in the forenoon. She found a burning wreck and no possibility of any survivors from within the blazing pool of petrol that surrounded the stricken vessel. Her blackened boats still hung from her davits. She took note of the position and radioed back that there was no need of a lifeboat or further support. Belfast radioed Barry and notified the standby tug that the wreck would not be approachable before the week-end after which it would need to be sunk or removed from the sea lanes.

Belfast entered the details in the log and recorded the official position of the sinking as 51 degrees 16 minutes North, 3 degrees 43 minutes 30 seconds West. No survivors from a possible crew of forty-five. Contact with

Portishead Radio confirmed that the only tanker over-due and reported in the Bristol Channel on 15th January was the Inverdargle due Avonmouth 16th January. Per-mission was granted to inform next of kin.

Angela was preparing afternoon tea for Miss Peath John when the telephone rang. It had to be something out of the ordinary for Miss Peath John was not telephoned during the afternoon. All her calls had to be a.m. or be-fore dinner and never after nine-o-clock.

Angela answered it.

'Hello, this is Miss Peath John's home. Angela Vickery speaking.'

'The voice was weak.

'Is that you Angela love?'

'Lizzie? Is that you Lizzie?'

'This is Lizzie here love, I'm afraid that I have some very bad news......'

Lizzie's usual warm voice was choked almost to a whisper.

'I've just had a telegram from the Ministry.'

Angela felt the strength drain out of her and she sat down awkwardly on the polished hall chair.

'Oh Lizzie, oh Lizzie my dear.'

'David's ship.... David's ship has been reported sunk by enemy action in the Bristol Channel on the morning of the 16th January. Apparently every effort was made to look for survivors but it is feared that all the crew have been lost.'

'Oh my God, Lizzie. Do you want us to come down?'

'No my dear. There's going to be some kind of memo-rial service but I'm too numb to take it all in at present.

Is poor Annie there?'

Angela bit back the tears and fought hard to control her voice.

'No, She's.....she's gone out to buy David a pair of cuff-links with his initials on for a welcome home present. She was sure he'd be back this week.'

'I ought to speak to her myself. Shall I telephone later?'

'I'll tell her Lizzie and then we can make arrangements for getting together soon.'

'Do you think that will be all right. It ought to be me.'

'No Lizzie love, you mustn't go through this again. Please leave it with me. I'll be as gentle as I can.'

'I know you will dear......Oh Angela, I saw it. I saw the ship all burning. It was terrible. I can't get it out of my mind. It's been on fire for days. I can't go out of the house...'

'We're here if there is anything we can do for you and your husband.'

'I know dear....I know. I must go.'

She put the telephone down and Angela was very aware that she was weeping as she did so. Angela herself was very shocked. She took a deep breath and found herself a bit trembly. She thought of their father very nearly killed and now Annie's David lost. Whatever else could this terrible war bring?

Miss Peath John found Angela sitting there ashen-faced and quickly realised there was bad news.

'Your father?' she enquired gently with her head held to one side.

'No, Annie's David.'

'Oh, the poor lamb. And she's only just married.'

'His tanker was blown up only a few miles from home.

There were no survivors. That was his mother on the telephone.'

Miss Peath John knelt beside Angela and put her arm around her.

'My home is your home and Annie's too should she care to stay here. She's going to need a lot of support. Please count on me.'

Angela looked into the kindly face that offered so much and realised what a true friend her employer was. She nodded and summoned her strength. Miss Peath John took her arm.

'I meant what I said. Annie is welcome here for as long as she wants.'

'She might want to go back to the Weir or to mother in Watchet. We'll have to wait and see.'

'Would you like me to be with you when you break the news. A little extra support might help.'

'Thanks, but I think it better be me at first. Can I call you if I need you?'

'Of course you can my dear. As I said, please lean on me if you need me. We've been a good team, you and me, and if I am able to help your sister in her distress I would be very glad to.'

The wait for Annie's return was one of the most harrowing periods of Angela's life. She rehearsed what she intended to say a dozen times over but failed to find any way of lessening the impact or softening the blow. Angela knew full well how much Annie loved David and what a match they were for each other. Annie had never hidden her rapture or been reticent in showing her feelings. The loss was going to be shattering. Lizzie was right when she said 'poor Annie'.

Within the hour Annie returned wearing a lovely smile and clutching a small gift-wrapped parcel.

'I've found just the right ones with an embossed D on each one. Look, they even had some pre-war wrapping paper left to make it special.........Angela, why are you looking like that?'

Angela swallowed and held out her arms to her sister. Sensing something was wrong, Annie looked alarmed.

'What is it Angela? What's happened'

Angela gripped Annie by the shoulders and spoke quietly and seriously.

'I'll not try to use any silly words. Lizzie has just telephoned. There was a telegram from the Ministry. It said that David's ship has been sunk in the Bristol Channel and that there were no survivors. Oh, Annie love, I'm so very sorry.'

Annie broke away, the colour draining from her face. She started to laugh, stopped, then became intensely excitable.

'No, no, there's been some terrible mistake. He's coming home shortly, any time now. Look, I've bought him a welcome home present! No, it's all wrong. No. NO! NO!'

She screamed. The scream fled along the hall and impacted again and again in Angela's head.

'Lizzie will telephone again and we can make arrangements to go down to the Weir. There will be a memorial service. I'll come with you. I'll get in touch with mother. She'll want to come.'

Annie was still shaking her head.

'I'm not going anywhere. My place is here in Bristol to wait for David. Any day now he'll come knocking on that door. He'll check here first before going on down to the Weir. He's not lost, he's, he's just been delayed. No, I don't believe it. They just haven't found him yet. He'll have been picked up by another ship. That's what has happened. He's been picked up by another ship and the Ministry people have got it all wrong.'

Angela gathered her little sister in her arms and kissed her.

'It's going to take some understanding Annie. You'll need a lot of time. I'll help you all I can and Miss Peath John wants to help too.'

'You'll see, he'll come back. It's ridiculous to say there are no survivors. How do they know? This is all a terrible mistake.'

'Oh, Annie love, the ship was blown up, it was torpedoed. I'm afraid David's gone.'

Annie leaned back against the hall wall and started to talk to herself, pressing the gift-wrapped present to her chest.

'I'll go down to Avonmouth and make enquiries. Ships have picked up survivors. Plenty of ships are coming up the Bristol Channel every day. Someone will have picked him up. Someone will have news. Yes, that's what I'll do. Bristol too, I could watch out from Sea Walls and if a ship comes up the river go down to the Basin and ask if any survivors have been brought in.'

She shivered and glanced imploringly at Angela.

'They'll find him won't they?

Angela looked at the broken little figure that was her sister and felt such love and compassion she could barely speak herself.

'I'm....I'm sure that you will be the first to know if

there is any news but Annie, I don't think that the Ministry would have sent telegrams if they weren't doubly sure. It would cause dreadful problems.'

'I know they're going to find him. It might take a day or so but I know they'll find him. Oh, Angela!'

Angela lead her sister into the sitting room. Miss Peath John had prepared a stiff drink and a hot water bottle.

'Drink this Annie and Angela will sit with you awhile.'

She looked grim-faced at Angela and shook her head as she whispered.

'Say no more, it's the shock.'

In the days that followed, Annie retreated into herself. She was far from coherent and Angela decided to telephone her mother, Lizzie and the Anchor Hotel to say that she was definitely not well enough to make any journeys at present. The days turned into weeks until one day Annie came downstairs looking much brighter.

'I think I'll go out for a little walk today.'

Angela agreed but suggested that it might not be a good idea to go too far on a first outing.

'Shall I come with you?'

'No, I'll be fine. The fresh air will do me good. I'll just go along the footpaths on the Downs. I won't be long.'

Despite the signals, Angela and Miss Peath John were not ready for the personality that emerged from Annie over the next months. She became secretive, tearful, exuberant, devious and awkward, all facets of quite a different Annie to the kindly, gentle girl she had been before the news. On that first outing, a policeman had returned her after eight hours having found her wandering inside the security fencing of the Oil Depot at Avonmouth. How she had got inside the complex was a mystery as was why she hadn't been challenged by the sentries. The policeman was a kindly man.

'She said she was looking for her husband off some ship. We could see she wasn't one of the regulars. It was when she said that they'd got the telegram all wrong we realised she was having problems.'

There were raids on Bristol that summer. Angela joined the ARP and was deployed as a fire-watcher. Annie came with her on several occasions and with a job to do, was sensible and alert, much more like the old Annie. Of course they were after BAC at Filton and in September they found the factory and bombed it. However it was in November that they came in earnest. From the flat roof on the top of Cheyne House, number 51 Upper Belgrave Road, they could see the tightly packed squadrons of twin-engined bombers with broad wings crossing the city. This time it was the City Docks, the shipyards, the old town and the Bristol Bridge area. The whole sky was alight with raw fire, search-lights stabbed through the drifting masks of smoke and the stuttering flutter of hundreds of incendiaries could be seen growing from the roofs and buildings of the city below them. On top of the highest building in Bristol they felt right in the middle of it. Toward the end of the raid three twin-engined bombers passed very low overhead with a trail of incendiary bombs zig-zagging down the sky behind them. They seemed to fall all down the Whiteladies Road towards the Cotham area. Then a lone aircraft swept just over their heads causing them all to duck. The detonation that followed was thunderous, a great rolling peal of sound followed by a rain of earth, debris and glass.

Angela shouted and pointed.

'That was too bloody close for comfort! Can you make out where they fell?'

'On the Downs, right opposite the Terrace. Looks like there'll be quite a bit of damage to Miss Peath John's and those close by.'

After what seemed like hours of rocking noise and pulsing aero engines it went quiet and the sound of the all-clear could be heard wailing up from the city. The following day, the full impact of the raid became apparent. A lot of the buildings in the old town had been smashed to pieces including Annie's hotel. The City Docks had been badly damaged and hits had been recorded on Charlie Hill's yard. Casualties were estimated to be well over a hundred killed and many more badly wounded.

There was damage all down the Upper Belgrave Road. Windows were out and one house almost opposite the craters had lost a lot of stonework on the upper story. Miss Peath John was lucky to get away with smashed windows and a spattering of burnt mud.

Tragic though it was, it brought home to Annie that people were being killed in this war and that she wasn't the only person to be afflicted. She became intent on playing her part and put her catering experience to good effect by volunteering for duty in the emergency canteens. Soon both sisters were busy with every spare moment they had. Annie felt she was doing something to help and decided not to take up her mother's offer of a room at Watchet. Lizzie was just pleased that Annie had work to do. Time spent kicking her heels at the Weir would do no good at all and in the circumstances she felt that Bristol, however dangerous, was the best place for her.

Both sisters saw the King when he came on 16th December. He looked drawn but resolute. Angela heard many comments about his visit and told Miss Peath John.

'They were saying that if the King was happy to stay and take it, we could take it too and damn Hitler.'

Annie stayed busy, often returning in the early hours of the morning. Her team had worked miracles, providing hot drinks and meals in situations of near devastation. She saw some terrible sights as folk were dragged from the rubble and debris of once sturdy buildings and rescue workers trembling with the effects of sustained effort in almost impossible situations. She was everywhere there were problems and always in the front line of clearing up after raids. The last bad raid was on the night of the 12th-13th April 1941 when the City Centre, Cannon's Marsh and the Broad Quay were hit. Annie's team set up shortly after the all-clear at the bottom of Baldwin Street. As the death-toll rose once again above the hundred mark, she saw the ambulances and stretchers clearing away from the area and the fire-fighters weary from their work. At no time during all this did she seem to fret about David and both Angela and Miss Peath John began to think that she was over the worst of her grief. If and when life returned to a more normal routine they felt that there was a chance Annie could take up her life again.

After the summer of 1941, there were no more major attacks and it seemed as if Bristol was over the worst. True there had been thousands killed or injured but the spirit of the city had not been broken. There were areas flattened and streets in ruins. Buildings were propped up with great baulks of timber and temporary huts and sheds appeared everywhere almost overnight. One such temporary building was erected at the bottom of College Green and became a British Restaurant. Annie applied for the position of shift manager and became a member of the staff.

One incident did hit Annie particularly hard. In the July, the Toronto City was torpedoed and reported lost with all hands. Details were scanty as to where she was but it was rumoured that she was not far from home. One of Annie's work-mates lost her husband on board. Annie had come home and told Angela.

'I was so sorry for her. It very nearly happened to me.'

Despite the sinking of the Montreal City the following year and the Bristol City in 1943 with an appalling loss of life, Annie remained adamant that David would still arrive one day on some ship. In every other way Annie seemed to be quite rational. She worked hard and dealt with the thousand and one everyday problems that a busy restaurant posed and there were some in those difficult days. Miss Peath John advised caution.

'Deep down, she knows only too well what has happened. This is her way of dealing with it. We should be patient and not try to force her to admit the truth. It will surface in God's good time.'

Angela was still worried about her overall approach to life.

'Look at the way she works, flat out all the time. She's not had a break since the first air-raids. It's not normal.'

'It's her way of dealing with the grief. My advice is to leave her well alone. There'll come a time when she'll accept it. Could be this week or a year. We're here for her if she needs us and her mother is happy with that.'

Angela sighed.

'You're right of course, but I feel that by encouraging the fantasy that David is alive, we are prolonging her illness and not working towards her taking up a more normal view.'

With VE Day, Annie's steam ran out and she started to take days off from the restaurant. There didn't seem to be the impetus there had been and she stayed at home more and more until she received notification that her services were no longer required. A week later she made enquiries at the Shipping Office in Avonmouth whether there had been any news of survivors from the Inverdargle. As chance would have it there were several locals among the deck crowd signing on at the time and they knew the names of all the local vessels that had been lost during the war. Mike, who was about to sign as Bo'sun held up his hand.

'No news of the Inverdargle love. They'll contact you if there is. You go on home now.'

He shook his head and as Annie wandered disconsolately away, screwed up his face at his shipmates.

'Poor kid! Bastard war!'

Two nights later Annie wandered across to Sea Walls wondering how long it would be before someone had news. She knew in her heart that David was still alive. Another incident gave her hope. It came in the form of a letter from the current landlord of The Ship in Rotherhithe Street, London. He'd found a note pinned under an old notice board addressed to a Mr Pollard of the steamship Jasper. It informed him that his motor car, a Morris, which had been garaged close by, had been destroyed in the bombing of Surrey Docks. The envelope had been annotated 'To await arrival.' As he obviously had not arrived and the war being over, he thought he ought to pass on the news if possible. Enquiries soon discovered that Mr Pollard had left the Jasper and gone on tankers at the beginning of the war. Not to be thwarted he'd made further enquiries at the headquarters of the British Tanker Company in Glasgow who, although not directly responsible for the Inver tankers, were able to discover that Mr Pollard had been reported missing after the tanker Inverdargle had been torpedoed in the Bristol Channel. His next of kin was given as Mrs A. Pollard of Porlock Weir, Somerset. Hence the letter. It read:

'Dear Mrs Pollard, I'm sorry to inform you that your husband's car which he left garaged close by, was destroyed during an air-raid on the nearby docks. The previous landlord left a note for him but obviously he didn't collect it. Your husband probably had the insurance details safely put by. I'm sorry. I'm sending this to your Porlock address and hoping that you will get it.'

'There, that proves that information will find it's way back to me. I'll keep this for David. He'll be sorry to have lost poor Greensleeves.'

It was Miss Peath John who suggested that Annie take a holiday at home with her mother and so it was that Angela arranged the details. Her mother was naturally very concerned to hear that Annie was still having problems and was delighted to offer help.

'Watchet was where you both grew up. If any place can bring her back to reality it should be here.'

'What about contact with Lizzie?'

'Oh, I'll talk to Lizzie and we can arrange for a stay at the Weir. Lizzie's been very positive and a wonderful strength to her husband. I think she's strong enough to cope.'

'She knows doesn't she?'

'Yes love, she understands.'

It was agreed that Angela would take her down by train with the excuse that she wanted to relive the pre-war holiday journeys. They would go in September and stay on until Christmas or thereabouts. Annie was not fooled by any of this. She knew why they were doing it and why she was to be escorted. The thing she found annoying was that they considered her faith in David to be a fantasy. Why couldn't they accept, as she well knew, that her David was alive and would find his way back home. She knew that all the big ships would call at Bristol or Avonmouth and that was the place to be to receive news or to welcome him home. It was no good being at Watchet, only a few coasters and the occasional paper boat called there. The Weir was lovely but too far off the beaten track to have news of sailors arriving in the UK. No, Bristol was the place to wait.

The journey down by train jogged her memory as it rocked along the track, first past the bomb damaged and forlorn, torn street-ends of urban Bristol under Totterdown and then out into the bruised countryside still criss-crossed by war-time allotments, army dumps and camps. Taunton still wore her camouflage, all too apparent in the buildings and sheds of Norton Fitzwarren and it wasn't until they were well past Stogumber that the more obvious tawdry trappings of war were left behind.

Despite this, the first tinges of colour in the trees and the burnt gold and hazy purples of the moors started to work their magic and Annie found herself looking out of the window more and more as they slowed into Williton and stopped to wait for the down train. The crossing gates closed and some cows lurched over the lines, some stopping to gaze curiously at the rear of the train just beyond them. She'd forgotten cows. She'd forgotten the countryside. It was like turning back to an earlier chapter in a book.

'Of course,' she thought, 'I've been away for some time. Perhaps it isn't such a bad idea to take a break.'

She gazed hard through the window as the train jerked into motion and the cottages started to blur by beyond the dipping and rolling embankment. Within a minute or so the train leaned through the cutting in the red-earth cliffs and Watchet harbour slipped into the frame. It looked absolutely the same, reassuringly the same and just as if there had been no war and no raids and no deaths. She was back where her story had started.

Both mother and father were on the platform and Angela steered Annie into a big hug from both of them. They weren't quite sure what to expect but were delighted to see that Annie looked well despite the dark circles under her eyes. She seemed buoyant enough and after greeting them with genuine delight started to chatter as if there was nothing in the air at all. Angela exchanged glances with her mother and announced that she would be departing on the next train which would be in about an hour.

'I'll have to get back. Miss Peath John has been very good but she really can't manage for long on her own.'

Her mother squeezed her hand.

'Lovely to see you my dear, There's not really time to go home and have a cup of tea so lets walk down to the Esplanade and have a chat.'

She slipped an arm about Annie and Angela looked up at her father and grinned.

'Remember when we shipped out with you on the old Dancer and Annie and I rustled up those amazing pasties?'

Captain Vickery's mouth curled into one of his characteristic smiles.

'Best oggies I ever tasted. They were poor days but we had a bit of fun didn't we?

He lowered his voice.

'Do you think I ought to have a word with Annie, you know, about David's death? I did write a long letter to her but I think she ignored it.'

'You'll have to be careful Father, She's blanked it right out and even working through the bombing hasn't changed her. We've all tried.'

'I'll be very gentle. There are several widows and widowers here in Watchet. One lad we know had a bad war and returned to find his wife had been buried without him knowing. He'd been in a hospital in Germany and had been posted missing himself.'

'Perhaps if Annie could meet others who have been hurt she'd make the leap into reality and could grieve for David. This situation is so frustrating and I'm sure is doing Annie no good at all.'

'We'll do our best.'

The tide was out and the harbour mud glistened in the weak afternoon sun. The wharves were empty and there were few folk about except for Tommy Peel with a great folder of posters under his arm and the tall figure of Captain Allen standing by the railings. Apart from them the scene was unusually deserted with all the overtones of a busy port and a bustling holiday centre markedly absent. Angela noticed that some of the upper house windows were still clad in 'black-out' and there were piles of sand-bags about. It would take some time to wholly obliterate the war, even here where there was little damage done.

Annie kept glancing at her mother as if to reassure herself that she was really back. Whilst she knew there was a hidden agenda, she also felt loved and cherished and was genuinely glad to be back in familiar surroundings. The buildings shouted to her of childhood as, unchanged, they witnessed to a solidarity that had elsewhere been destroyed. She had been a little girl here and had found her true love here. Here she would find the courage to take her further. She was glad the war was over. So much death, so much suffering. It had all come so close to her.

They walked along the Esplanade and turned into Swain Street. They had started to sell ice-cream again in the little shop opposite the bridge. Only a few were sold each day and they were not for everyone. One could get them in the Parade at Minehead too but it meant eating them behind a curtain in the back of the shop. Even in the countryside, things were still scarce and rationing was likely to continue for some time.

'We'll have one before you have to go back. It doesn't look as if it's open today.'

Angela looked rueful.

'We used to be pigs for ice-cream in the old days didn't we?'

They crossed the bridge and turned on to the platform. There were only minutes before the train announced itself with a whistle on the far side of the road-bridge. It drew to a steam-drenched halt with a hiss and a judder of brakes as the three carriages presented their wooden running boards to the edge of the platform. The hiss continued as four or five passengers alighted and Angela climbed aboard and let down the compartment window by its heavy leather strap. Annie was standing between her father and mother and looked relaxed. She hoped that this would do the trick and that Annie could then begin to live her life from a fresh beginning. She quite accepted that a measure of responsibility was hers as it always had been but now that Annie was safely back with family, albeit for a short time, she hoped that her father would be able to bring the weight of his years and experience to bear and bring about the longed for change.

The train jerked and pulled her steadily away, leaving her alone in the single compartment. She stretched and put her feet up along the sprung bench seat. It was a strange life. She had never found the one who could have made a difference to her life and Annie had lost the one who had made all the difference for a few brief years. 'Better to have loved and lost than never to have loved at all' ran the old jingle. Angela had to concede that Annie had been marvellously happy before the war but had suffered desperately since the fatal news. Whether her years of happiness outweighed her own stability was a question indeed.

Note: U-33 was depth charged and sunk by HMS Gleaner in the Firth of Clyde on 12 February 1940.

CHAPTER FIFTEEN

That he loved his daughters was undeniable. He'd always found them willing, tractable and quite charming. Ever since they were little girls, he'd hoped that they'd be happy with life and all the early indications were that they would meet every eventuality with spirit and character. He'd been glad when little Annie had met David. He seemed a fine man and well able to provide for her every need both financially and emotionally. The problem was that following the loss of the Inverdargle with all hands, Annie failed to grieve and held to an absurd belief that David was still alive and would return. True, some lads did return from the jaws of death but after five years it was highly improbable that David would come back.

He sighed and wondered just how to tackle the issue. As a seaman he knew the chances of escaping from a burning tanker were nil but talking of the horror of being cremated alive was not the way he wanted to convince Annie. The more he thought about it, the more he came back to the plan he envisaged at first. He would introduce Annie to Peter, the RAF lad who'd been widowed. In sharing their stories and their anguish, they might find some solace and a mutual appreciation of each other's plight. He was a sensitive lad and likeable. Captain Vickery smiled.

'Might even make a good husband for my Annie when she finds herself.'

That evening, he discussed it quietly with Mrs Vickery. She however posed another question. Should they tell

229

Peter what the problem was or leave them to share their experiences and likely answers. If Peter was primed, Annie would know soon enough and feel that she'd been set up. If Peter was left believing Annie had been widowed at the beginning of the war, his responses would be the more weighty and might therefore be more convincing. In the end they came back to the question of the ethics of engineering the meeting in the first place. If Angela had failed in five years of living in the same house, what chance would they have in a few weeks? Perhaps the locality would help. It had certainly helped him after the old Domino had been shot up.

The weather was kindly. Autumn was leaching the colour from the unstable greens and splashes of mottled yellow and gold enlivened the familiar slopes where clusters of blackberries were still as tantalizingly out of reach as they ever were. The strength had drained from the sun and the shadows that stretched across the jewelled meadows were longer. For the first few days Annie walked the familiar paths and beaches of her childhood. Paths where she and Angela ranged as children and beaches where she and David helped each other to clamber across the steep ridges of sea-torn grey rock and fallen cliff face. It did her the world of good. Her parents were happy to let her go and there were no lectures or serious talks. They had not even talked of visiting Lizzie, though she knew that she would have to visit the Weir before she went back to Bristol.

It gave her time to reflect. As for many young folk, the war had bitten an enormous slice out of their lives. For some there would be scars that would take years to heal and for others it was a matter of dealing with the missing years and picking up the threads of old careers or starting new ones. She was lucky, she had skills and experience which meant she could earn her living wherever she chose to settle down. Not back to the hotel in Nicholas Street, that had gone or to the Anchor where the tension of living close to Lizzie would prove difficult. No, she would return to Bristol and wait for news of her husband which would surely come through there, the centre of the region.

On the way home one day she was passing the Bell and although it was considered unladylike to go in unaccompanied, she turned in and followed the little passage through to where their father had once taken them after a trip in the Dancer. Then they had drunk some cordial but now Annie thought she'd like a brandy. A small brass bell stood on the little counter on the left and Annie gave it a shake. Clutching her purchase, she stepped into the dimly lit parlour and sat down. There were several young men there talking quietly. Two were in uniform. As she sipped her drink she realised they were sharing experiences that were still fresh in their minds. It would be some time before the war would be out of people's systems. She eavesdropped.

'I was still in a shallow dive, flat out chasing this Jerry fighter when the bloody engine caught fire. Couldn't see a thing. Down to about three of four hundred feet. Managed to get the canopy back. Too low to bale out. Sort out somewhere to land. Difficult to see but there was a flat enough field ahead. Came in too fast and pranged it. Next thing I knew was seeing the ground bobbing up and down from a few feet up. Couldn't work out where I was. Discovered I was over the shoulder of a German soldier who had risked his life to get me out of a burning wreck. Spent three months in a German hospital where they stitched me up with those new-fangled clips. Stopped some terrible scarring, see! German sergeant was one of the AA gun crew that shot me down. He came to see me in hospital twice.'

'You home for good now?'

'Yes, demobilised and got my civvy suit. Some of the lads are staying on for a while but the Doc' says my flying days are over.'

'I think I owe my life to one of you chaps. We was torpedoed off Cape Finisterre an' spent four weeks in a lifeboat. The weather was terrible and we had no idea where we were. Couldn't get a fix an' when we did finally get a sun, we was too weak to pull. It were one of those Catalina flyin' boats that found us. Waggled 'is wings at us an' sure enough, a ship come and picked us up the next morning. We was too weak to climb up the nettin'. They 'ad to come down an' carry us up one by one. Took us into Gib'. It were six weeks before we got back.'

Annie couldn't help herself.

'You mean if someone is picked up at sea, it might be some time before they can get back to the UK?'

'Serpently. One of my mates was picked up by a ship outward bound to Australia and he never got back for eight months. No fault of his, and no-one worried about it. He said it was the best holiday he'd ever had.'

Annie bit her lip.

'My husband was reported missing at sea and I believe he could still be out there somewhere. I know he'll get back if he can.'

'When was this?'

'January, 1940.'

They exchanged glances and fell silent before one of them coughed and spoke up'

'That was a pretty terrible winter. I hope things work out for you. What was the name of his ship?'

'The Inverdargle.'

'She were a tanker weren't she?'

'Yes.'

'Sunk down Porlock way.'

'Yes.'

'Would you like another drink Misses?'

'Here, allow me.'

The pilot rose to his feet and went out into the passage. Annie felt it was in order and smiled a little nervously.

'Thanks.'

He returned and placed a brandy on the table. Annie looked up.

'I'm not in the habit of...'

'I can see that. You're very welcome. This war has messed us all about. Your good health.'

As they started to talk again, Annie felt a new surge of hope. What if her David had been picked up by a passing ship and taken to a distant port? And what if he had to save up enough money to pay for the fare home. It might take some time but she was sure that he'd get in touch as soon as he could. She drank up and thanking the young men, walked out into the afternoon.

She was not looking forward to her visit to the Weir. It wouldn't be easy for either of them regardless of their different perspectives. There was too much of the old days present. Too much of the summer shingle and the dappled tree lined way to Worthy. Too much of the distant, ochred obduracy of Hurlstone Point crouching at the end of the bay. The memories were sharp, poignant, dear. This was their country, the place where they had made their vows. She couldn't understand Lizzie and she was sure that Lizzie wouldn't find her view at all acceptable. They had moved in two different directions, each accepting their way.

Lizzie tried to make it easy for her. She was out in the road as the Western National bus pulled in outside the Ship.

'Annie my dear.'

'Hello Lizzie.'

They hugged and then stood back to look at each other. Lizzie looked a little older and perhaps a touch slimmer. What she saw in Annie was a look of resolution and determination that did not bode well for what she had prepared to put to her. Nevertheless, they walked back to the cottage arm in arm and felt the ties that had bound them together.

Annie stayed over that night and slept well. After a good breakfast, she walked out and wandered across to Turkey. She noted the beach-stone pill-boxes and thought how wicked it was that the war should have crept up on their beach. No doubt they would remove them as soon as possible. Apart from that the Weir hadn't changed. There were still a few yachts and motor boats moored within the Dock and the little coal-yard was still tucked away beyond the wharf. The Ship and the Anchor seemed as popular as ever though she wouldn't be going in to see anyone. She hadn't expected Lizzie to follow her out and so it came as a bit of a surprise when she caught up with her at the end of Turkey cottages.

'Do you mind if I come with you?'

Annie was a bit unprepared for the way in which Lizzie took the initiative.

'I come down here quite a lot. I had to force myself at first. Being a mother in a war is one thing but being a mother when your baby has been taken away is something you can never really come to terms with. In a way I don't want to forget but sometimes the pain is more than I can bear. I can still see that great pall of smoke down there beyond the Gore. It was there for days and I don't think that it will ever really go away. Of course days follow days and years follow years and there are others to think about. Grief to comfort and mouths to feed.'

Annie looked at her wanly. She went on.

'We all have our ways of coming to terms with death. It is enough for some to bury themselves in work and blank out the hurt until it dulls with time. Others fish the years for the shared joys and trials and keep the flame alive in their hearts. Some are angry and some are bitter but I fear that they are hurting themselves more than they should. My husband worked and I have dwelt on all the blessings of those years. Do you know, I find more and more each time I think about it.'

Lizzie stopped and picked up a pebble.

'One life among so many thousands. Your David and my David was very special. We shall not forget all that he gave to us both. All that he made us. The ripples from one pebble can be infinite.'

She flung it far out into the sea.

'All that he was will still be with us until our dying day and perhaps for others he touched also.'

She smiled.

'It's time you lived your life now. Put your grief behind you and while preserving the memories, plan for a new future. We'll need all the brave young people we can get to take us forward from this war.'

Annie had always respected Lizzie and had also found great warmth and love there. She also respected her opinion but in this matter she felt unable to respond in the way Lizzie expected.

'Dear Lizzie, I know my mother has spoken to you about my feelings and to you they might seem at odds with the world. I've thought about it a great deal but have to tell you that I can't accept that David has gone. I can't put my finger on it but have the strangest feeling that he is alive and may come home at any time. Oh at first I know it was my refusal to come to terms with it but as time has gone by this feeling of certainty has grown and grown. It's not logical I know but I have the strangest conviction that he survived. Do you understand?'

'No my dear, I'm afraid I don't. It's hard I know but I think you will come round to accepting his death in the end. It's not a nice word and I hated to hear it but I'm afraid it must be faced.'

'I shall never give up!'

'Nor I cease from loving him but we ought to face up to facts. He would not want us to bury ourselves.'

Annie swung round vehemently.

'I shall never accept that he is dead. Never.'

Lizzie realised that perhaps she had gone too far too quickly. She tucked Annie's hand under her arm and turned her back on the Gore.

'I want to cook a nice piece of cod for tonight. Any ideas for a special stuffing or sauce?'

Annie knew she had been blunt and perhaps hurtful and so thought it best left alone. If and when they met again, things might be different.

'I've got a super recipe for a stuffing with onions, apples and herbs if you'd let me try.'

The two of them made their way along the top of the shingle ridge past the now abandoned pill-box and turned along the harbour wall for the bridge. Joined by love for the same man they were as far apart as two human beings could be. Sensitive to each other's plight they felt helpless to alter the course they had plotted. Both thought the other tragically wrong.

The meal was a success. So many meals were restricted and boring, cobbled together by necessity from rationed essentials. It was easier in the country but still difficult to lay on a memorable dinner or a satisfying luncheon. It was all too easy to gobble up a week's ration in one go. Annie had stuffed the fish with her special recipe and served it with an equally special sauce. It was a delight upon which all could agree and, of course, served the purpose of lifting the conversation from the aftermath of war.

Annie made her excuses after tea and caught the five twenty-five for Minehead. She would get a connection at the Avenue and catch the Taunton bus for Watchet. She alighted in the Parade outside Boddy's and walked slowly down towards the top of Blenheim Road. The air-raid shelters were still in the middle of the road and there was an air of austerity about. True there were no more gas-masks in evidence but the lack of vehicles, the few lights and the drabness of the pedestrians made a poor show. She crossed by the hospital and made for the Western National bus office. The Taunton bus would not leave for an hour, time to walk on down the Avenue and have a look at the sea front. In common with all seaside resorts they had started to clear up the beach, remove the posts and clear the slipways. Similarly she'd read in the West Somerset Free Press that the army was clearing North Hill of shells and mines and the road across would be opened shortly. There'd been some kind of training camp up there and the Americans had used the hill for their tanks.

The beach was deserted. To the westward the bulk of North Hill reached into a still sky and it turned noticeably colder. It wanted only a couple of hours to dusk and already the last few folk were leaving the Promenade. Compared with the colour and bustle of the pre-war years this was sad. She wondered if ever the life would return to the town but it somehow suited her mood. She hadn't found the meeting with Lizzie easy.

'Mrs Pollard? Mrs Pollard is that you?'

She snapped out of her reverie and looked across to the road. A solitary red sports car was parked opposite the telephone boxes.

'Mrs Pollard?'

She turned and walked over. It was the young pilot from the Bell. He stepped out of the car and opened the door.

'Allow me!'

Annie climbed in gratefully.

'That's what you said the other day.'

238

' So I did. Would you care for a lift?'

'Rather! There's not a bus 'till seven.'

'Do you mind, there's just one more thing to do before we can go home.'

He looked at his watch.

'I want to see a friend of mine. He's due any minute now and we'll catch him if we get a move on. He stabbed at the clutch and they set off up the Avenue at a good pace. Instead of turning up Friday Street and heading out on the Alcombe Road he slipped up past the Wellington and on up Bampton Street, up Cher Steep and right on to the Hopcott Road. A fast turn left took them past Higher Hopcott and up the rough stony track to the heather moor where the little car bucked and slid on the loose stones before coming to a rest by the path's edge. He looked at his watch again.

'It should be any minute now.'

He grinned and switched the engine off.

'No, I'm not trying to kidnap you. I really will take you home but if I'm not mistaken my friend should show up now. Ah, here he comes.'

Annie looked about her. The bracken-covered hillside was deserted. Then she heard something. A vehicle, an engine perhaps. Her new friend was grinning and pointing. Level with them and still way out over the Bristol Channel beyond North Hill came a solitary aircraft. It banked and passed over the town towards Bratton Ball where it circled and gained height. The throaty roar of the Merlin engine in the still evening air betrayed it as a Spitfire.

From as high as a speck, it dived, flattening out over Wooodcombe from where it twisted and turned, rolled and looped in the most amazing display Annie had ever seen. It almost danced in the air. Once Annie held her breath as it climbed almost vertically before slipping back tail first into a spin. After that the Spitfire circled, dipping its wings over the Bratton area before heading straight for them. With a tremendous roar it floated at tree height above the young pine plantation and swept up the hillside only feet above them. They waved furiously.

'He spotted the car. I thought he might if we parked up here. It was either here or out on the Warren Road.'

Annie was impressed.

'Who was that?'

'Ron Madeley, in a Reconnaisance Spitfire. It's a PR IX. They strip all the guns out of them to keep them as light as possible. Then armed with a camera, they go behind the lines to photograph for Intelligence. Ron's been doing it for the last two years. Sad thing is, he's been told he won't fly any more after the end of this month. Too many silly pranks. It was bravery during the war but foolhardiness now. They said he was psychologically unfit to fly. You saw him, what do you think?

'I thought he was brilliant!'

'His dad lives on the edge of Woodcombe. That display was for him. He won't have another chance. He said he'd look out for me if I had the car. I said I'd put it where it could be seen. Smashing chap, won two gongs in Germany. Wizard pilot. What a waste of talent.'

Annie's eyes lit up.

'Fancy seeing us from the other side of Minehead.'

'Easy with a red car in the open. He's used to spotting Tiger tanks camouflaged in copses. Here, we should go or your bus will have got home before us.'

Annie discovered she could talk to this young man. He displayed a gentle assurance. He was polite and at the same time, seemed to have a twinkle in his eye which belied his obvious experience. If the conversation she'd overheard in the Bell was anything to go by, he'd had a rough time but it wasn't apparent in his manner. She liked him.

They slid down the rough sandstone track to the top of the tarmac where the car found some traction. Trees crowded the steep bank and leaned across the road as they slowed to turn on to the by-pass for Alcombe. There was little traffic. Annie wondered how he had managed to get petrol. It wasn't easy.

'How can you run this now that you aren't in the RAF any longer?'

'I can't is the quick answer but I've got half a dozen jerry-cans at home. When that's gone I'll be the same as everyone else.'

'How long do you think this rationing will go on for?'

'I think it might get worse before it gets better. The war has done far more damage to our economy than the average person realises.'

They turned at the Washford BBC station and accelerated towards the hill. The two five-hundred foot masts reached into a darkening sky and the red lights at their tops warned aircraft of their presence.

'It would be just like Ron to fly between them just for the hell of it.'

Annie grinned.

'Love to see it.'

'So would I!'

They pulled up outside the Doniford Road house.

'This is it, isn't it?'

He swung out of the car and moved quickly around to open her door. Annie smiled.

'Thanks a lot. It's made a lovely end to my day.'

'Yes, it's been smashing hasn't it? Thanks to Ron and all that.'

She hesitated by the gate.

'Bye then.'

'Goodbye Mrs Pollard, I hope we shall meet again.'

He stepped into the car and drove off smartly towards Doniford. Annie walked up to the front door and let herself in. At the end of the hall, her mother was just coming out of the kitchen.

'Lizzie was on the telephone. She said you were on your way. Were the buses all right?'

'I had a lift from Minehead. An RAF chap in a red sports car.'

'That will be Peter Lewis. He lives in the end house. Number 34 I think. We used to see him when he came home on leave. He's demobbed now. He was shot down right at the end of the war.'

'He seems a nice man.'

'He is. Your father sees him sometimes in the Bell.'

Annie suddenly felt tired. She hadn't travelled very far but there seemed to be extremes of experience within the day. From Porlock Weir to Hopcott was only a matter of some eight miles but today they were leagues apart.

'I think I'll go up and read for a while.'

'All right love, I'll look in when I come up. Goodnight.'

Annie was asleep almost before her head touched the pillow. As she dropped off, the Spitfire lifted again over

242

her head and vanished into the evening sky. Below her
Mrs Vickery was delivering a cup of cocoa to her husband.

'She's met Peter.'

He met her glance.

'Then let us pray for them both.'

CHAPTER SIXTEEN

It was a beautiful early October morning. A pale sun was having difficulties with the heavy dew and the windows were all streaming with condensation. Peter had awoken early. Habit was the prime mover but his head wound had been troubling him and he felt the need for movement. He stretched and went downstairs for a cup of tea.

Stirring it idly, he allowed his mind to range over the possibilities that lay in front of him. A few more weeks leave would soon trickle away and then there would be a need for a job. Two of his chums had opted for teaching. They were offering a year's Emergency Training. It sounded attractive. It had been one of the possibilities he'd considered before the war. Flying was out. There were thousands of pilots out there and not enough jobs to go round, besides he'd never pass the medical with his history.

He sighed and took himself to the bathroom. Looking in the mirror, he brushed the palms of his hands up his cheeks against the stubble and reached for his razor. Living here alone was no joke either. He missed Hazel desperately and had to admit that of all the problems that was the worst. For weeks he had thought that it would have been better the other way around and he had been killed. He pulled himself together of course. Moral fibre and discipline were there for a reason. He should get on with it and count his blessings. He'd been to his parents for a while but they could only offer the same formula. A stiff upper lip was how his father had put it. Strange how all these phrases added up to the same thing, you were on your own and you'd better make the best of it.

Mrs Pollard was another question. Captain Vickery had mentioned that his daughter was coming down for a few weeks. Apparently she had been involved in Civil Defence work in Bristol right through the war. Her job had been with the Mobile Canteens and afterwards she had worked at a British Restaurant. Now that he'd met her, he had to admit she was a real beauty. He thought he'd heard Captain Vickery say that she had lost her husband in the first months of the war but he seemed to remember that she had mentioned this in the Bell the other day. Didn't she say that she thought he was still alive? There was conflict here. Was she just hoping or did she have some evidence that he had survived. It had been a bit like that for him. When he had come home it was all dealt with and all there was was a hump of earth sprouting a few blades of grass. He knew only too well how difficult it was. Still, if he bumped into her again, he'd not be upset. She was, after all, the one ray of sunshine in what could be a very bleak winter ahead.

Shaved and dressed, he wondered about calling. He'd seen nothing of her for some days and was beginning to question whether she'd gone back to Bristol. In the end his courage failed him and he decided on some letter writing after which he'd walk on down to the Bell for a pint. There was a teaching course starting in mid October at Redland College on The Promenade in Clifton. It might be somewhere close to where Mrs Pollard lived. Somehow the thought of offering her a lift back to Bristol seemed an attractive proposition.

He set off and was soon crossing the railway line and

the sidings that lead to the Eastern Wharf. There were a few figures on the corner of the harbour by the railings and he recognised them as mainly retired seafarers. Many of the old lads took a stroll along the Esplanade before settling for a pint in the Bell or the West Somerset. He'd passed them before her realised that one of them was Captain Vickery

'Ahoy, young Peter, what's on then?'

Peter stopped and waited for the captain to catch up.

'Just going to post some letters and then pop in for a pint.'

'I'll join you.'

'You're welcome.'

They walked together along the Esplanade and turned into Swain Street. Peter thought he ought to raise the subject that was on both their minds.

'Saw Mrs Pollard the other day.'

'Annie said she had met you.'

'Haven't seen much of her since. Has, has she gone back to Bristol?'

Captain Vickery smiled tightly.

'No, can't get her out of the house. We'd thought this holiday would do her good but after the first few days of getting about, she seems to have stuck. Why don't you call and take her out in that car of yours? Blow some of the cobwebs away.'

'I'd love to but I've got to say that I'm a bit hesitant if she's waiting for her husband to come home, I mean, if she still believes she is married...'

Peter thought he might have gone too far.

'You know about that then?'

'She was saying the other day that she felt he would

come back, that he was still alive despite what everyone said.'

Captain Vickery sighed and steered Peter by the arm into Market Street.

'I'll be frank with you. Ever since his tragic death, and it was tragic so near home, she has failed to grieve. Somehow she has blanked it out and refuses to discuss it. She went over to see her mother in law the other day. We thought that if anyone could put her on the right road it would be her. She failed despite opening her heart to her. None of us know what to do.'

'I think it's different for the folk left at home. In the squadron we saw a lot of death which, as the Wing Commander used to say, has a habit of being permanent. Often we saw them die. We were there. Annie had to imagine it and that I feel is where the trouble lies. It was a bit like that with Hazel, my wife, when I was shipped back, it was all over and I wasn't there. I was left to imagine what happened.'

Peter broke off. Captain Vickery ushered him into the Bell and they went in to the parlour on the right of the door. They sat for a while in silence. Then Captain Vickery called for two pints and laid his hand on Peter's shoulder.

'I'm not saying that young David wasn't one of the finest chaps you could wish to meet. He was. But I know and his mother and father know that he was killed when the tanker he was on was torpedoed. There were no survivors and there never could have been. No lifeboats got away and the sea was covered in blazing petrol. Believe me, he's gone poor lad.'

Peter took a long drink.

'So Mrs Pollard, Annie, is a widow?'

'I'm afraid so, officially and legally. She has a small legacy but she's never touched it. Take it from me, she's a lovely, honest, straightforward girl. It would be a tragic travesty if she were to pine her life away hoping for the impossible.'

He looked grim for a moment.

'There are no resurrections outside the Bible. Life is for the living.'

Peter spoke earnestly.

'Do you think she would listen to me?'

'Not at first. I'd be very careful but she might grow to trust you and enjoy your company. Then, who knows?'

'I'll call then.'

'You do that. She needs to get out into the world and start her life again. You are just the man to do it. In fact I think you are probably the only man who could do it. Just go easy.'

Captain Allan and Captain Webber entered.

'Bugger me, 'er's got one in already. Two pints Jack!'

They settled down to recollect storms long blown out and trips hard-pressed in the uncertain waters of the Bristol Channel. Soon there was talk of the Trio and the Kelso, the Coronella and the Naiad and the other local vessels proudly remembered in Watchet.

'Didn' 'ee take they girls o' yourn to sea wi' 'ee in the old Dancer?

'Bloody 'ad to. Couldn't pay a crew!'

Peter smiled and raised a hand in salute before slipping out. Captain Vickery nodded to him.

It was fresh on the Esplanade. A cold wind was blowing from the north-west and although still sunny, a short choppy sea was slopping aggressively against the Eastern Breakwater. The Rushlight, having yielded up her cargo of coal dust, was rocking against the wharf and a blue-clad figure was washing down the foredeck.

Peter began to see a course in front of him. Although his own sadness was still very real, he felt that he could move on with someone like Annie. And if he could help her overcome the stumbling block in her own life, albeit very gently, they might just discover a companionship and perhaps even love. Was he dreaming or was all this a possibility? Certainly Captain Vickery seemed to think there was a chance. Then there was this teaching course at Bristol. If he made haste he might be able to get on it and be in the right place to support Annie as the months unfolded. Was it too soon for him to be thinking of moving on the relations front? If he was to help Annie, he needed to start right away while she was in Watchet. He knew it could all go dreadfully wrong and he didn't want to hurt the poor girl. God knows she'd suffered too much already.

By the time he regained the Doniford Road he'd made up his mind. He would write straight away for the teaching course and see if there were any suitable digs about in the Clifton area that would enable him to walk to the Promenade. He wasn't familiar with Bristol but if Annie had lived there for some time, she might be able to help him find somewhere. This would be his approach. As for the short term, well, tomorrow was Friday and the West Somerset Free Press would give details of all the socials and dances in all the local village halls. There was bound to be one that would appeal.

The more he thought about it the more he felt that he

was on the right road. Hazel wouldn't have wanted him to remain alone. He remembered what a fun-loving, extrovert character she was and how she enjoyed life to the full. No, she'd not want him to remain in mourning for years. Besides, rattling around in a large semi-detached house that was all paid for was no joke. It was lonely and when he returned to the silence each day he had to admit he hated it. He thought seriously for a moment. Even if Annie could not love him as she had loved her man, and it was obvious that she did, the companionship would be sufficient. He'd be happy with that. Love would be a bonus or perhaps something that might grow with the years. Annie seemed a gentle, vulnerable girl who had been dealt a poor hand. He just might be the man to alter all this and give her a chance to find a fresh life.

At least his bloody demob suit fitted reasonably well. Some of them were terrible. He could afford to go to Taunton and buy a new one if he wished but with the course ahead thought it better if he wait and see what the accommodation situation was like and whether he would need to conserve resources. There were a few hundred pounds in the bank but that was all there was and until he was earning a salary, he'd have to be prudent.

As he knocked on the door of Annie's house, he thought that it was not every young man in his position that had the blessing of the girl's parents. Nevertheless he was certainly not confident of the outcome. Annie might turn him down.

Annie herself answered the door.

'Oh, hello.'

'Hello Annie, I was wondering if you are free, we

might go to the Regal Ballroom tomorrow night. Reg Howard's band will be playing. I'd be honoured if you would come with me.'

'I don't really know if I ought.'

'I'll drive you there and bring you home afterwards.'

'I'll have to see what father says.'

'By all means.'

She opened the front room door and announced, 'It's Peter, the RAF chap I met the other day. He's asked me to go to a dance with him.'

Peter could not hear the reply. In what seemed only a minute Annie returned.

'They seem to think that it would be a good idea. All right then Peter, I accept.'

'I'll pick you up at seven thirty then.'

'Yes, I mean thank-you. I'll look forward to it.'

It had all happened so swiftly, it took a few minutes to accept that it had happened at all. He was back down the drive and walking along the road before the penny dropped. She'd accepted. She'd come with him!

Now it was up to him and whether he could break the spell that had locked her away for so many years. He would have to be extremely careful. The last thing he wanted to do was to go in with a pair of hob-nailed boots and spoil it all. She deserved the utmost consideration not the least for her loyalty and fidelity. It would be sufficient at this time if he could just get to know her a bit better and allow her to see that he was above all a gentleman.

It quite took his breath away. She looked absolutely topping, dazzling in fact. A shadow of guilt swept over him as he found himself stunned by Annie so soon after the loss of Hazel. Of course there was conflict here but as he had learned in the hard school of war, life was precious and every minute of value. She was wearing a long ivory dress that contrasted with her dark hair and complexion. Her arms were bare and to guard against the evening chill, she had on a long wrap of brushed wool that was wound about her shoulders.

'Will I do?'

'Absolutely stunning.'

'We won't be too late will we?'

'I shall bring you home whenever you wish.' H e ushered her into the waiting car and carefully closed the door making sure that her dress hadn't been caught in the step. Easing gently down the road he turned the corner by the school and set off on the familiar road to Minehead. For a minute or two he felt tongue-tied. It was Annie who spoke first. He'd anticipated her drift.

'You understand that this is perhaps a little difficult for me. My husband hasn't come home from the war yet and I feel a bit disloyal coming out like this, I mean I'm sure he wouldn't mind me going out once in a while but I mustn't make a habit of it.'

'I quite understand.'

'I'll be blunt, you won't get any ideas will you?'

'I hope that you will come to see me as a friend or at least someone you can relax with. Your father knows I am not the frivolous kind.'

'He said you were a man to be trusted which is why I felt able to come out with you.'

'There! That's the serious bit over. Let's try to enjoy the evening. We've both had a difficult war.'

He felt that he might have gone just a little too far on

this first sortie but as there was no adverse reaction he pressed on with the personal intention to have a good time and to enjoy the privilege of escorting this lovely girl to a dance.

He parked alongside Henry Wood's furniture store just a few yards up from the Ballroom. There were few cars about but no spaces left outside the Regal. Opening her door he took her arm and together they walked back to the Ballroom. The sound of a saxophone echoed across the pavement.

He paid and they walked down the long passage towards the sound. The little bar on the left was alive with folk and there were couples sitting chatting at the tables in the alcove. The Ballroom itself was a blaze of twinkling lights from the large revolving ball of glass facets that hung from the centre of the ceiling. The band, conducted by Reg Howard himself, was delivering a catchy melody from just before the war and several couples were swinging around the empty floor in an exuberant quickstep. The atmosphere was intimate but happy and he felt that it was the right place to take Annie on their first outing.

'Would you like a drink?'

'Could I have a port and lemon?'

'Certainly.'

He found a table on the edge of the floor and pulled a chair out for her. She settled down and within a minute was watching the most extrovert dancers as they took the dance to its limits.

'Here we are. Your very good health Annie.'

He put the drinks on the table and lifted his glass in a formal tribute. She smiled a little nervously.

'Don't get any ideas that I can dance like that. I'm pretty rusty. In fact I haven't been dancing since before the war.'

'I'll let you into a secret. I haven't either but we'll just see how things go. I'm sure we can manage the waltzes and the quicksteps, the foxtrots might prove a bit of a challenge though.'

The next dance was a waltz and he thought he'd better take the initiative.

'May I?'

'Oh, thank-you.'

He guided her out on to the floor and took her hand in his. It was the first time he'd held a girl's hand for more than a brief second since Hazel and again he felt the stab of guilt. Annie's hand was small and firm and she grasped his with a confidence that bolstered his faltering courage. As they moved out on to the floor together he felt a growing confidence that this was right and that perhaps in some way they might be able to plot a course through the uncertain mists that clouded their vision at present. They moved well together and Annie was quite flushed when they returned to their table.

'Ooh, I'd forgotten how nice it could be.'

'It was good wasn't it?'

'I still feel a bit disloyal though. I mean, dancing with you instead of David.'

'I know, I feel a bit like that myself. It's difficult to adjust.'

'I feel you understand.'

'I do, Annie, but we have to go on living. To bury ourselves alive is not the answer.'

'Just as long as you know that I'm not free. I have to

make that clear to you.'

'You probably know, I've just lost my wife. I too am very much at the beginning of things. It's a new world out there and we ought to tread gently. I respect your situation.'

He knew that was badly put. He wished that he was a bit more articulate and could frame his thoughts with more eloquence but he was on new ground and was presented with a situation that needed a degree of tact and understanding that was at the edge of his experience. Oh, he had strong feelings for this gentle, vulnerable, damaged girl but just how best to proceed without jeopardizing his chances he didn't know.

They had several more dances together and managed not to fall over each other's feet. In fact they moved with some grace and Annie found herself being led into some steps she'd only thought she could do. It gave her some confidence and she recognised to her amazement that she was enjoying herself. She smiled up at him. As she did so the bolt shot through his heart and he realised that he had fallen quite hopelessly in love with her. That picture of her with her head tilted back, smiling up at him was the moment that he knew. He was destined to be involved from the first. There was never any alternative. He was committed.

They drove home through a moonlit landscape. Past the lifted bulk of Dunster Castle, round Big Firs Corner and through the still village of Carhampton. Annie was silent but there was the ghost of a smile about her mouth. He thought he detected the first glimpses of happiness robbing the long years of duty, frustration and anguish that was the inevitable legacy of an early death. It was early days. He knew that he must be, oh so careful.

'That wasn't too bad was it?'

'I think I enjoyed it.'

'I'm so pleased. I did too.'

The car purred on through the overhanging branches of Dragons Cross to the sharp Washford turn and all the while the moon like a pale medallion swung alongside them turning the road into a bright ribbon of silver foil unwinding before them. All too soon they were descending St Decuman's Hill with the harbour and town spread below them. Far out across the Channel the Flatholm light winked its reassurance and the sea sparkled a million million jewels so tiny and transient they defied all attempts to pull into reality. The town was asleep below the dark shadowed roofs and tiny streets. He felt intrusive as the car seemed to thunder through the silence. He drew up outside the house.

'Well, here we are. Thank you for a lovely evening. I really enjoyed it.'

'Thank-you Peter, it was kind of you.'

'Allow me.'

He jumped out, opened her door and held out a hand. She entered into the drama and took his hand and he led her to the door of the house. As he held her hand again he wondered if his feelings were apparent to her. The feel of her hand in his was electric. He was fearful that he might give himself away. She bowed in mock courtesy.

'Thank-you, kind sir.'

'Thank-you Lady Annie.'

He held her glance, perhaps a second too long for she turned and opened the door and vanished inside. It was the end of their first outing together.

Had he muffed it? Had he spoiled his chances of trying again? He hadn't made any plans for another sortie. Should he have perhaps said something about seeing her again? He would just have to call.

He left it for a couple of days and spent the time sorting through his meagre pile of belongings. He still had the scraps of childhood lying around in the form of a school tennis racket and a cricket bat with a frayed handle. Hazel's parents had kindly taken her things away with them so there was precious little of her left in the house except the one or two items that were of sentimental value and would be hard to part with. It would be easy to pack if this course firmed up. He felt strangely unsettled and knew the reason. Just why it all had to happen as it had was one of those mysteries of life that defied explanation.

With his serviceable gear all packed and a heavy heart he set off for a last walk around Watchet. If the letter came it would require him to start right away. The Bell was full and so he retraced his steps to the West Somerset. The long carpeted lounge bar was quiet with the exception of a group of ex-servicemen talking at the far end.

'How we ever won the bloody war with some of the clowns in charge is a puzzle to me.'

The speaker was a tall, fair-haired chap with a cynical air.

'I mean, we were ordered to the wrong targets, landed on the wrong beaches, fetched up at the wrong destinations and as far as I can see, shot lots of the wrong people.'

'Aw, come on, it weren't as bad as that!'

'It was on the ship I was on. At Salerno we shelled a battery that wasn't there and failed to find the beach we were ordered to support. On my next ship we lost the bloody convoy we were supposed to escort and when we did finally catch up with it we failed to notice a U-boat on the surface which had been following it for hours. Of course we did spot it in the end and managed to get an echo after she'd dived. Dropped several patterns and up came all sorts of stuff among oil-fuel and rubbish. We were credited with a kill but it was more luck than judgement.'

Another lad spoke up.

'I was on an escort based at Belfast when we were ordered to rendezvous with an incoming convoy off the Devon coast. Our job was to escort the tankers to Milford for unloading. To my surprise we anchored off Porlock Weir. The next morning the Jimmy says, "Lovely little village, Clovelly." I says, "No!" He says, "Over there, village of Clovelly." I says, "No! If you put me ashore here, I could walk home in ten minutes. That's Porlock Weir." The Jimmy goes off to talk to the skipper and the result is we up-anchor and move back down the coast to Bideford Bay. The skipper, he says, "You know this coast then?" and I says, "Born here Sir." "Bloody good job!" he says.'

Peter felt at home among them but couldn't find a story to add. Perhaps his crash had been a case of over-stressing his engine and pushing it too far. Or being silly enough to fly into an anti-aircraft battery. His briefing had outlined their possible positions. Of course the stories would persist and there would be many more to come as the services demobilised and found themselves living more sedate lives. Certainly the war took many lives in shocking circumstances but for some lads it was the most exciting time of their lives and they would never find such drama again. As for him, they could keep the drama and the stories. Once shared, they could lie in the past. There was a new life to be carved and that would take courage too.

He smiled, nodded and finished a pint at the bar before taking himself back along the Esplanade. The tide was out and the banks of mud glistened about the twisting stream-bed as it turned around the Eastern Wharf before finding its way out through the harbour entrance. The Rushlight had gone on one of its thousands of voyages across the Channel for coal-dust for the mill and the other boats lay at all angles waiting for the tide to creep again into the harbour. It was still and there was an air of emptiness about. This was no good, he'd have to go back to Annie's house and try again. It was all most unsettling.

On the way, he decided to sacrifice his last reserves of petrol and offer to take her on a picnic over Exmoor. The year was fast dwindling away and there would be few more opportunities to do something like that. Perhaps down to Tarr Steps or over to Oare. Lynmouth might be nice.

He knocked.

'Hello Peter.'

'I was wondering, as the days are getting shorter now, you might like to go for a picnic, say across to Lynmouth. We might not get another opportunity before the weather gets worse.'

She smiled wanly and then became pensive.

'Lynmouth, oh, no I don't think I could go to Lynmouth. It's, it's sort of special in my mind. We went there after we got married. No, not Lynmouth.'

'Well perhaps down on the Barle or the Exe. Tarr Steps for instance?'

'It's very kind of you Peter, but I think I'll give it a miss if you don't mind. In fact I'm thinking of going back to Bristol shortly.'

Peter didn't want to lose the initiative.

'It's on the cards that I shall be going to Bristol soon too. I'm waiting for news of a teaching course at Redland College. It's designed for ex-servicemen and I think it will suit my needs.'

'Oh that will be nice for you.'

He felt that she was only being polite.

'Perhaps, perhaps we could drive up together. We'd be company for each other.'

'Yes, if you let me know when you'll be going. I think Redland College is on the Promenade. That's not far from where Angela and I will be. Yes, That will be fine. Let me know then and I'll be ready.'

She smiled again.

'Sorry about the picnic but it was the wrong place. You weren't to know. Like you, I expect you have a lot of memories. It's difficult not to tread on them. Give me a knock when you know about Bristol. I'd be happy to travel with you.'

Peter walked slowly home. It was going to be a lot more difficult than he reckoned. Perhaps it would be a battle he couldn't win. Still, he knew he must try. The house seemed empty. It always did. If this course did come up, it would be the right thing to do. At least he'd have company and the comradeship of those who had similar experiences to his own.

When the letter dropped through the letter-box it came as a shock. It was one thing to plan but another to find plans turning into hard reality. He tore it open and quickly scanned the contents. He was in. His pre-war qualifications were sufficient. He started the following Monday. He'd stated a preference for Geography and there was, apparently, a need for Geography teachers. His next subject was Maths which suited him fine. So it was decided, he was to become a teacher. His first impulse was to share it with someone and to fly around to Annie but he checked himself.

'I mustn't go dashing round like an excited schoolboy however much I want to share the news with her. Easy does it Peter.'

He strolled over early in the afternoon and knocked only to discover that Annie had taken herself off for a walk.

'She won't be long Peter, I suggested that she take a breath of fresh air. She'd been cooped up all day.'

'Where do you think she's gone?'

'Across to Splash Point I expect, or even along to Doniford.'

'Do you think she'd mind if I went after her?'

'I'd be grateful if you did. She does too much brooding on her own. Perhaps getting back to Angela might be a good plan after all. At least there's a degree of normality in that household. That Miss Peath John sounds a sensible type.'

'I've not met them.'

'My eldest daughter Angela works as a housekeeper to this lady in Bristol. They've been looking after Annie on and off for a while.'

'I'm starting a teaching course in Bristol next week. I hope to see Annie there.'

'You have my blessing lad. I think you know the score.'

'I do Sir, but it's not going to be an easy road and I can't help thinking that I may not win in the end.'

'Faint heart lad! You know what we think.'

'My feelings are sincere. I want you to know....'

'Go on, you might catch her before she leaves the fore-shore. She went that way.'

She wasn't difficult to find. The tide was out and the only figure on the beach, though distant, was easy to spot as she crossed the outcrops of truncated rocks, bright pools and ridges of lingering shingle. He set off in haste. Although always in sight, she took a good ten minutes to catch up with. He was quite out of breath when he fell into step beside her. They turned about and started the homeward leg.

'Thought it was you out here.'

'I was out for a walk and a think. Father pushed me out but I feel better for it now.'

'I know, he told me he'd recommended a walk. I called just now.'

'When are you going to Bristol?'

'I start on Monday morning at the College.'

'Congratulations.'

'Thanks. There's a lift for you to Angela's if you want it. I shall leave on Sunday morning. I'll need to look for some digs too if I'm to stay.'

'Angela might be able to recommend somewhere. She

knows the area pretty well.'

Will you introduce me to her?'

'Yes, I'm sure she'll want to help.'

'Do you often walk on the beach?'

'Used to a lot as a child. Angela and I spent hours down here and along the coast towards Blue Anchor.'

They meandered slowly back along the beach stopping now and again to pick up an ammonite or a bright piece of alabaster.

'Fascinating coast isn't it? I mean all these fossils just lying here for the finding.'

'There's a whopper just where you caught up with me. As big as a kitchen table. Often thought I'd like to have it in the garden.'

'You mustn't think like that. Leave it there for others to marvel at.'

'It's too heavy to lift anyway. I've tried.'

She grinned and he saw what a pretty girl lived just under the surface of her stance. It was difficult to treat her as a married lady when he knew full well that she had been a widow for five years. Of course he respected her feelings and had her husband been about to return from the war would never dream of behaving in the way he had. Even in allowing him to walk with her, take her out and escort her surely meant that a part of her knew that there was no likelihood of David ever coming home. It was a puzzle.

'I'll collect you about ten on Sunday then.'

'Right, I'll be ready.'

It was going to be a new start. There'd been lots of moves in the RAF, in fact he'd been shifted from place to place so often it had become the norm. But this was different. In a way he was going back to school again. He wondered what it would be like.

Annie waved to him as she turned into her gate. If only they were going up as a partnership instead of a friendship.

'Still,' he mused, 'I've got to start somewhere and friendship is an excellent basis for a long relationship. We shall see.'

Sunday dawned fine and the morning grew bright with the multi-coloured trees painting the landscape with rich splashes of copper and bronze. The air sparkled invitingly with a freshness and vitality that invigorated. It was good flying weather and for the first time since his crash he felt he'd like to take his kite up for a fling about the sky. He looked forward to the drive. He'd fold the hood down and feel the air on his face. Yes, it would be good to motor on a day like this.

He hadn't bothered to make any enquiries about digs by telephone. The College had listed several addresses for newcomers but he thought he'd wait and see whether Angela knew of anyone. This was perhaps a way of keeping a bit more involved with Annie and an excuse for finding out where she lived. Perhaps it was a bit obvious but it was all he had at the moment.

Annie was ready when he drove up at the end of her drive. He'd turned the car and was facing towards Doniford to make a speedy good-bye. Wedging her suitcase behind the seat he tucked her coat in and slammed the door. They drew away from the curb, Annie waving, and gathered speed along the empty road past the drawn curtains of his house and soon into the scattered houses of Doniford itself with its military camp set back towards the sea.

'Will you be warm enough with the hood down?'

'Fine, thanks, I prefer it.'

'Brilliant day for a drive.'

'Lovely colours!'

They roared up to St Audries and thundered between the dressed stone walls of the estate, under the bridge that connected the deer-park to the Quantocks and around the sharp bends that wound through the dying foliage. The road leaped at them, a leafy trackway that dipped and plunged its way through beds of tumbled leaves that swept into the air as they passed. He found it quite stimulating and from the rosy glow that soon appeared on Annie's face, felt that she was enjoying it too. Before he left he'd prepared a few sandwiches and a flask of coffee. They were behind his seat on top of his grip.

'Would you like to stop for a while and have a cup of coffee?'

'Not really,' she shouted over the engine, 'I'd rather get back as soon as possible. Besides, you'll need the time to go hunting for digs.'

He had thought that they might have stopped for a quiet minute or two and shared a coffee. Holford would have been ideal. However if it wasn't to be, they'd crack on and make good time.

There was not a lot of traffic about in Bridgwater and they soon left it behind. Brent Knoll loomed on their left and then it was the run across to Churchill Rocks and the long climb up to Redhill. Soon Dundry Hill became visible with its prominent church tower and Peter knew that they were almost there. The whole journey had taken under the hour, not surprising when the car was capable of eighty miles an hour not that they'd been doing that.

He had thought that they'd probably topped seventy-five on a couple of occasions.

'This is Bedmister Down. Turn left as you go down the hill. I'll show you.'

They crossed the bridge and turned into Hotwells.

'Left here and then first right after going under the Suspension Bridge.'

They slowed and Peter turned into Bridge Valley Road climbing between the pebble-encrusted outcrops of over-grown conglomerate. The trees were a mass of blazing gold and behind them the long form of the bridge stabbed across the river on its towers, like an accusing but deli-cate finger. He could see that Annie was pleased to be back. She was animated, even excited and pointed out the various landmarks as they drove past.

'There's the zoo along here on the right.'

'And that tower thing there on the left is the top of a ventilation shaft for the railway tunnel underneath.'

'Stop here. That's where Angela lives. That's Miss Peath John's house.'

Peter parked on the edge of open grassland dotted with trees and shrubs. A string of large bomb craters was al-ready well grassed over.

'These are the Downs. They stretch right across to the gorge.'

Peter switched off the engine and stretched. He looked at the substantial house that Annie had indicated and was impressed.

'Quite a lot of house for Angela to look after.'

'If it's all right, I shall be staying to help.'

He lifted her bag from the back and carried it across the road. A smiling woman in her early thirties appeared at the door. She hugged Annie and turned to him.

'It's Peter isn't it? Thanks for bringing my little sister back.'

'It's my pleasure. It's been a splendid drive.'

'I'll put the kettle on. Miss Peath John will be pleased to meet you.'

'You don't happen to know of anyone who might have some digs I could stay in?'

Angela wagged her finger at him.

'Come in and have a cup of tea first and then we can sort out the details later. Yes, I do know where you could go. Lovely family. I'll tell you all about it in a minute.'

She reached out and squeezed Annie's arm.

'Super to see you love.'

They passed inside and went into the sitting room. A silver-haired lady rose to greet them. Peter recognised her qualities immediately. She shone with confidence, authority and a persuasive gentility. A lady of the old school, charming and yet distinguished. She held out her hand.

'I'm very pleased to meet you Peter. I trust you had a pleasant journey.'

'Yes, thank-you Ma'am.'

'And Annie here, you've brought her safely back to us?'

'I trust so.' Peter bowed slightly.

'Good, good, then we can all have some tea. Angela has prepared luncheon and I hope that you will join us before dashing off to settle your affairs.'

'Thank-you, I'd be pleased to.'

'Now then, what was the west-country like on this sunny autumn day?'

Angela excused herself and slipped out leaving Annie and Peter to share the glories of the way. Annie perched on the arm of the chesterfield and chatted cheerfully about the journey mentioning several things that he had missed. She looked almost unreal, still slightly flushed and bright-eyed. There was no trace of the anxiety that had been so prominent in the days before and he ventured if the return to her sister might be a strong factor in her recovery. He wondered if he ought to talk to Angela but there would be time for that in the future if things went well.

Tea was served in delicate china cups and saucers, a far cry from the flask and bakelite cups he had prepared for their break. They chattered easily for a while until Angela re-appeared and announced that luncheon was ready in the dining room. The table was laid for four and luncheon prepared in dishes on the sideboard. Angela helped Miss Peath John to the table and drew back her chair. Peter stood by to help Annie.

'Do help yourselves.'

Luncheon consisted of cuts of salmon with a herb sauce, garlic potatoes garnished with parsley and fresh steamed vegetables. Angela served Miss Peath John and Peter watched Annie as she served herself a tiny portion. He had to admit he was hungry and the meal looked absolutely delicious.

'This is wonderful. Thank-you so much.'

'You're very welcome. Don't get any ideas that I'm connected with the black market. The salmon came by train from a friend of mine in Scotland.'

Peter laughed.

'We used to find all sorts of things on the various bases

and airfields we were stationed at. We called it local produce. Sometimes our beef was venison!'

Conducted skilfully by Miss Peath John the conversation drew everyone into an intimate group. They touched on Peter's early days in Hurricanes, Annie's work during the bombing and Angela's experiences selling rope to sailors. After a while the talk centred on the house itself.

'It's beautifully built.'

'It ought to be. It was constructed by a builder for his own use in the 1890's using the best available materials and craftsmen. Look at the quality of the dressed stone and the carving on the mullions as you go out.'

'It's much grander than the houses in Watchet.'

'Clevedon has a number of similar ones. They are classics of their kind, roomy, manageable and not too difficult to heat in winter. I put an extension on the back of this one in the twenties that enabled me to be private even with a house full of guests. They hold their value too. I was asked only the other day if I would care to accept an offer of over a thousand pounds more than I paid for it but then prices are beginning to move a little now that the war is over. We oughtn't to be talking of money. My father used to say it was vulgar to mention money!'

Peter suddenly became conscious that time was flying by and he hadn't begun to think of where he was going to lay his head. He rose.

'I ought to be thinking of moving. There's much to be done. Thank-you so much for your kind hospitality. I really enjoyed it.'

He looked across to Annie.

'Perhaps I could call again?'

Angela jumped in.

'Yes, do call whenever you are passing, you'll be most welcome. Oh, and your digs. If you go around the corner into Sutherland Place you'll find a house with a green door and a large shamrock knocker. Mrs Teresa Daws has a room to let and she's used to looking after gentlemen. There's all your meals if you want them and your laundry as well. She's a really nice lady. You'll get on fine. Just say that Angela Vickery has recommended you. Her last gentleman worked at BAC and was there for two years.'

He again glanced across at Annie, hoping to catch her eye.

'I'll be off then. Good-bye.'

'Good-bye Peter and thanks again for bringing Annie back.'

He stepped out into the afternoon. His faithful red charger was still parked on the grass on the other side of the road. He left it there and set off to discover Sutherland Place and the shamrock knocker.

CHAPTER SEVENTEEN

Peter became a regular visitor in the early days of his course. He took the digs around the corner and was very settled there. The College proved stimulating too; a couple of other pilots had signed on and I think that if the truth were told, a lot of their homework was done in the Coach and Horses and the Port of Call. He called often and we soon became used to his cheery greeting. Annie however, continued to hold on to her view of things and poor Peter became more and more frustrated as his every attempt to take her out was thwarted.'

Angela smiled ruefully.

'I have to admit that as the time went by I became very attracted to Peter and looked forward to his visits as much as Annie began to dread them. She liked him well enough but was still fiercely loyal to her memories.'

She glanced up.

'I suppose I fell in love with him which put me in a difficult position. Part of me wanted my sister to be drawn out of her melancholy and to find the right partner but the secret part of me wanted Annie to continue with her fantasy and Peter to look to me instead. It was awful. I felt absolutely dreadful.'

Jill held her breath.

'He was a lovely man and a complete gentleman. Look, I've kept his photograph all these years.'

She proffered a snap from the pile of papers before them. It was yellowing and there were creases on the edges as if it had been kept in a pocket folder for some years as indeed it had. A young man looked up at her. He wore a blazer and an open-necked shirt with a cravat. A quizzical smile played around the corners of his mouth.

Jill handed it back.

'Was he as tall as David?'

'A bit taller and a bit slimmer I think. They were both fine men. Life isn't always fair.'

Angela sighed and brushed her hair from her forehead.

'I think that Miss PJ knew of the situation that had developed under her nose because one day she took me aside, smiled sadly and said "Oh what tangled webs we weave."

'However there was little time for either of us to worry over much about Peter for in December, just before Christmas, Annie vanished. Miss PJ sent for the police and Peter and I scoured the Downs and the Avonmouth and City Docks as I had done before. When we sat down and thought about it, we realised that Annie's disappearance coincided with a wireless broadcast telling of the thousands of displaced persons that were flooding into the country and indeed were making their way back to destinations all over Europe. It was Peter who had the idea that we should cast our net wider. Whether it was a psychic lead or a near miracle he found her on the fifth day at Folkstone, tired, hungry and exhausted. She'd been meeting the boats from France and posing the eternal question. When Peter finally caught up with her she'd said, "I thought, what if he had been interned somewhere and been in a camp? He would only now be making his way home." Peter finally persuaded her to leave with him by promising to leave David's name and description with the immigration authorities at the ferry ports. When they finally arrived home by taxi from Temple Meads, Peter had to carry her up to her room. I vowed then to keep well out of the equation. Annie needed Peter more than I did.'

Angela looked up and caught Jill's eye.

'I could dash on right through this story and tell you it all amounted to nothing but there's a lot of life and a lot of courage to be seen first. Annie recovered but missed that first Christmas after the war. It was bright but poor. Nothing much had got through to the shops by then.

The most amazing thing was the lights, lights in the streets and lights in the shops. It was brilliant after years of black-out. At Easter, she began to wander again and could be found trailing about on the Downs asking folk if there was any news of her David. Most of the neighbours knew her of course and so were kind and pointed her back home. One or two were not so kind and sometimes Peter asked if he could go with her. He did too, taking her arm and guiding her across to Sea Walls nodding to folk left and right and all the time reassuring her that everything was being done that could be done. He still loved her and I think in his heart felt that given the right set of circumstances he might bring her to the point where she could mourn the loss of her husband and start life afresh.

Peter qualified that June and had a certificate to prove it. I remember it was a day of high skies and fluffy clouds and we all went out on to the Downs to celebrate. Miss PJ had bought a bottle of champagne and I provided some salmon sandwiches, again by train from Scotland. Peter told us about the presentation on the steps of the College. A Bristol head had addressed them. "Don't think that you are teachers," he'd said. "In thirty years you'll be teachers and so I salute the teachers you will become. Upon you rests the responsibility of shaping the generations to come. You mustn't fail for your country needs you as much as it did in 1939." Miss PJ puffed, "He forgot to mention the fun, we're going to need some humour in the future!" She was right too, and I think Peter recognised what she was saying.

If Peter was a little serious on that occasion he could be forgiven for he asked Annie for a private moment. I remember her looking up and smiling at him. They walked off for a minute or two before returning and joining in with the chatter. I was about to ask Miss PJ what she thought was going on but she raised a finger and I knew. Peter had come to the final question and had asked Annie if she would come with him now that he was about to take up a post. She'd given the expected answer and Peter had accepted that the relationship would never develop as he had hoped. Later he spoke of her courage and her loyalty and how, sadly he knew that there would never be any hope for any other person in her life. Peter called for the last time toward the end of August. He'd been appointed to teach Mathematics and Geography at Wedmore School under Mr Herridge. Apparently in the interview Mr Herridge had asked Peter about the geography of the Mendips. Peter had done an essay on the Highlands of the Southwest Peninsula and so felt he'd answered well. He said it was a lovely country school on the edge of the village with splendid views. He'd got his eye on a house in Cheddar and had put the Watchet house on the market. We agreed to keep in touch but it was hard to see him go. He seemed settled and was man enough to make decisions. I missed his cheery smile. I don't know if he ever realised how I'd felt. If he did he never showed the slightest sign. Annie knew how much he cared about her but could never put another in David's place. I think she was relieved when he declared himself and was able to give him a straight answer.

The winter of 1947 has become a legend. Only if you lived through the strikes, power cuts, lack of fuel and strict rationing that went with temperatures down as far as 16 degrees could you understand how bad things were. Mr Atlee spoke to the nation on the wireless and told us we were in a crisis. We knew that well enough, even Miss PJ's supplies dried up and Annie and I went wooding down in the Gorge bringing back enough to make faggots, Somerset style. We even fell back on some of the old sailing ship recipes. Miss PJ seemed to enjoy them, or so she said. Many of the tricks we learned on the old Dancer came in useful. When her mind was busy or when there was a job to be done Annie was fine. It was when she had time to think that things started to go haywire.

The snow stayed on the Downs right through the spring, not that you could call it a spring. When finally the weather did start to improve, Annie became very unhappy and spent a lot of time just sitting by herself. Predictably it was Miss PJ who suggested that Annie see a doctor. Reluctantly she went and was diagnosed as depressed or as they put it in those days, in need of a complete rest. The doctor suggested a spell in hospital, not for bed rest you understand, but to receive support and care. She didn't fight and within the week went to Barrow Hospital for a period.

We visited her regularly and Miss PJ suggested that

she see a specialist. Whilst Annie was indignantly determined not to be classified as ill or odd she thought it might give her the chance to discuss the probabilities of David's survival with someone outside the family. She had no evidence of his death other than assumptions made at the time. She'd also heard of many more rare escapes from terrible circumstances. She went over some of the questions he'd asked when we saw her afterwards. "What makes you so sure he survived?" She had to admit it was only an inner feeling. The specialist pointed out that at least she ought to admit he was missing and that after a decade even the law makes decisions on such cases. "I'll be hard on you." he'd said, "after the war there were tens of thousands of people missing with no trace, in Russia, millions. I think if you can't accept death, you must accept missing as the appropriate term and plan your life accordingly."'

'Did it help? This interview with the psychologist.'

Angela shook her head. She suddenly looked worn as she relived the pattern of her sister's illness.

'No love, She spent a month in hospital and then went for a rest-cure in Bournemouth but on her return persisted with the same old insistence that David would somehow return to her. Miss PJ was consistently kind and suggested that we concentrate on making Annie as comfortable as possible and humour her ideas. And that's what we did. We rubbed along through the years trying to ignore the more bizarre incidents and suggesting as many diversions as we could think of to normalise the situation.'

Jill reflected for a moment. Angela had been steadily moving through the years and she had questions to ask.

'What about old Captain Vickery? What was his reaction to all this?'

'Father was far from well. By the end of the forties, he developed a chest complaint. It might have been to do with his injury but mother said it was probably more to do with standing at the tiller for hours in all weathers as a young man. He died at Watchet in 1950 and Annie and I went down to St Decuman's for the funeral. It was a cold, rainy day. Why is it that so many funerals are held in the rain? We all needed the sunshine that day but it wasn't to be found. Mother still lives at Watchet but she's pretty frail now. Her friends keep in touch and I go down to see her fairly regularly. She was invited here but she remembers the Watchet of her early days and prefers to be there.'

'And how did Annie react?'

'We thought at first that she might like to go down and stay with mother, to look after her but she wasn't very happy about that. She came down with me when I visited but apart from that, she preferred to be here.'

'Miss Peath John was a fantastic friend wasn't she?'

'The best anyone could ever have. She was a gem. The day I accepted a post here was the best decision I ever made. She adopted us all really.'

'And what happened to her?'

'It came as a bit of a shock when she died. We had no idea that she was ill. She was always so concerned about others that we never thought that anything could be wrong with her. She went downhill very quickly. It was pneumonia the doctor said but added that she would have died within a month from her problem anyway.'

'Oh the poor lady. When was this?'

'It would be 1957. Yes, '57 in the summer.'

Angela sighed.

'It's still like she's here. Not a ghost you understand but the pleasant memory of a good friend. I often think of her and find myself asking what she would have done under the circumstances.'

'Did she have any relatives?'

'Not living. She left me a letter and asked me to visit her solicitor. Still have the letter. She left fifty percent of her estate to the RNLI but the remainder to me. The house was mine too. I was very touched. Here, let me read it to you.'

She reached out to the table and selected an envelope.

"My dear Angela,

You may recollect a conversation we held a long time ago when I decided I could trust you. I am leaving the house to you together with the residue of my estate after certain bequests have been made. It will probably surprise you and be a responsibility you didn't ask for. However I know you'll use it wisely and in the way I would wish.

You will understand I know when I say that the greatest joy in my life was discovering the practice of kindness.

Possibly because life is never fair it enables some of us to show compassion and kindness in almost all circumstances. We are all a part of the living world and we all make significant contributions to each other's lives. Our mark is permanent, our way indelible and we cannot erase a day of it. There's a list of folk I help at the solicitors and sufficient of the vulgar stuff to continue doing so. I'd like it to remain private please. Use the house and the residue as you think fit. God bless you and look after that sister of yours for me.

Yours with love,
EPJ"

Angela looked up and spread her hands.

'You can imagine how I felt. I was quite overcome. When the solicitor told me what I had responsibility for I was even more taken aback. There was near fifty thousand pounds not counting this house and some property in Scotland that yielded a regular rent. He was quite explicit and showed me just what Miss PJ had been doing to help several families. I retained him there and then and we have been working together ever since. The money for the RNLI was sufficient to build several boats and I saw to it that the first to be launched was named after her.'

Jill reached for the letter and scanned it.

'I've never seen anything like this before. What a shock it must have been. Did you have no inkling at all that she'd do something like that?'

'Not one bit. I thought that she might leave me twenty pounds or something if I survived her. I never expected her to go off like that.'

She sighed.

'She was a wonderful lady. There aren't many as fine. Look, here she is at eighteen. This was painted in India.'

She handed Jill a small silver travelling frame containing the picture of a pensive, sensitive girl with a mass of auburn curls and blue eyes. She was wearing a white dress with a lacy fill-in at the throat. If there was just a tinge of sadness about the mouth it was hardly discernable.

'She was beautiful.'

'Beautiful in spirit too though I think she could be practical and worldly when the need arose. She wasn't a weak lady.'

Angela leaned back in her chair.

'There was a lot for me to learn but bit by bit I managed to sort everything out. She'd been helping people for years, some anonymously. I was surprised when I learned of one or two folk but I kept my mouth shut and continued to follow her wishes. I remember the solicitor's remark the first time I made a gift on my own initiative. He said, "Miss Peath John would approve. Well done!"

Annie stayed reasonably stable for the next few months but in February 1958, she became ill after staying out all night on the Downs. What possessed her, well, I know what possessed her to stay out in the bitter cold. It was just one walk too many and she developed a dreadful chest. If she'd had the will to fight it she might have made a recovery but she seemed to have lost all heart.'

Jill brought her hands together and touched her thumbs to her lips. She began to feel the emotion that moved with the story like a tide lifting and slipping as it swept inexorably along.

'So it was over two years ago she died. It must have been a terrible time for you.'

'Yes, early March on a cold blustery morning with the snow flurries dancing up the windows. I'd put the boiler on all night to keep the house warm so it was cosy enough inside. She'd been in a fever all night and I sent for the Doctor soon after dawn. He came before surgery started and said that she ought to make a recovery if she had the will.

However her temperature remained high and by mid

morning her pulse quickened and she became bright-eyed and unusually talkative. I thought that the crisis had passed and she was going to relax and start to get better.

Then she looked at me.

"I'm tired Angela," she said. "So tired."

I remember suggesting that she try to rest.

"I'm tired of hoping and tired of searching. It's all so hopeless and no-one believes me."

I tried to reassure her but she smiled at me and stopped me.

"Stay with me a while Angela and we can be like we were when I was a little girl. I always looked up to you, you know. Do you remember the congers below West Street beach and how we were frightened of them? Oh, Angela I'm not frightened now. I think I can see David. He's hiding. Tired now Angela, so tired, so tired."

I held her hand and hoped she would sleep. When she closed her eyes and started to breathe more easily my hopes rose. Then she just failed to breathe in and the tension drained out of her. She died peacefully by my side. It was like dying myself, like losing the best part of my life. Oh, how I loved her.

For weeks afterwards I tormented myself with all kinds of remorse. Had I done enough for her? How constructive had I been during her illness? I cursed all the times I'd been exasperated with her and regretted all the times I'd not listened more attentively when she needed me.

But I had the responsibilities left to me by Miss PJ. In effect I now was Miss PJ or rather Miss AV and there was much to be involved with.'

'So you lived here alone?'

'Not quite, for a year I shared the house with two elderly ladies who had been jettisoned from a local hotel for being too eccentric. They were wonderful and I found my life again by loving and giving as Miss PJ had done. These two were characters! They had a naughty sense of humour that was probably why they were thrown out in the first place. The older one used to make hoax telephone calls to pompous people and station herself where she could observe the fireworks. She had the manager of a local furniture store roll out the red carpet for the Duke of Edinburgh who was to call to inspect an armchair for his office at Buckingham Palace.'

'What happened to them?'

'They went to live in Jersey. They still send a card at Christmas.'

'Did you ever hear from Peter again?'

'Yes, he sends a card too. I didn't tell him about Annie's death for some time. I don't know what prompted me not to. He's married now with a boy of his own. After two or three years at Wedmore he went to America. A school in Alabama. In fact I think he is still there. Yes, I still think of him. I often wonder about the cross-roads of life and what would have happened if I'd gone down a different path. However, as Miss PJ said, it's the problems that create the opportunities to be kind. Perhaps I was on the right road all the time.'

Angela stretched and rubbed her eyes. She yawned then apologised.

'How rude of me. You must think I'm dreadful rambling on like this.'

'Not at all. It's the story of a life and I feel honoured to hear it. I think I admire Annie's grit and her determination to hold on to her memories. They must have been very real to her and David must have been a very special person.'

Angela nodded.

'Her memories were her reality. Nothing in her life after the news came could tear away her conviction that he was alive. It sounds irreverent but she made a God out of him and believed in his resurrection. Such is the stuff of gospels.'

'And when did she first give folk reason to believe they had seen her? After, I mean...'

'Oh, I'd almost forgotten the reason you called. April I think, a girl in school uniform called with such an accurate description I almost shot out to find her. Then just before Christmas, several glimpses on the Downs and on the driveway here. On Christmas Eve a couple called to tell me that they'd seen a woman walking through the front door here without opening it. And then there was a lady from Pembroke Road who saw her several times and called to ask after her. From their pictures of events, it was Annie. I don't fret about it now. I know she is free of her pain and her search is over. If she appears as a ghost, it is as a pattern caught in time and not my Annie in distress. All that is over.'

Jill heaved a sigh and glanced at the table with its faded photographs, letters and papers, its albums and post-cards. She felt heavier but not dulled by the impact of all she had listened to. What could she do other than pray that Annie rest in peace. It was so personal. A life laid bare, a life scattered on the table.

'So now you have it all. Our complete family story with its triumphs and tragedies, its comings and goings. Dear Annie, poor Annie was so wounded she never really recovered. Not all the wounds of war were inflicted on the battlefield. There was much suffering at home too, a lot unseen and unsung. There were many thousands of war widows though I shall never quite understand why Annie could never accept it. Then, I never had a husband and that says a lot doesn't it? There, come through and I'll put the kettle on!'

Jill rose slowly to her feet. She smiled and then thought better of making any remark. Angela went through into the kitchen and Jill trailed after.

'Why her,' she thought. 'Why should the laws of the spiritual world, if there were such things, conspire to draw her into the drama? Why should she have been privileged to hear this sad story? Was that the end of it all?'

Something told her that it wasn't.

CHAPTER EIGHTEEN

Jill moved stiffly over the crisp grass conscious of the continual roar of close traffic as it pressed around the corner by the top of Pembroke Road and pushed up Upper Belgrave Road. She wondered how much time she had left and if Martin was enjoying the exhibition. If she knew anything, he'd be chattering nineteen to the dozen and not worrying about their rendezvous. She'd been dreaming. The cold air wrapped itself about her and her breath hung on the morning like a pale drifting balloon. She walked around the bomb craters now tree-filled and criss-crossed by well used up and down paths. Brambles twisted among alder and young rowan and the rime persisted on the finest tendrils. A few more mature trees clawed the cold sky with long scratching fingers. It wouldn't move much above freezing all day.

The house was flats. Three or four name-plates were attached to the right hand side of the door and there was one of those answering devices through which one could talk without coming face to face with the occupants. She wondered what Miss PJ or Angela would have thought. It was obvious that the house had changed hands. The thought crossed her mind.

'I wonder if Angela is still alive. Let's see, she'd be in her nineties now. Probably not. There's likely a lifeboat out there called the Angela.'

The sitting room window where she'd heard the story all those years ago was netted and she couldn't see in. She speculated if the present owners of the flats knew anything more than that the house was Victorian, well built and had a later annexe on the back. More to the point, did Annie still reach out for the front door?

She stood there for a while and for a while time blurred and she heard again the voice of Angela telling the story in her soft West Somerset accent. She remembered how sad she had been to hear about Annie and David and the family. She'd not forgotten, or dismissed the saga. It was all still fresh in her mind. She'd kept it and pondered it, feeling disloyal if ever she'd been tempted to share it with anyone.

There was no sight of Annie this time. Perhaps in the scheme of things she had long gone and all traces of her past traumas removed from time. And yet there was that small nagging feeling that in some way her being there was of some significance. She couldn't put her finger on it. Still, here she was and as far as she knew she would never make the same pilgrimage again.

She shivered, partly the cold. What was she doing out here? Satisfying some old whim? Pandering to imma-ture feelings that should have been put away with her nursery toys? The adult in her started to rationalise. She shivered again, partly that feeling, that remnant of child-hood, never lost.

An old man came unsteadily down the road on the wrong side. Traffic ignored him as he tapped his stick uncertainly against the broken stones at the edge of the Downs. He was inclined rather than bent and his left arm hung limply by his side. No, it was an empty sleeve. An old cap with ear-flaps was pulled well down against the weather and a heavy scarf protected his face from the cold.

By now, Jill was standing right opposite the house.

Quite why she had become focussed on this figure rather than the other faster moving walkers on the Downs she couldn't say. He seemed awkward yet positive and obviously knew where he was bound. Perhaps a morning constitutional recommended by his doctor though on a cold morning like this he'd be better off in bed.

His voice was strong and carried a marked American accent.

'You don't happen to know who lives there do you?'

'It's flats,' Jill returned. 'Flats now but many years ago it was owned by a lady called Miss John.'

She felt a bit ridiculous adding the extra information and hastened to justify herself.

'I used to be a student here in the early sixties. They weren't all flats then.'

'Just one lady then?'

He rested on his stick and looked into her eyes. He was old but bright eyed above the scarf twisted about his face and neck.

'Just the one then. As far as you know.'

Of course she knew more. A lot more.

He went on.

'I reckoned I got the right road but I'm not sure if I've found the right house. I'm making enquiries about family from a long time ago. It's probably far too late.'

'Depends on how far back you want to go. When I visited the house, as I said in the sixties, a lady lived here who had been housekeeper to Miss John. Miss John left the house to her after many years of service.'

'And she was called Angela wasn't she?'

The voice was steady but a trace of excitement had entered it. Jill's mind raced. Perhaps an old friend from the States who knew Angela and had lost touch.

'Yes, Angela, Miss Vickery. I met her here but not Miss John of course.'

'Were you a friend of hers?'

'In a way, she once shared a confidence with me. It's a long story but I do know a bit about her up to the time she took over this house.'

She looked again at the old man. Angela's friend Peter had gone to America. Wasn't he keen on Annie but she had refused him. It couldn't be Peter could it, after all these years?

'Did you know Angela?'

The old man heaved a great sigh and tilted his head to one side.

'Oh, yes I knew Angela. I talked to her here on the Downs many years ago. I knew Miss John too, though we referred to her as Miss Peath John.'

'Then you knew Annie too. Annie, Angela's sister.'

'Yes, I knew her and loved her.'

His voice became brittle. He coughed and continued.

'She was a beautiful girl. I've never met her equal. No, never.'

Jill remembered as if it were her own history. Peter had proposed on the Downs, here not far from where they were standing. She'd turned him down because of her love for David.

'So you've been in America for years?'

'Until my heart tugged me back. I should never have stayed in the first place. It was a mistake.'

Jill felt more certain.

'This is the first time I've been back since the sixties. The house is now flats and so I presume that Angela must have sold up or died.'

'Did she say anything about Annie? Did she keep in touch with her? Do you know what happened to Annie?'

'Yes, but do you not remember that Annie lived here with Angela? You visited here didn't you?'

'I brought Angela here by car once at the beginning of the war. She promised to look after my Annie.'

An icy dart shivered through Jill's spine. Her breath choked in her throat. It wasn't Peter.

'What happened to Annie?'

The voice was not as strong as it had seemed. Jill faltered, then recovered and tried.

'She died at the end of the fifties. She'd not been well for some time. Angela told me that she went peacefully in the early year.'

The old man covered his face with his hand and began to sob.

Jill held him.

He pushed free and looked at her earnestly.

'Tell me what you know. Tell me everything.'

'I only know what Angela told me. After Annie was widowed early in the war she persisted in believing that her husband was still alive. She did catering work during the war but afterwards settled here with Angela who looked after her. I'm afraid her belief turned into depression and she became ill.'

'Oh my God. Did, did anyone believe her?'

'No, Angela and her parents tried to tell her that thousands were in the same situation but she still clung to the idea that her David had survived. She was unshakable to the end.'

'God!'

'I don't know whether I ought to mention this but at the time of her passing and shortly afterwards folk saw her. I did too. I think it was a measure of the emotion felt at the time. To all accounts she was a remarkable girl.'

'She was.'

Jill felt a deep concern rise within her.

'I think you ought to sit down. Let's sit on the wall over there.'

She waited for a gap in the traffic and guided him across the road to sit on the wall outside the house.

'What if? What is your name?'

'Jill.'

'What if, Jill, what if she was right and David wasn't killed on that tanker in 1940?'

Jill remained quiet and looked full at him.

'What if he was picked up before the rescue ship arrived and taken out of the area? Then what if he was transferred to a bigger ship and taken to America?'

She knew it wasn't Peter but who could have news of David after so many years? Were there other people who knew of this disaster? The rescuers perhaps, or relatives of David from Porlock.

He started to speak, slowly at first as if it was a well rehearsed speech. As he continued he became more animated and distressed.

'Just before the torpedoes hit, David and the starboard bridge look-out went out on to the bridge wing to look at the nearby coast. They were only a couple of miles off the village where David was born. You can't believe the explosion as tanks of aviation spirit are ignited. It blew them a hundred feet into the air. Both men were injured but David probably not as badly as the seaman.

They landed in a lake of burning petrol and suffered severe burns before diving under the surface and managing to reach the edge. A V and W destroyer picked them up clinging to a damaged deck raft. She was only in the area by chance and had diverted to see if there were any survivors. Not being able to cope with extensive injuries she signalled for assistance and managed to attract the attention of an American liner outward bound from Liverpool south of the Smalls. She carried a surgeon and had the facilities to operate. Both men were transferred by boat to the liner. Two days later the seaman died of his injuries. David was operated on but remained close to death for a week. Once in New York he spent four months in hospital.

It was high summer when he was discharged and given leave to return to the UK as a distressed seaman. This automatically gave him a passage home and this is where the problem began. David was, to put it plainly, disfigured. He'd lost his arm and was unrecognisable to all who might have known him. Not reasoning straight, he decided to lose himself in Up-State New York and set off for the mountains. The thought of being a cripple and exciting sympathy was unbearable to him. He recollected a time when he and his wife were on their honeymoon and she remarked how she felt pity for a crippled man. He decided not to return. "Better," he said, "for her to think I died months ago rather than nurse a wreck for the rest of her life."

He lived from hand to mouth and finally came to stay in a small settlement east of Tupper Lake in the Adirondac Mountains. There he managed to make a living as an illustrator supplying drawings for nature magazines. In later years he made quite a reputation as a wildlife and landscape artist and sold a lot of his work. His conscience got the better of him in the end as he understood that his feelings had been selfish and he'd lost the one person, the one person who would have loved him whatever condition he was in. Knowing that he may well be too late, he nevertheless took a ship for England and set off to retrace his steps and find out if his Annie was still alive.'

Jill reached out and took his hand. She looked at him. He was crying.

'Will you forgive a foolish old man? Will you? Angela must have told you how much hurt I caused. Annie knew. Oh, she knew I was out there just as I knew she was there waiting for me. I was too stubborn, too blind, too hurt and too selfish.'

'David! You're David.'

He nodded and rubbed the back of his hand across his eyes.

'David Pollard, old and stupid. David Pollard with the hurt of my trusting faithful wife on my conscience.'

Jill spoke out and added.

'Faithful she was, faithful and believing to the end. Oh my God, she was right! She stuck to her guns for the whole of her life despite any amount of sympathy and help. God, they even sent her to hospital!'

'Don't. I feel so desperate.'

'Angela told me the whole of it. They were always close. She kept all sorts of things, photos and the like. I think I have most of the story.'

'Would you, would you please be kind enough to share it with me?'

Jill slipped her arm about his shoulders and he leaned against her. There wasn't very much of him despite his heavy coat and scarf.

'I've got to go back to the time when I first caught a glimpse of Annie here by the door. I followed her and Angela knew somehow that I could be trusted with the story. She invited me in and shared her life and the life of her sister with me. In some strange way I always believed it was for some purpose.'

'I broke her heart. She knew I was alive but I was too frightened to come home. It was all too easy to run away in a war. Tell me all you can.'

Jill recounted as gently as she could all she remembered of the story. She couldn't help but marvel at the situation. She was the only living person who could tell it and she was telling it to the one for whom it mattered the most. It was the reason why she'd heard it in the first place and it was the reason for her being there. She knew that now.

David listened quietly, nodding and murmuring to himself. Occasionally he looked up like a wistful child. Jill felt older than her years.

'Do you think she forgave me? Do you forgive me?'

Jill looked him full in the eye. She pulled the scarf away from his shattered face and kissed him firmly.

'Yes, David. Yes, I think that's why I was here waiting for you.'

He looked up and attempted a brave smile.

'You were, weren't you? You were here. You look a little like her you know. Something about the eyes.'

Jill stood up.

'Come on, we're going to get a warm drink and something to eat.'

'I'll stay for a while if you don't mind. You go on. Perhaps we'll meet again one day. And thank-you.'

She left a little reluctantly. She somehow felt a sense of responsibility for him. As she walked back up the road, past Belgrave Terrace towards Wesley Place she looked back. David was kneeling on the pavement, his head bowed. She felt it was a private moment and hurried on her way.

The Port of Call was busy and she was half way into the Portside bar when she remembered that she was to meet Martin in the Mall. She was late. The quickest way would be to retrace her steps and continue up the Promenade and across the grass by Gloucester Row. As she passed the house there was no sign of David. He'd vanished. A thought flashed through her mind. Did it happen or was it all just a fantasy, an extended day-dream?

She finally made it, a little breathless and a little more late but found that Martin had not yet arrived. Sinking into a chair she ordered a coffee and started to relax. What were the chances of it being coincidence? It was just too fantastic. Who would believe it anyway?

Martin found her sipping coffee and was full of apologies.

'Brilliant exhibition. I'm afraid I got involved. Sorry I'm late.'

Jill smiled and handed him the menu.

'You pay for lunch then, wicked man.'

'How was your morning?'

'I went across the Downs. Saw a few places we've known.'

'Did you see that famous house of yours?'

'I did as a matter of fact. It's flats now.'

'And did you lay a few ghosts?'

Jill paused.

'I suppose I did in a way.'

She looked up. Should she try to explain?

'I'm having the garlic chicken, what will you have darling?'

'Oh, the same please.'

She smiled back at him but her mind was elsewhere. Someone had to be there when he came back. She was glad she had been able to do that. She glanced at Martin. No stories here thank God. She reached out and patted his hand. She wondered who she might tell? Perhaps no-one. Perhaps it was too private for that or was it all 'magination as her mother used to say?

After dinner that evening they strolled out on to the Downs. It was still cold and the sky loomed yellow with the glow of a thousand street-lights. It all seemed very familiar. They came back past the grey bulk of the water-tower towards the top of the Blackboy Hill. Jill glanced up to the top of Cheyne House, the highest in Bristol and took a deep breath.